VAMPIRE TRANSGRESSION

VAMPIRE TRANSGRESSION

MICHAEL SCHIEFELBEIN

 ST. MARTIN'S GRIFFIN ✹ NEW YORK

www.stmartins.com

Book design by Jonathan Bennett

Library of Congress Cataloging-in-Publication Data

Schiefelbein, Michael E.
    Vampire transgression / by Michael Schiefelbein.
        p. cm.
    ISBN-13: 978-0-312-37439-6
    ISBN-10: 0-312-37439-9
    1. Decimus, Victor (Fictitious character)—Fiction. 2. Vampires—Fiction.
3. Gay men—Fiction. 4. Georgetown (Washington, D.C.)—Fiction. I. Title.

PS3619.C36 V358 2006
813'.6—dc22

                                                                    2005044807

First St. Martin's Griffin Edition: September 2007

10 9 8 7 6 5 4 3 2 1

FUGITIVES TOGETHER

Ay me! For aught that I could ever read,
Could ever hear by tale or history,
The course of true love never did run smooth.
—*A Midsummer Night's Dream I, 1, 134–136*

1

Victor Boudreaux followed the tall woman through the wrought-iron gate and up the steps to his townhouse. She wore a knit dress, short and backless. Wobbly from drinking, she stumbled. As Victor steadied her, he pressed his face against her bare back and inhaled the sweet metallic scent that oozed through her damp skin. Her blood aroused him as though it rushed from her veins to his crotch.

She jumped at the touch and then chuckled as if to apologize for the start. "God, Victor, you're freezing."

From behind, Victor brushed aside her hair and kissed her cheek. "Here, let me get the door." He dug a ring of keys from the pocket of his leather pants, spotting the door key instantly, despite the faint porch light. Darkness only sharpens a vampire's vision.

Inside, the unlit entry hall puzzled him. Where the hell was Paul? He wasn't supposed to be out feeding on his own. They'd agreed that Victor would bring someone back from the club—

someone for both of them to feed on. Paul's new rebelliousness was growing tiresome.

"How beautiful," the woman said when Victor clicked on the table lamp. She moved through the archway into the living room, where sconces glowed on either side of a life-size portrait above the fireplace. Victor followed her to the painting.

A Roman painter had finished the portrait of Paul just before their return from the Eternal City in April. Against the painting's dark background, Paul nestled in a club chair, one lanky leg draped over the side, his arm crooked across the back, his head resting on his big hand. His hazel eyes gazed shyly at the viewer. An odd gap in his left eyebrow and a large nose marred otherwise classic good looks. But these flaws, along with long, sandy hair falling on broad shoulders, lent him an intense sensuality. He looked like the free-spirited artist that he was. His face and the patch of smooth chest exposed by his unbuttoned red shirt matched the cold marble of the mantle below the portrait. His complexion had grown paler and paler since the night of his transformation a month before the painting was begun, until it reached this pristine quality—like cloudy molten glass that had finally solidified into porcelain.

"Yes," Victor said, with the pride of ownership. "He is beautiful."

"Who is he?" The woman turned to him. Her features were large, but striking. Her slender throat seemed to throb audibly to Victor. She tugged at the purse strap on her shoulder and blinked at him drowsily, determined to maintain the coquettish air she believed had allured him. At the club she'd spread her fingers to display the rings she'd purchased at an antique store by the Georgetown canal. Victor's breathing had quickened at the sight of the veins discernible beneath the soft skin of her hands. And her eyes had widened on registering his excitement.

"Can't you tell?" Victor said. "It's a painting of me."

She flashed him a look of amused disbelief, then drew her lips into a pout. "Do you even remember my name?"

"Karen," Victor said. He caught a whiff of Paul's patchouli soap and glanced toward the entry hall. Paul had mastered the technique of moving through space at the speed of thought, evading even Victor's seasoned perceptions. There was no sign of him now.

Karen smiled, flattered that Victor had paid attention to her name after all. "What a gorgeous place," she said, glancing around the spacious room filled with custom designed Italian furniture in white leather, the walls raging with red and black swirls of the abstract paintings Victor had pillaged from the studio of a talented victim near the Piazza Navona. Paul confined his own art to the rooms on the second floor of the townhouse. He'd become protective of it since his transformation into a vampire, as his own creative vision also underwent transformation. "I don't know where the work is heading," he'd told Victor. He worried that it would reveal too much of what he was, at least to intelligent viewers. Victor humored him even though he found Paul's fear baseless. Who could see the hand of a vampire in a painting?

"We both like it here just fine," Victor said, nodding to the portrait.

"Oh, I see." Karen smiled knowingly. "He's your lover?"

"Yes."

"You obviously have an open relationship."

"I do what I want." Victor caressed her throat. The pulsing flesh made his fangs begin to descend, and he drew back his hand. He wanted to feed upstairs, away from the large bay window that looked out on the dark Georgetown street of townhouses riddled with windows for potential voyeurs.

But she grabbed his hand, kissed it, and started to kiss his mouth. He jerked away to keep her from the shock of the icy lips that marked all vampires and pulled her body to him. Her muscles relaxed in his embrace, her flesh softening and swelling as she pressed into him.

"So, where are the toys you told me about?" she whispered. "I'd love to play with you."

"They're upstairs."

Victor had nothing but scorn for the thrills sought by the bored rich who patronized the private club he ran next door. Some craved only the occult, crowding around a table for drug-induced consultations with the dead. But most needed the S and M instruments he stored for their amusement in the basement of the club and in the guesthouse next to it. He kept his own selection in the shuttered room upstairs for the guests he selected to bring into his own home.

He could show them real torture, if it weren't so dangerous to kill guests. He and Paul had both come close to pouncing in the excitement of S and M sessions. But they'd always saved their lust for later when they could spend it on a victim. There was nothing more exciting than passion that climaxed in feeding. And, for them, all passion concluded that way. Even in their own lovemaking, they tore at each other's throats, teasing themselves with vampire blood—recycled from their victims and chilled into a life source for the undead—blood that could only whet their appetite without sating it.

Karen's hand on his crotch snapped Victor out of his reverie, and he led his guest up the narrow stairs to the third floor. He unlocked a door and drew her into a dark room where he kissed her until she panted, mumbling something about his cold skin. Then he lit a candle. The shadowy outline of a bed appeared, chains dangling from the ceiling above it. On a kitchen-sized table next to it, the steel of sex toys glimmered in the candlelight. The room smelled musky, and the sound of their steps was muffled by carpeting and heavy drapes.

Without a cue, Karen slipped off her dress and proceeded to the bed. Victor disrobed and followed her.

For half an hour, he used implements from the table according to her pleasure—nipple clamps, handcuffs, a studded dildo. She moaned and swooned, while he fought his impulse to attack and have done with it. When he turned her over, he found a crucifix tattooed on her left buttock and recoiled.

"What is this?" he said, squeezing the tattoo.

"You like it?" she said, her voice muffled by the mattress. "I think it's the supreme act of S and M."

"I think you're full of shit."

"Don't tell me you're offended, Victor."

"He was a political prisoner. The Roman government made an example of him. Like it did with thousands of other rebel Jews impaled along the highway. It didn't excite him."

Two thousand years ago, Victor had stood at Joshu's bloody feet after the crucifixion—Joshu, his name for Jesus of Nazareth. He had stood there hating him for his mad rush to embrace a martyr's death.

"Everyone gets off on it," Karen said, reaching back to yank the engorged flesh bobbing over her.

Enraged at her, enraged at Joshu, he entered her from behind, the crucified Joshu flashing before his eyes. As he rammed her, he nuzzled her neck, inhaling her blood, and finally flipping her over for better access to her throat. Against her shuddering belly and warm breasts, he fought to remember his new rule: no draining to the point of death, only some blood from several victims, no corpses to dispose of and police investigations to circumvent. Losing only an ounce or two of blood, the victim lived—and forgot everything.

But Victor's desire flared uncontrollably and his mouth sought the woman's pulsing jugular. Then, just as his fangs descended, he heard Paul's voice in his mind: *Remember what you said, Victor. Remember our agreement.* And then he felt Paul's cold presence behind him, and thought, illogically in his state, that he'd teach him a lesson for his rebelliousness. As he thrust more deeply into Karen, Paul approached the bed. He touched Victor's shoulder. He kissed Victor's head.

"Who is that?" Karen blurted. "My God, you scared me. Are you the lover?"

Sensing a disturbance in Paul, Victor stopped pumping, now able to concentrate. "What's the matter?" he said.

"Hey, boys, the more the merrier," Karen said, squirming beneath Victor. The pungent scent of her aroused body hung heavily in the air. "It's all right, lover boy."

"Victor," Paul whispered.

Victor climbed off Karen. He clutched Paul's arms and tried to read his pained eyes, perfectly clear to him in the darkness.

"I fucked it up," Paul said. "I went too far, and then I couldn't finish him."

Victor stroked Paul's cheek. "Why did you wait so long to tell me? Where is he?"

They left Karen behind to find her own way out of the house. Paul lacked the concentration now to fly to the spot so they walked down Q Street, past Tudor Place, the Georgian mansion built by Washington's granddaughter. They crossed quiet Wisconsin Avenue, where traffic had buzzed until two A.M.—an hour ago—and where shop lights still glowed in the Georgetown retail area. The muggy August air rose like a wall before them. To their keen senses, the nearby Potomac reeked of sewage and decayed fish.

They followed a cobbled section of P Street to the edge of the university. The familiar Gothic spire of Healy Hall jutted into the yellowish night sky painted by the city lights. Along the stone wall demarcating the campus, beneath an oak, the boy lay unconscious. Victor glanced up at the row houses across the street. The windows were all dark. He knelt down to examine the victim. His throat oozed, but he still breathed, as impossible as it seemed after losing so much blood. He was twenty or so, a pretty boy with white-blond bangs. His T-shirt, embossed with a decal of the rap singer Eminem, was sopping with blood.

"I followed him from a pub back to campus," Paul said. "He's probably a new freshman."

"Why did you go this far?" Victor peered up at Paul, who stood against the tree, unable to look at the boy. He was dressed in a black tank top and black jeans, good camouflage in the night, but probably useless since his broad, bony shoulders were so white they seemed to glow.

Paul shook his head. "It felt like a seizure. Just like the old days. I lost control. I thought they were history, Victor. I thought you said . . ."

"I didn't make any promises. What do I know about epileptics who become vampires?" Victor turned back to the boy. "Let's finish the job."

"I can't. The seizure . . ."

"You can. Come on." Victor grabbed Paul's hand and pulled him down.

For a moment Paul squirmed. Then he seemed to gather strength. He stared serenely at the young face, as though it were a mountain spring, and stooped with Victor to drink from it. They alternated in siphoning the jugular, first Paul, then Victor. Hearing the boy's heart slow to the danger point, they stopped.

"We don't have a choice now," Victor said, his lips stained with blood. "Here." He lifted the boy's wrist to Paul's mouth. "Get the last trickle."

Paul pierced the wrist, savoring it, then lapping contentedly while Victor sucked at the boy's throat. Both stopped just short of the final dull beat of the boy's heart. Blood from a corpse would poison them.

Hot and excited from feeding, they knelt over the body and kissed, their lips wet with blood.

"I guess we leave the body here," Paul said, glancing around the dark street.

Victor nodded. "Moving it would be risky. We'd draw attention."

"I'm sorry, Victor. I fucked up."

Victor kissed him. "Let's get out of here."

They hurried down the dark sidewalk along the wall, crossing the street at an unlit corner. A lone car whizzed through the intersection, the bass of its stereo booming. Victor turned back to look at the driver, a man with some kind of cap. He seemed oblivious to them.

They didn't talk until they'd cleared Wisconsin Avenue and turned down Q, their street, lined with trees and dotted with the charming streetlamps on all the residential streets of Georgetown.

"I don't get it," Paul said. "I thought with the transformation, the seizures were over. Especially after all these months."

Victor shrugged. "We're in new territory."

"You don't know anything?"

"How could I know anything? I'm not an epileptic. I only know what happened to *me* after the transformation."

"You don't get sick," Paul shot back. "Your wounds heal instantly. What do you mean you don't know? Vampires aren't supposed to have seizures."

Victor stopped walking and turned to Paul. "What happened?"

Paul shrugged. "I grabbed the boy. I covered his mouth and started feeding. These voices started, I don't know, chanting or screaming, and I lost control."

"Voices?"

"Voices. A whole chorus of voices. I couldn't stop drinking. Then I froze. I couldn't take in another drop. But I'd gone too far. If someone found him, he could regain consciousness long enough to talk."

"Did you ever have seizures like that before the transformation?"

Paul shook his head. "No. But it felt the same as a seizure. Like I was outside my body or something."

They found the front door unlocked when they arrived home. Karen was probably too angry or drunk to care about protecting their property. She'd printed a sloppy note in lipstick on the mirror above the entry hall table: "Let's do it for real next time, boys."

After inspecting the house to make sure she was gone, they unbolted the basement door and descended the stairs. The radiation of the approaching dawn tightened their skin and drained them of energy. They needed their tomb.

A single lightbulb dangled from the rafters. Around the brick walls stood metal cabinets filled with flowerpots and bags of potting soil. They had been left by the previous owner, an elderly woman with Alzheimer's whose children had put her in a high-dollar nursing home. They waited until she died to sell Victor the townhouse at the hefty price of 2.5 million. But what was money to someone who'd amassed a fortune from the victims of two millennia?

The old woman's husband had built an oblong room in the cellar for wine. Brick walls and a steel door secured the store of vintage bottles and kept the temperature constant to preserve their flavors. Victor unlocked the door, and they entered the chamber without turning on the light. Even meager artificial light stung their sensitive skin as daylight approached. Side by side in the chamber rested two sarcophagi, the lids sculpted with the images of the noblemen who'd lain in them. Victor had hired thugs to steal them from the crypt of a medieval church in Florence, discarding the dusty remains. The ordeal in getting them shipped to the States was well worth the effort. The alternative was two modern coffins, whose accidental discovery by a curious guest would draw attention. No one would blink an eye at exotic collectibles imported by two rich fags. Besides, after centuries of sleeping in monastery crypts, Victor felt secure in the stone casket. And Paul didn't know the difference.

Victor bolted the door. Then he took Paul in his arms. "Are you feeling better now?"

"Fine. Just the usual predawn jitters."

"The seizure's probably just residual. Something that has to work its way out of your system."

Paul shrugged as though he didn't doubt it for a moment.

"Why did you go off alone? After we agreed to feed together."

"I couldn't wait, I guess. I didn't think it would be a big deal."

Victor let the comment go, despite his irritation. Maybe this rebellious phase was part of the process. How would he know? He'd never had to assert his independence because he'd never lived with another vampire. The rules didn't permit it. The rules they had broken.

"It's been wonderful," Paul said drowsily. "Everything you said it would be."

"Georgetown?"

"This life. Everything."

"The world's at our feet."

"I don't want the world. Just you."

With a vampire's ease, they lifted the stone lids from the sarcophagi and hoisted them back over themselves once they'd crawled into the tombs. Victor pressed his hand against the side near Paul's tomb and sensed Paul returning the gesture. Within moments, they both slipped into a sleep that carried them far beyond the fierce reach of dawn.

2

Victor Decimus was his true name, too archaic for modern times. He came of age during the reign of Rome's second emperor, Tiberius. Like all the males in his patrician family, he left his father's villa outside Rome to perform military service in the provinces. He served first in Gaul, then in Judea, under the governor Pontius Pilate. He scorned the backward Judean province, as well as its fanatical Jewish subjects—with one exception. A Jew who claimed his heart high in the desert crags and who then haunted him for the next two thousand years.

That first encounter happened after a night of revelry. Victor had fled the squalor of Jerusalem in search of fresh air. He found the sinewy youth dancing naked and in rapture, his circumcised cock flapping like a rope. He watched the boy lustfully, waiting for the moment to take him, as he had just taken the whore in the city below. But that was not to be. It was never to be. For the boy, despite his own clear longings, pledged himself to a puny Jewish divinity. Joshu was his name for the boy, short for Joshua, his Hebrew name. His followers came to call him Jesus. And though Victor, with a ruthlessness perfected on the flesh of Romans and provincial subjects alike, might have forced open Joshu's legs, he could not find the will. Joshu's uncanny power over him had robbed him of it.

But it did not rob him of the rage he directed toward residents of Jerusalem. His rampage left a path of devastation through the city. However, the rapes and murders were not committed with impunity, despite his rank and family name. Pilate sought to apprehend him, and Victor fled to the lair of a seeress named Tiresia. Tiresia bestowed on him her own nocturnal existence, which she traded for a new, glorious existence in the Dark Kingdom. There, vampires may ascend after two hundred years of stalking the earth and after replacing themselves by transforming a willing human being into a predator of the night.

Until recent years, Victor had no interest in taking his place in the Dark Kingdom, content to punish Joshu and his God by abusing the most dedicated of their adherents: holy monks. Since the inception of European monasteries before the Dark Ages, he had insinuated himself within sacred cloisters, posing as a monk to prey on the bodies and souls of his brothers. Every conquest was a blow against Joshu, who continued to haunt him in apparitions over the centuries, futilely begging him to accept his brand of salvation: submission to a frigid god to win a place in a static heaven.

At the same time, he could not choose the Dark Kingdom until he found the perfect lover, who would replace him on earth for two hundred years and then join him for eternity in a realm where they could thrive once again under a golden sun. He thought he had found such a lover in Paul. But Paul could not relinquish him, not even for so brief a span compared to eternity. And now two vampires lived side by side in violation of the incontrovertible laws of the Dark Kingdom.

Bold in this rebellion, Victor had conceived the idea of establishing his own perverse realm: a club called Dies Irae. In a way, he had picked the name back in the Roman monastery where he and Paul met. The monks of San Benedetto had hired Paul to illuminate a handwritten book of the Gospels. Late one night, Victor kept Paul company in the monastery's scriptorium while Paul studied illuminations in an enormous medieval volume. He ran across the Latin phrase and asked Victor what *Dice Ira* meant. Victor, born in Rome during the reign of Augustus, laughed, correcting Paul's pronunciation of his mother tongue: *Dee-ez Earray. Dies Irae*, Day of Wrath. It was the Catholic Church's term for the Last Judgment when God pitched randy sinners into the flames of hell. Victor joked that the phrase would be perfect for the name of a club that catered to the godless.

So after Paul's transformation into a vampire a year ago, when they wanted a home for their new life together, he couldn't resist the Georgetown property listed on the Internet. A church. A consecrated church. He'd turn it into a shrine to sin and decadence, and he'd call it Dies Irae. It would rise like a fist in the face of Joshu's god. A perfect gesture for the perfect taunt: "We'll see who's in the judgment seat now."

The club had already acquired a widespread reputation among wealthy S and M and occult devotees. Victor had culled patrons from both groups by infiltrating exclusive clubs in New York and enthralling them with his prodigious abilities as master of both human subjects and the black arts. Women and gay men succumbed to his fiercely handsome face, brawny physique, and commanding presence. Heterosexual men from the sex clubs liked to watch women submit to him. Heterosexual men from the occult clubs respected his conjuring powers, which he possessed as a vampire but attributed to years of study and practice.

Those who visited the club visited as nonpaying guests, there for Victor's amusement. They stayed in a Victorian row house adjacent to the club, which matched the house on the opposite side where he and Paul lived. Victor had purchased both homes under the name Boudreaux, his Latin family name being too cumbersome. Since no money changed hands, the club was technically a private residence not subject to zoning laws. Police stayed away because guests confined their orgies and rituals to the thick brick walls. If neighbors guessed the activities inside, they wisely kept their guesses to themselves.

"Do you know what today is, Victor?" Paul said. It was a Monday night. He lay naked on their mattress, his hands clasped behind his head, gazing up at the eight-foot bedposts. They spiraled like the Bernini columns of the baldacchino in St. Peter's Basilica. The custom-made bed had recently arrived from Munich, along with a massive wardrobe and matching chests of drawers made of walnut from the Black Forest.

"Of course I know. Your anniversary." Victor grinned and nosed Paul's crotch. Paul's penis remained half engorged after their lovemaking. It rested against his belly, content and sated, like a drowsy animal that could no longer hold up its head after eating its fill. Victor kissed it.

"One year ago tonight, on the steps of Basilica Julia," Paul said.

"In the rubble of the Roman forum. I never thought anything good would come of that place again. Not after Rome fell to the damned Visigoths." Four hundred years into his nocturnal existence, Victor had watched the Barbarian's fiery raids from the Capitoline Hill above the Forum.

"The moon was full," Paul said wistfully. "It was beautiful. Like a glowing stone. Then I drank from you." He touched Victor's left nipple, the source of the blood that had transformed him. The tender brown flesh lay like an island in a sea of dark hair on Victor's chest.

"Do you have any regrets?"

Paul smiled. A soft stubble covered his cheeks and his hazel eyes looked sleepy still, although he and Victor had climbed up from their dark resting places over an hour ago.

"No more stretching out on the beach with the warmth of the sun on your skin." Victor caressed Paul's smooth chest.

"Like there are beaches in Kansas," Paul said.

"Well, picnics then. With . . . your family."

Victor could not bring himself to say the names of Paul's

mother, sister, and brother, typical representatives of the shabby American working class. It amused him that an artist of Paul's sensibilities could emerge from such an unpolished family.

"I miss them," Paul said. "It's been two years since I've seen them."

Victor shrugged. He got up, pulled a purple silk shirt from the wardrobe, and started dressing on the white bearskin rug next to the bed. "We've been abroad. They know we've been busy opening a club. They also know my sad, sad skin disease forces me to have a nocturnal schedule, and that I need you to run things during the day."

"Will I ever see Kansas again?"

"Who's stopping you?"

"Kansas by night. There's a beautiful thought." Paul quietly watched him dress. "What about the letters, Victor?"

"What about them?" Victor turned back the cuffs of his shirt.

"They keep coming." Paul picked up a folded sheet of parchment paper from the nightstand. "This one came in the mail yesterday. No return address, of course."

"So what? Ignore it, like all the rest."

"They all say the same thing. I practically have the words memorized." Paul unfolded the letter and tossed it on the sheet.

"Exactly."

"What can these people do to us?" Paul drew up his lanky legs against his chest. His body was livid against the wine sheets and dark headboard.

"Nothing." Victor combed his thick black mane without the

benefit of the cheval mirror in the corner, a gift from the well-meaning furniture maker for the large order. He had not produced a reflection in two millennia.

"You don't know that."

"No, I know nothing of penalties for broken rules. I don't know what the Dark Kingdom can or cannot do to vampires who threaten the goddamned eternal order. If such an order exists."

"The Dark Kingdom is a realm created by the forces of the universe as an alternative heaven for vampires." Paul assumed a formal British accent as he recited the words from heart. "On earth vampires are not allowed to associate because to do so would concentrate their destructive power. The reward for a solitary earthly existence of not less than two hundred years is an eternity of bliss."

"Sensual bliss," Victor corrected him.

"Yes." Paul continued the recitation. "An eternity of sensual bliss. Upon creating his replacement, a vampire must immediately enter the Dark Kingdom. Violations of this law are not permitted. Violations will be corrected."

"How many times have you read that tripe?"

"The letters keep coming. In the mail. Under the front door. Even e-mail."

Victor laughed. The fussy letters reminded him of something a school librarian would send to students with overdue books. He had no idea what agency of the Dark Kingdom dispersed the typed boilerplate, but he imagined an office of ineffectual bureaucrats wringing their hands over Paul and him.

"You think it's funny. But there must be some reason you've never encountered a vampire couple."

That thought had often come to Victor since the letters started, and it always sobered him. What had happened to those who violated the rules? "We have our own territories," he said. "We're loners by nature. I just happened to fall in love."

"And no vampire before you ever fell in love?"

Victor glared at Paul. And he could see that Paul knew why. Anger flashed in his eyes.

"I know. All right?" Paul said. "If someone falls in love, he makes the big sacrifice. Two hundred years of separation from the man who transformed him. And I'm too fucking weak to be away from you that long."

Victor couldn't bring himself to make his own admission: he could not stand the risk of losing Paul to some new love during the two-hundred-year absence. No law said that Paul would have to join him in the Dark Kingdom after the required period on earth, and he might just decline to do it if a replacement came along.

"To hell with their rules." Victor ran his fingers through Paul's long sandy hair. "What can they do to us?"

Victor left Paul to his painting and exited the house through the front door, climbing down the iron steps to the sidewalk. Up and down the lamplit street stood three-story Victorian row houses with dormers, bay windows, and turrets. A few less ornate houses from the Federal period punctuated the rows of painted brick, and an occasional columned mansion—heavily landscaped with wisteria, oaks, and magnolias—claimed large corner lots. Directly across the street was a brownstone apartment building covered in ivy, many of the windows glowing.

Next door to the townhouse, separated from it by a gated mews, Dies Irae loomed like a Gothic fortress among the charming residences. Giant towers with battlements flanked the stone façade, which rose to a lofty peak. The hefty oak doors were miter-shaped, as were the stained windows, including an enormous one in the center of the façade. Prickly shrubs skirted the building behind an iron fence with arrowlike palings—as if the foreboding walls of stone were not enough to discourage intruders. To the right of the Gothic structure, also separated from it by a gated mews, stood the townhouse designated for Dies Irae's guests, with its steep, peaked roof.

Victor entered Dies Irae through the door in the left-hand tower. The square room inside served as a vestibule. Glowing candles in iron stands flanked the archway that opened into the central building, but the beams of the soaring ceiling were barely visible. From inside the club, a piped recording of Gregorian chant swelled. Then one voice screeched above the sweet tenors, accompanied by a frantic electric guitar and throbbing bass: *You want it, don't you? But you'll pay a price. Can you pay it? Fuck! You've got to pay it.* Victor passed beneath the arch.

Lurid in the glare of torches along the walls, the expansive stone space before him was webbed in oak dark with age. Oak columns supporting oak arches divided the nave into three unequal sections, the middle section taking up two-thirds of the space, the side sections forming aisles. The columns traveled up the wall to the roof where they met beams, connecting in the center of the pitched vault. Oak trim formed geometric designs on the vault and within the apex of each ceiling arch.

The long nave was divided into three seating areas. Near the entrance on the left side of the nave was a bar. High shelves behind it held liquor bottles and full wine racks. Arranged near it were a dozen heavy mahogany tables with high-backed chairs upholstered in scarlet damask. On the opposite side of the nave was another seating area arranged with horsehair sofas, overstuffed armchairs, and game tables draped in indigo velvet. Some fifty yards away, in the front of the nave near the apse, was a dining area with tables and chairs like those near the bar. They were arranged around a stage at the base of the high altar.

In the very center of the nave, glowing under a massive iron candelabra that hung from a beam, a grim fountain gushed. Rising from the center of the fountain was a painted statue of St. Sebastian, lashed to a pillar, his hands tied above his head. His handsome face was turned to heaven, as if he bravely offered his soul to Joshu's God. He wore only a loincloth. Arrows pierced his white chest and belly and thighs. Water tinted to look like blood streamed from his wounds into a pool, where a stone nymph knelt in naked adoration before him, her head tilted back as she drank from one of the bloody streams.

Through the haze of incense, a reredos, riddled with niches of plaster statues, rose in the distant apse. A hundred candles glowed on the reredos. Lighting them required a lengthy ritual on ladders each evening. At the pinnacle hung a life-size crucifix, the corpus naked and bleeding, the genitals exposed, the face grimacing in pain. The crucifix was a declaration to Joshu: I can take any memory of you now because there is no blood in it. It is only dust.

Victor approached the bar, where a pair of bare-chested men necked. He made a little small talk with them while he admired the stocky new bartender, dressed in a monk's robe—the Dies Irae uniform. He also greeted two newly referred heterosexual couples gathered around a Ouija board in the seating area across the nave. Then he traveled up the nave to greet two more such couples dining at the base of the high altar. Both of the women wore bright, jeweled necklaces instead of tops, and their full breasts glittered. The smell of the braised lamb sitting before them gagged Victor—most cooking odors did before he fed—and he excused himself, retreating once again to the vestibule where he ascended the staircase that led to his office in the church's choir loft.

He sat in the leather desk chair, where he could peer through the wall of glass he had installed to separate the loft from the church below. It was one-way, the reverse side like a black sheet to guests gazing up. From their niches in the high altar, the plaster saints—all painted scarlet—stood at attention before him. The crucified Joshu awaited his cruel pleasures.

25

Checking his e-mail on his desk computer, he found several messages from people on the East Coast who'd heard about Dies Irae from friends and wanted to make reservations. A woman from New Jersey described her favorite sex acts in graphic detail. One routine involved a dog. Victor could see the woman was eager to shock. He deleted the note. He also found the usual spam from dealers in S and M and occult products. They'd been given his address by guests who wanted their favorite toys in the club's stock. Victor quickly browsed through the catalogs.

He was scrolling through some accounts when the club manager, Mark Seepay, showed up for the usual nightly meeting to discuss staff, supplies, and guests.

"The woman we were expecting got in tonight from Europe," Mark said, standing near an armchair facing the desk. He was Asian, in his late twenties, with high cheekbones and a bright, confident gaze. His monk's robe, opened in a V over his smooth chest, accentuated his broad sloping shoulders. Victor had lured him from his night manager position at the Washington Hotel. He was quite competent, but malleable.

"A single woman?" Victor looked up from the account on the screen. Individual guests were rare at Dies Irae, self-sufficient orgy groups being the norm. No single woman had ever walked through the doors.

Mark nodded. "I had Horatio put her in the smallest room on the top floor." Horatio Adams managed the guest rooms.

"And what did she list as her vice?"

Mark smiled. A trio of studs gleamed in both of his ears. "She gets off on playing goddess or something. Whipping men. Making them beg to fuck her."

Victor liked the picture he was getting. He liked the prospect of turning a goddess into his slave.

"Her name's Sonia Mesjke. She's originally from Eastern Europe. Romania, I think. But she said she's lived in Rome most of her life. Her voice gave me the chills. Maybe it was the accent."

"Remind me how long she's staying."

"She said she'll be in Washington indefinitely. Wanted to stay here as long as she could. I told her we have a one-week limit, so she reserved the room for a week. Said she'd make other arrangements for the rest of the time."

"Fine." Victor had little interest in the whims of eccentric world travelers—beyond the amusement they provided for him and the variety they brought to his feedings.

"And we're all set for tonight's performance. The stage is—" Mark hesitated. "Shit."

Victor looked up and followed Mark's gaze to the window. Downstairs, a man in a Roman collar and clerical shirt stood in the center of the nave staring at the two amorous men at the bar. He was husky, with a dark beard and long hair pulled back into a ponytail. Next to him stood an athletic young man of twenty-five or so, with a shock of blond hair. He also wore a Roman collar.

"I told him to stay the fuck away," Mark said, "two times now."

"Who is it?"

"Some Jesuit priest and his assistant. He says he has to talk to the owner of the club. He sounds pretty uptight and preachy. I told him this is a private residence and he's trespassing. He dared me to call the police on him. Maybe we should."

Victor continued to watch the pair. Clearly uncomfortable, the young priest glanced around the club. A woman in a low-cut dress and a bustier waved to him from the Ouija table, and he averted his eyes. "What's the name of his church?"

"Saint Ignatius."

"Of course," Victor said, guessing that the church was named after the founder of the Jesuits, St. Ignatius of Loyola—a self-tortured soldier turned priest. Victor had endured recitations from the saint's writings during many a monastic meal.

Victor typed in "St. Ignatius Church" and the location on the Google site and the church's Web page popped up. The church was located just off Rhode Island Avenue in northeast Washington. The Web page indicated that Father Albert Gimello was the pastor and Father Kyle Durham the associate. Kyle—what a sweet name. Victor glanced up at Seepay and said, "Send them up."

The employee disappeared without another word.

Victor got up and watched Seepay lead the pair of priests toward the vestibule. He stepped away from the window and sat in the center of a sectional leather sofa in the corner, his arms stretched along the back, his legs crossed. When Mark appeared at the door, Victor nodded to him by way of dismissal. Mark exited and the two priests stepped in.

"What can I do for you, Father Gimello?" Victor said. He

brazenly admired Kyle, taking in the high, bubblelike pectoral muscles beneath his black shirt and the muscular thighs typical of soccer players.

Gimello noted Victor's interest and smiled scornfully.

The older priest's dark, rough looks were not unappealing to Victor, but his self-righteous intensity destroyed any potential attractiveness he might have had.

"So," Gimello said, "you already know all about us? And we don't even know your name."

"What do you want?"

"May we?" Gimello gestured toward a pair of high-backed chairs with tapestry seats resting along the wall. He and Kyle positioned them across from Victor and sat down. He turned to Kyle. "Go ahead, Father Durham. Explain."

Though nervous, the young priest seemed prepared for the question. He cleared his throat and turned his gray eyes on Victor. "The Jesuits built this church," he said.

"I'm aware of that," Victor said, amused by Durham's earnestness.

"It's still sacred ground, with a history sacred to the order and to the church. And this was once a consecrated building. It still is, technically, since there's no way to revoke such a blessing." Durham spoke as though he'd rehearsed the presentation of grievances. "Some believe there's a forgotten relic of Saint Ignatius in the high altar." He nodded toward the window.

"You want it back?" Victor said. "Is that what you're here to tell me?"

Gimello suddenly noticed a sculpture of three nude male figures on a pedestal against the back wall. The center figure
stretched his arms in delight while a kneeling figure performed
fellatio on him and a figure behind him bit into his throat. Dis-
gusted, the priest leaned forward in his chair, his hands on his
knees. "What we want, sir, is an end to the defilement of hallowed
ground. Christ himself was present in that altar for two centuries.
The holy sacrifice of the Mass was offered daily in that sanctuary.
Your desecration of this place is like a sword in the heart of the
Blessed Virgin, the Mother of God."

"I doubt she much cares. Virgin or not."

As though to keep calm, Gimello studied his young assistant
for a moment, then turned back to Victor. "Will you, for the love
of God, stop what you're doing here?"

"What is it I'm doing?" Victor said. When Gimello began to
answer, Victor raised his hand. "Let Father Durham tell me. What
is it that we do here, Father?"

The young priest furrowed his brow, sweetly, Victor thought,
like a toddler grappling with a matter over his head. His small
features, white-blond hair, and clear complexion expressed the
sort of masculine innocence Victor had encountered over the
years in athletic novices not prone to introspection. "People have
unlawful sex on the property," he finally said.

"Really?" Victor said, "What makes you think so?"

"You think the neighborhood doesn't know what's going on
here?" Gimello blurted. "The kind of people who come and go?
Sounds that come from this place? And we can see for ourselves

the defilement down there." Gimello pointed toward the crucifix on the high altar. "You crucify Christ again, each and every day."

"Fuck you and your Christ."

Father Kyle shifted uncomfortably, but Gimello calmly scrutinized Victor. "You seem to have something personal against Christ," he said. "I can assure you, Christ never rejects those who come to him. He offers freedom to the pure of heart."

Victor's blood pounded in his temples, as it did whenever he heard the Joshu he knew turned into a great icy god. In his unrelenting memory, he still smelled Joshu's perspiration and musky flesh. He still saw the mischievous gleam in Joshu's sensuous eyes and the savage grace of Joshu's sinewy limbs as he danced naked on the cliffs above Jerusalem the day Victor first spied him. But what did he care? Bent on a mission to rattle worldly institutions, Joshu had succumbed to them. He'd become the figurehead on a ship called the Holy Apostolic Church.

"I hear Christ was hung like a bull," Victor said.

Gimello grinned defiantly, refusing to be scandalized. "He'll win you over yet. Maybe that's what you want. Maybe that's why you've got his image displayed down there."

Victor's impulse was to clutch Gimello by the throat and crush his larynx. Instead, he chuckled. "You know, you've got quite a bit of nerve, Father. Barging into a private residence. Demanding to see the owner, as though he owes you something. Now that you've done your priestly duty, I don't expect to see you around here anymore."

As he stood to signal the end of the interview, a heavy beat began pulsing through the sound system, followed by the screech of a steel guitar. In the church, red lasers flashed to the rhythm.

Beams strobed on the stage below, where two men dressed as monks carried out an altar. Then two bare-chested body builders dragged out a college-age boy wearing only a black thong over his crotch and long black gloves. His hair was bleached and spiked. His eyes were lined in black.

The priests stood, their attention on the stage, where the muscle men now grabbed the boy's arms and stretched him against the altar, while the monks took turns whipping his torso with cords. Red gashes soon streaked his chalky flesh. Over the throbbing electric bass, a voice screeched. *You want it, don't you? But you'll pay a price. Can you pay it? Fuck! You've got to pay it.* Bright beams continued to strobe on the stage.

His eyes riveted on the scene, young Durham froze in place. Gimello watched him with a righteous expression, as though he were thinking, *See for yourself how depraved this place is. Take it all in.*

On the stage, the muscle men hoisted the bleeding boy onto the altar. They stripped off his thong, caressed his crotch, and then wrapped a cord tourniquet-style around his now-erect penis. As their heads rhythmically bobbed above the victim's crotch, the monks circled the altar, swinging censers. Smoke swirled above them. The pace of the fellatio sped up as the music crescendoed. The monks stopped, made the sign of the cross, and raised their hands as though they were offering a sacrifice. As the boy shuddered in orgasm, one of the muscle men drew a knife from his belt and plunged it into the boy's throat. The stage went dark.

Gimello stood still as a rock, but Durham recoiled, his face pale.

As the applause of a dozen people pattered through the chamber, a floodlight washed over the stage. The victim, his throat intact, struggled to his feet. His erection persisted, despite his obvious weakness, the muscle men at his side to steady him. The whole troupe of performers bowed, and the light once again vanished.

Gimello glared at Victor. Without uttering a word, he signaled to Durham to follow him out of the office. Still pale, Durham hesitated a moment at the door and cast a troubled glance at Victor before exiting.

When Victor came back from feeding at four in the morning, Mark was waiting for him outside his office. He was pale and excited.

"What's wrong?" Victor said.

"Someone's dead."

"One of the guests?" Victor assumed that a sex game had gone too far.

Mark shook his head. "I've never seen her before. She's in the basement."

Victor followed Mark to one of the playrooms beneath the church. A naked woman with curly blond hair lay on the floor, her flesh livid. Victor stooped to inspect the double puncture marks on her throat. For a moment he thought that Paul had foolishly brought a victim here and once again lost control. He changed his mind when he noticed words scrawled in red across the wall. DIES IRAE!

3

Paul stretched his legs on the emerald green sofa, a sketch pad on his lap. A breeze through the studio windows carried the scent of rain. A late summer storm was brewing. But Paul was lost in his sketch, unaware of the rumbling thunder.

The sketch was of Alice, his mother. He planned to turn it into a watercolor and send it to her for Christmas.

The sketch captured the sharpness of her eyes, the strength of her square jaw, and her intelligent brow under short, wavy gray hair. Her face glowed with the health that Victor had infused into her during her visit to Rome the year before, dribbling his blood into her mouth when she collapsed with a heart attack. But something essential was missing. Maybe her crusty sense of humor. Or maybe her trusting affection. Maybe he had reproduced the fear he imagined she would feel in his presence.

Fear also marred the eyes of the people in the paintings on the walls. Above the mantle, a little boy on a swing cast a troubled, sidelong glance at the viewer. Paul had stolen into the boy's room one night through an unlocked window. He had painted the boy from memory, posing him on a swing, only imagining his opened eyes. And what he imagined in the boy's sidelong glance was dread.

The same dread appeared in the eyes of the other subjects hanging on the walls: an old woman peering from her front window, a man with a tattooed neck sitting at an outdoor café, a male model bleeding on a sheet after a sex game. Even the abstract characters in one painting, aswirl in blues and reds as they gyrated on a dance floor, moved from fear rather than pleasure.

Agitated, Paul laid the sketch pad on the marble tabletop near the sofa. He got up and walked to the window, peering out at the lightning high above the brownstone across the street.

The warm, humid air felt good on his cool face and hands—his body temperature never climbed above ninety degrees. He closed his eyes and pretended he was basking in the sun's rays again.

An explosion of thunder rattled the windows. Suddenly, he felt someone's presence behind him. His fangs grew slightly as they did whenever he felt threatened.

"Are you Paul?" a woman with a thick foreign accent said.

Paul turned to find a stunning woman of thirty-five or forty standing at the studio door. She had an ivory complexion and raven hair pulled back into a single braid. Her almond-shaped eyes were dark as licorice and fringed with long lashes. Her face, sprinkled with freckles, was broad, with high cheekbones and a strong mouth. Her expression and erect posture gave her a self-possessed, even regal air. A simple black tunic draped the curves of her full figure. Lapis stones adorned her neck, wrist, and fingers.

"This is a private residence," Paul said. "How did you get in?" He was amazed he hadn't heard the woman climb the stairs. He could detect the sound of a mouse behind a wall on the first floor. Of course, when he was lost in thought, noises fell into a murky distance.

The woman smiled serenely, exposing neat white teeth. "I'm so sorry. The door was open downstairs. I thought this was the guest house." Her voice was deep for a woman, her pronunciation deliberate, as though to compensate for the accent, which seemed Eastern European. "My name is Sonia Mesjke." She approached Paul and extended her pale, freckled hand.

The hand felt cool, even to Paul. "Oh, you're the guest from Italy. You don't sound Italian."

"I moved to Rome from Romania many years ago."

"When Ceausescu was in power?" Paul remembered reading something about the tyrant's bloody police state in the 1980s.

Sonia smiled sadly, as though the subject was an unpleasant one. Paul did not pursue it. "How did you find out about Dies Irae?"

Sonia laughed. "How does anyone? As they say, word travels. Especially among people who seek stimulating amusement in a very unimaginative world. I enjoy mastering men. Perhaps you enjoyed being mastered."

Paul laughed at her boldness. "Who knows?"

No doubt Victor would enjoy the prospect of forcing the dominatrix to submit, so odds were high that the three of them would end up in bed. Before his transformation, just the thought of Victor fucking someone else would have set him off. But now their bond could never be threatened by relationships with humans—as long as they remained humans. If Victor ever tired of him, if he ever wanted to create another mate . . . but Paul never gave that possibility serious thought.

Sonia studied him, as though she could read his thoughts. "Do you have a cigarette?" She glanced at a half-full ashtray on the coffee table.

Paul had started smoking after his transformation. As a mortal, he'd smoked only grass from time to time to get in a painting mood. Now he figured what the hell. It wasn't like he'd get emphysema or lung cancer.

Paul pulled two cigarettes from the pack in his breast pocket. As he lit hers, Sonia gazed into his eyes unabashedly.

"These are very intriguing," she said, glancing around at the paintings. "You painted them all, didn't you? I noticed the easel." She nodded toward the easel and paints in the corner of the room.

"Yes."

Paul watched with apprehension as she approached the painting of the little boy. No one but Victor had seen the paintings. And Victor swore that Paul only imagined the fear in the faces.

"This child has known some pain, I think."

"Pain?" Paul said.

Sonia exhaled a stream of smoke. "He wants something he can't have. He wants to feel power." Sonia cast him a kind glance. "That's how I interpret it. Of course, I've known children like that. Gypsies in Romania. Refugees in Rome, from Albania. There is so much pain in the world."

Paul wondered if Sonia's family had suffered under Ceausescu. She spoke and carried herself like an aristocrat. Maybe her parents had fled the Communist regime, managing to protect their wealth in Italy. She had to be rich to jet to S and M clubs around the world.

As Sonia inspected the paintings, she nodded in admiration. "You're not from this part of the country, are you?" she said.

Why did Paul feel that she already knew the answer? She seemed to take in everything about him, everything about the room. Of course, the guests who found their way to Dies Irae were not run-of-the-mill eccentrics. They rigorously scoped out places before traveling to them, networking among themselves about tolerance levels for drugs, prostitution, and their most dangerous games. No one had died yet at Dies Irae, but one woman had come close. She liked to be choked as she reached orgasm. Victor had nearly asphyxiated her.

"No. I'm from the Midwest. Kansas." Paul felt the familiar reticence to discuss his blue-collar family with sophisticates who might look down on them.

Sonia didn't pursue the subject. She made small talk about the beautiful monuments she'd seen on descending into Washington and on Georgetown's charm. Then she remarked on the unusual

location Victor had chosen for his club. "A church. Very original!"
She stubbed out her cigarette in the ashtray.

Paul shrugged. "Victor used to be a monk. He hates the fucking church now. The location's his way of getting back at it." This
was no secret. Victor liked to shock his guests with the revela-
tion. What did he have to worry about? Victor had left San
Benedetto intact—all the monks safe and sound inside the
walls—unlike monasteries where he'd caused mayhem before
departing.

"What a coincidence," Sonia said. "I was once a nun."

"You?" Paul was surprised.

"It is true. I entered a convent in Rome when I was just a girl.
My father wanted me to marry a fat Romanian from an old family. The convent in the Apennines was my means of escape. I
learned surprising practices living among those nuns."

"Like what?"

"Beautiful rituals of the black arts. Titillating forms of sexual
torture. You might think that strange. But the Roman church is
full of sadomasochism. What else makes people line up to eat
someone's body and drink his blood?"

Paul smiled.

"And I have seen many churches in Bucharest and Rome with
gruesome statues of naked, bleeding Christs. Pleasure in pain is
primal, I think. The Roman church has tapped this primal urge.
Saints who scourged themselves. Martyrs who embraced tortur-
ous deaths. The pious people kiss holy cards with these images.
They deprive themselves of food. Beat themselves."

"But they do it because they're sinners, don't they? They want to punish themselves."

Sonia laughed. "That's what they say."

Paul liked the new guest. She showed no hint of the vague intimidation that vampires unconsciously provoked in most people.

Sonia touched Paul's arm. "Perhaps you would be willing to paint my portrait while I'm here? If your schedule permits. I'm very curious to see how you would render my image."

The request caught Paul off guard. His fear of exposure suddenly flared again. "I'm sorry," he said awkwardly. "I make it a policy not to paint our guests."

"I quite understand."

Did he detect a strange hint of triumph in Sonia's smile—as though she knew she had touched a nerve? Paul shook off the impression as paranoia. How could she know his reasons for concern? And why would she wish him discomfort?

"Let me show you to the guest house," he said with a graciousness intended to compensate for the awkward refusal.

"How kind of you."

Their conversation was pleasant as they made their way to the guest house. After Paul showed Sonia around and led her to her room, he slipped into a hooded windbreaker and set out in the rain to feed. It was early, but hunger gnawed at him. He usually waited until after midnight, when most people were in bed and he could enter houses with little trouble. Public places were too dangerous, and if anyone came upon him while he fed, he would have to attack.

On P Street two streetlamps were out. The houses near them, shrouded in oak foliage, showed no sign of activity inside although their porch lights burned. Row houses lined one side of the street. On the opposite side rose two large brick mansions with mansard roofs and shuttered windows. As Paul approached the first mansion, he inhaled the strong scent of blood. The house contained at least three people. Bars protected all the dark windows on the front side, but maybe the owners weren't so careful in back. With his new strength, bars gave way easily, but why add an unnecessary obstacle?

He eased open the iron gate and followed a stone walk to the rear of the house. He found a garden lush with shrubs, hostas, and vines trained on trellises. In the center of the yard, a flock of yellow and red mums crowded around a birdbath. Two large magnolias hid the yard from the neighboring homes. From the edge of the yard, he could make out the windows above a screened porch. A chandelier glowed in what was apparently a hallway window, the only window without bars. With little exertion, he sprang to the roof of the porch. The leap tickled Paul's testicles the way bouncing on a trampoline had in his high school gym. He glanced around, confirming that the magnolias protected him from view, and tried the window. It was locked, but with a quick, powerful jerk he had practiced now on many bolts, he quietly broke the latch and slipped through the window, throwing off his hood and wiping his wet face with his hands.

Pseudo-Impressionist paintings in heavy, ornate frames hung on the hallway walls between four doors. An oriental runner padded his footsteps as he approached the first door, partially ajar, on the right. A metallic scent wafted from the room. The door creaked as he entered. Someone stirred in a canopied bed. He froze until the occupant settled again. Softly moving through the dark room, he discerned the face of an old woman on the pillow. Her scalp was visible through her thin, white hair.

When he clamped his hand over her mouth, her eyes flashed open and she moaned, tugging at his hand. But the moment he sank his fangs into the loose, doughy skin of her throat she stopped, paralyzed by his will. Her blood was laced with medication from the brown prescription bottles on her bedside. The taste was bitter, but Paul was used to all kinds of pollutants now—drugs, nicotine, liquor, even cancer, which gave blood a charred taste. After siphoning two ounces of blood, he withdrew from her throat without trouble, licking the wound clean. The fang marks would remain, to be explained away by the old woman's son or daughter with a hypothesis about a broach prick or bee sting.

He exited by the back window, closing it behind him. At the front gate of the house, pain suddenly shot through his chest and arms. He couldn't take another step. Was he having a heart attack? Can vampires have heart attacks? His throat constricted as though someone clutched it, but he could not raise his hands to pry away the invisible grip. He grunted, willing himself to be free from the force, fighting to breathe. But it persisted, ratcheting Paul's panic so much that he tried unsuccessfully to yell for help, as if any human could save his life. Suddenly the pressure on his throat subsided. His limbs thawed.

He glanced up and down the wet street. There was no sign of anyone. Not even a single car passed by. Still, he felt that the invisible attacker was watching him—maybe from one of the dark windows across the street. Rattled, he set off down the dark sidewalk.

Outside the club, he lit a cigarette to calm himself. What had happened to him? First the out-of-body experience and the voices. Now this even more frightening kind of seizure. Were these the work of the Dark Kingdom? If so, the warnings he and Victor had received were not so laughable. Maybe the Dark Kingdom could kill transgressors.

He stared up at the gothic façade of Dies Irae. Why did Victor need this? Why couldn't they go off somewhere by themselves, away from mobs of people who could cause them trouble? Someplace off the radar of the Dark Kingdom. He focused his thoughts on Victor's handsome face—the intense eyes, black as gunmetal, the aquiline nose and full lips, the square jaw, shadowed in blue-black beard. Silently, he breathed Victor's name.

Within minutes, Victor joined him on the sidewalk. He wore a black leather jacket, jeans, and square-toed boots. A tuft of dark hair shot from his white shirt, wide open at the neck. He kissed Paul on the lips.

"What's wrong?" Victor said.

Paul told him about the strange seizure.

"Maybe the epilepsy . . ."

"No," Paul said. "This was different."

"They can't hurt us."

"How do you know that?"

Victor's expression turned grave for a moment. Then, shaking off his apprehension, he kissed Paul again. "Come on." He took Paul by the hand and led him to the guest house.

"It's too early," Paul said.

Victor flashed him a mischievous glance. "Horatio's in there with a horny young priest."

Victor had lured Horatio, a bleached-blond bodybuilder, away from a New York club where he worked as a go-go boy, gyrating on bartops in an adorable pink jockstrap. Under Victor's training, the dancer had proven to be a competent manager of the guest house. Not that his duties required much expertise. They mostly involved housekeeping, as well as being attentive to guests—bestowing sexual favors if they required them. Horatio was always happy to oblige.

"A priest?"

"The one who came with the lunatic Jesuit. The young soccer stud. At least he looks like a soccer stud. Apparently, he's changed his sanctimonious tune. I've seen him twice downstairs and so has Horatio. I saw them disappear together about half an hour ago."

They climbed the black iron steps of the row house where Dies Irae's guests stayed. Inside, the foyer was cavelike. Polished slate gleamed on the floor. Black walls rose twelve feet to meet dark beams and exposed timbers. The right wall extended past a staircase and down a long hallway that opened into the interior rooms. On the wall hung large photographs of naked, entwined figures—men with men and men with women. Track lighting shone on the bodies, stark white against black backdrops. Bloody stripes crisscrossed the backs of the models. Blood dripped from their groins and buttocks.

The row house had ten guest suites. The only one on the first floor was just off the foyer at the front of the house, next to a large sitting room, which in turn was next to a kitchen at the back of the house, well stocked with coffee and breakfast things that late-rising guests rarely availed themselves of before noon. The second and third floors each had four guest rooms arranged in a row off a long hallway. A tenth guest room was at the front of the English basement, across from Horatio's own room. Storage and laundry rooms were in the rear of the basement.

Paul followed Victor past the foyer staircase into the large sitting room, softly glowing in lamplight. Wallpaper with a leopard skin print wrapped the room. Matching upholstery covered the chaise lounge, sofa, and chairs. White furry rugs covered the dark marble floors. Candles glowed on the mantel, but there was no one in the room.

"They're in his room," Victor said.

Paul followed him down the steps near the kitchen and down the narrow hallway to Horatio's room. Without knocking, Victor opened the door, and they both stepped in.

Horatio's buttocks greeted them. The bleached-blond body builder knelt in the king-sized bed, the young priest's feet on his shoulders. When the door opened, he stopped thrusting and glanced back.

"Very nice," Victor said.

"Jesus!" The pair of feet slipped off Horatio's shoulders.

Horatio turned himself around. Two erections pointed at Victor and Paul in the midst of a large quantity of muscular flesh. The priest reached for the sheets.

Victor signaled Paul with a glance. They approached either side of the bed, Victor on the side of the priest. A look of frightened excitement spread over Horatio's face when he saw their fangs descend. He was used to Victor's games. The priest, his hair tousled, his chest still heaving, looked confused. Victor pounced on him, sinking his fangs into his throat. Smiling, Horatio watched, then laid back for Paul. His heart pounding, Paul nuzzled Horatio's throat, piercing the jugular. He had to muster every ounce of determination to pull himself away. Victor needed to feed on both men. If Paul drank, too, Horatio couldn't survive.

Paralyzed by the sting, Horatio's arms fell to his side, his lifeless blue eyes gazing at the ceiling. Paul assumed victims entered a state of complete unconsciousness once they'd submitted to his will, but he liked to think they experienced some vague pleasure in letting him feed. He liked to think it gave them the warm, comfortable feel of fellatio, or the feel a mother must have as her child suckled at her breast.

As he watched Victor feed on the handsome priest, caressing his damp, matted chest hair, he felt the usual twinge of jealousy. He'd had plenty of practice dismissing the feeling, but this time he found himself exerting more than the usual effort. Perhaps his own strong attraction to the stranger made him exaggerate Victor's. The thought reassured him and he finally shook off the unpleasant feeling and watched Victor feed.

The two healthy victims withstood more than the usual loss of blood, satisfying Victor's needs for the night. So the vampires left the naked men on the mattress, and set out for a walk. Clouds cleared and a moon emerged, full and white. At one in the morning, it had reached its zenith, where the sun reigned at noon.

They climbed up steep R Street to Oak Hill Cemetery, springing over the tall iron gates. Holly trees, oaks, and evergreens grew throughout the exclusive burial grounds. Obelisks, angels, and stone benches marked the well-maintained graves of prominent families. They strolled along a stone walk, breathing in the earthy scent of death that still took Paul by surprise.

They descended to the dark path along Rock Creek, used by joggers and bicyclists during the daylight hours. Recent rains had filled the creek, and it rushed noisily by them over its stony bed.

Paul took Victor's hand and listened to him talk about Washington politics, which Victor followed with amusement. Victor derided the inept president for his handling of the Iraq occupation. He suggested they slip into the White House and drain the man's blood.

"I guess the office of president doesn't impress you much."

"I've fed on the caesars, for god's sake," he said. "Why should I revere the puny president of an infant republic?"

Paul stared at the rushing water, uninterested in the topic.

"We'll be all right," Victor said, squeezing Paul's hand.

"They were trying to kill me," Paul said.

"They can't kill you. This is just a scare tactic."

"It's working."

"What do you propose we do?"

"Get out of here," Paul said. He lit a cigarette and flicked the match away, suddenly angry. "They never bothered us until you desecrated a church and advertised online to the world."

"You think I've offended their religious sensibilities?" Victor snapped.

"I don't know." Paul knew how ridiculous he sounded. "Why are you obsessed with this Catholic shit? I thought you left the monastery behind. I thought you left Joshu behind."

"The club amuses me."

"Yes, I know. Anything for your amusement."

"There's a solution."

Paul got hold of himself at this allusion to the one unthinkable way to ward off all threats: relinquish Victor to the Dark Kingdom for two hundred long years before finally joining him there. "No. It just shook me up. I'll be all right."

When he took hold of Victor's hand again, he reminded himself of Victor's vast experience of the world, his vast power to thrive in age after age of human history. With Victor he could fight whatever the hell dark powers ruled their universe. The pair of them were fucking caped crusaders—with the world at their feet.

The feeling of invincibility lingered as they made their way home and climbed into bed. Paul lay back and let Victor's mouth travel over his belly and chest. He writhed in pleasure with Victor inside him. Each thrust felt like a pledge of eternal defiance together.

As they lay in each other's arms, Paul mentioned the interview with Sonia.

"What did you think of her?" Victor asked, kissing Paul's hand.

"I liked her. Believe it or not, she used to be a nun. A first for Dies Irae."

"She's a vampire."

"What?" Paul thought he'd misunderstood.

"She's a vampire," Victor repeated.

"What do you mean?"

Victor clasped his hands behind his head and stared up at the ceiling. "I mean, I don't believe our new dominatrix will submit to me. She's one of us. Apparently she's decided to break the rules, too. The rules against association. Didn't you sense anything unusual about her?"

Paul reflected on Sonia's perceptiveness, her unusual ease in the presence of a vampire. He lay back on the pillow, trying to absorb the idea of being with others like them. "It's good news then. We don't have a thing to be worried about. Others break the rules and survive."

Victor said nothing.

"You're not happy about having her here."

"Why should I be happy?" Victor said. "This is our territory. We don't need competition. Or complications."

"How did you find out about her? Did she tell you?"

"She dragged one of her victims into the club. I had to dispose of the body. My first thought was that you'd lost control and dragged your prey here. But then I saw the calling card she'd left." Victor described the bloody message on the basement wall. "Then I knew it was a declaration of power. Like an animal marking territory."

"Jesus." Paul sat up in bed. "What did you say to her?"

"Nothing. She'd already gone to her resting place. Wherever that is. She must have returned there after your little conversation with her tonight."

"Why did she bring the victim here? What if she left a trail?"

"Exactly," Victor said, hostility in his eyes. "You're starting to understand."

4

Victor knocked on Sonia's door. But there was no answer. He didn't have his keys with him and had no desire to force the door to inspect the room. Why damage his own property? He found Horatio in the basement laundry room, scrubbing something in the utility sink under glaring fluorescent lights. His eyes still sensitive, Victor flicked off one of the lights. Horatio was used to this. He glanced up and then went back to his work. Victor slipped his hand into Horatio's pocket and pulled out a ring of keys. He noticed bloody towels in the sink.

"Whose are those?"

"The hairy fucker who got here yesterday. He likes to slice himself with a knife while a chick goes down on him. He told me all the gory details."

"Which key opens Sonia Mesjke's room?"

Horatio showed him with a wet hand. "She's gone. She went to New York for the weekend."

"That's what she said?"

Horatio nodded. There were dark circles under his eyes, probably from a late night with the young priest.

"Get some sleep, Horatio." Victor patted his firm rump.

He climbed the stairs to the third floor. Sonia's room was the one nearest the staircase at the back of the house. He turned the key in her door and thrust it open. The room held a queen-sized bed, a tall wardrobe, and overstuffed chairs covered in white damask. The chairs were splattered with blood. Victor sniffed it. It wasn't fresh. Earlier guests must have played too hard.

The lamps and a large mirror were shrouded with black scarves. A madras shawl was spread on the bed. A deck of tarot cards lay on the bed table. Victor recognized the ornate fifteenth-century Visconti design from his days in Milan during that period. Of course they were only reproductions, but the date inscribed on one of the yellowed cards was 1879. No doubt Sonia had acquired the deck when it was new. Perhaps she was already a vampire by that year, but perhaps not. Victor had no experience determining the ages of other vampires.

In a jar of fluid on the windowsill floated what appeared to be a human embryo. A rosary was wound around the jar. Near it sat several half-burned candles and a container of incense sticks. Apparently the embryo played a role in an occult ritual that connected Sonia to another dark sphere, though why a vampire needed such communication eluded him.

Sonia's wardrobe held a scarlet caftan, two saris, and several long tunics. The top drawers yielded nothing out of the ordinary—tights, camisoles, shawls. But under the shawls, he found a daguerreotype of Sonia and a young woman in plaid dresses with full skirts. Jaunty feathered hats perched on their curls. Looking exactly as she looked now, Sonia sat, and the young woman, who might have been nineteen or twenty, stood behind her with a gloved hand on her shoulder. Since vampires can't be photographed, Sonia must have become a vampire soon after this picture was taken. Victor had never aged since his transformation at the age of thirty-two, and he assumed that his condition was typical. The young woman in the picture was a stunning beauty, although a large birthmark—like a shadow—covered one full side of her face. Was this Sonia's sister? Or perhaps her lover, now a distant memory?

In the bottom drawer of the wardrobe, Victor found a strange assortment of gaudy necklaces, assorted rings—some with precious stones—a plastic name tag that said MARILYN, a necktie, a broken compact, a baby's bib, a dashboard statue of the Virgin Mary, a pair of cotton panties, and other assorted articles. The necktie, bib, and panties were stained with blood. Clearly, all of the articles served as souvenirs or, more accurately, trophies from Sonia's victims. At least one of the victims had given up her life along with her personal effects. Who knew how many other corpses in Georgetown bore her marks? Marks that could bring trouble to his door.

He pulled aside the heavy drapes and gazed at houses across the alley. Where, he wondered, had she found a resting place? The nearest graveyard, Oak Hill Cemetery, had no mausoleums—which would offer the most convenient refuge from potential intruders. Maybe she'd discovered the mausoleums at Congressional Cemetery or escaped each night to the caverns in the Blue Ridge Mountains, for a vampire a five-minute flight through the night air. She knew where he and Paul rested. This vulnerability had to go two ways.

On Monday night, Victor reviewed receipts for liquor and food, and entered totals on his computer spreadsheet. Most of the monasteries he'd inhabited over the past decade were computerized and he'd quickly picked up the necessary technical skills that would help him manage his bank accounts in Switzerland. His investments from centuries of robbing victims now passed the billion-dollar mark, but he managed money carefully—as his patrician father had taught him to do. He never knew when he might be forced to flee an area for his safety—perhaps when his rashness left a trail of blood for local authorities—and he had to have ready funds to set up house anywhere in the world.

Downstairs, customers sat at the tables around the high altar, watching the torture performance of the muscle men and the college boy. The music shrieked through the torchlit chamber—*You want it, don't you? But you'll pay a price. Can you pay it? Fuck! You've got to pay it.* Two long-haired Australian men—whom he had fed on the night before—left their table and disappeared into a confessional that now served as a sex booth.

In the seating area across from the bar, Sonia sat with Paul at a table. She'd returned from New York at two o'clock that morning. From his bedroom window, Victor had seen her emerging from a taxi. She'd probably taken the rapid train from New York, which left there after ten, well into the safety of night.

Victor watched her with Paul at the table. Despite her sophisticated bearing, her beauty had an earthy quality. Her freckled face and her great round breasts might have belonged to a Romanian peasant. She smiled as Paul explained something with animated gestures, a cigarette in his hand.

Under the power of Sonia's charm, Paul had apparently dismissed his initial concern about her reckless feeding in the club. No doubt she apologized and explained the scene as her bid for drama or mischief making. Paul was too trusting, too happy to discover this vampire underground. He probably took it as proof that the two of them could walk the earth without consequences for their transgression. Victor was not so sure. Authorities, whether human or supernatural, thrived on exercising their power. Joshu's God ruled Joshu's every move in the sphere he occupied—and Joshu's unyielding submission never stopped disgusting Victor. Authorities of the Dark Kingdom had to maintain their own supremacy. How they might exercise power, however, Victor couldn't begin to guess. He doubted their strength, but one never knew. He would like to hear the newcomer's advice, as much as he loathed asking for it.

When the show ended, Victor went down to them.

"What's this?" he said, indicating the glasses they held. Why pretend to drink wine here, something that vampires could not do without vomiting afterward?

Sonia raised her glass to Victor. He inhaled the aroma of blood in it. He sipped it, savoring it before swallowing.

"I collect it," she said. "It is much more convenient this way."

Victor pounded the table with his fist, anger overcoming his intention to solicit Sonia's advice about the Dark Kingdom. "Your convenience is putting us in jeopardy. Why did you bring a victim here?"

Sonia smiled, not the least intimidated. "It was my calling card. Didn't you like the joke? Dies Irae. The young woman's day of judgment had come."

"What do you want here?"

"Please, sit down. I'm happy to tell you everything you want to know."

Without letting down his guard, Victor took a seat.

Torchlight shone on Sonia's face. She seemed to study him with admiration.

Paul reached out for his hand. "Sonia was telling me about her life—the one before this life. She broke the rules, too, with her lover."

"Regina," Sonia said. "A girl I met in the convent."

Victor remembered the woman in the daguerreotype. But her costume had not been that of a nun, and neither had been Sonia's. Sonia quickly cleared up his unspoken confusion.

"We left the convent. We ran off together," she explained. "I eventually made Regina what I was, then refused to leave her. We were like you. Always running."

"And where is Regina now?" Victor said harshly, not liking her comparison.

Sonia shook her head sadly. "The powers claimed her. We couldn't resist them alone."

Victor snorted. Sonia's weakness was evident.

She glared at him. "They can hurt you, you know. The powers of the Dark Kingdom. The letters seem innocuous. But take them seriously."

Paul threw a concerned glance at Victor. "We just got a new letter. It ended with the words 'Final Warning' printed in red." Paul had found the letter that night on his easel.

Sonia eyed him gravely.

"What does it mean?" Paul said.

"That they will now resort to more serious measures."

"I don't believe it," Victor blurted. "How can these powers hurt us?"

Sonia gripped his wrist and whispered, "They can take your lives."

Victor stared at her long and hard, as though her intention was to threaten rather than warn them.

"She can help us, Victor," Paul said.

Sonia nodded. "You can survive if you take certain precautions. All fugitives must learn what to do and what not to do. But you can survive."

"I have no interest in just surviving," Victor said.

Sonia smiled and lit a cigarette. "I'm very happy. I go where I want. I do what I want."

"I repeat, what brings you here?" Victor demanded.

"I heard about your club. I heard about the two of you. I knew the truth. I wanted to help you."

"How many like us are there?" Victor said.

"Thousands. The key to *thriving*—does that word suit you?—is solidarity. Human underdogs have discovered that, haven't they? Gandhi's Indians, King's black Americans, campesinos in South America. It's not just a matter of ideology. There's true power in banding together against the controlling forces. It's the only way."

"I don't like it," Victor said.

"Of course not." Sonia chuckled. "It goes against the grain. When survival in the night has meant trusting no one, living like a lone wolf—I know this well. That is what the powers count on. They think we can't defy them because we don't know how to exist together, to combine our strength."

Victor gazed at her with contempt. "I didn't like dependency *before* my transformation. It's not the way of a Roman officer."

"We are not discussing dependency. We are discussing the power of numbers. We must trust one another. I can assure you. We must. I've seen what happens when violators go their own way." Her solemn eyes filled up. "My own lover did not survive when she left me."

"What happened to her?" Paul said.

Sonia shrugged. "Who knows exactly? I only know she is no longer among us."

"Then what keeps you here?" Victor said.

"I have found no replacement. The rules have not vanished." Sonia refilled the glasses and raised her own in a toast. "To trust," she said.

Paul raised his glass, but Victor's remained on the table. "Where is your resting place?" he said.

Sonia hesitated, resentful of the bullying. "I'm leasing a vacant mansion here in Georgetown. On R Street. Across from the cemetery."

"With two big magnolias in the front yard?" Paul said.

"Yes. It's called Calloway Manor."

"Yeah, that's it," Paul said, accepting a cigarette from Sonia. "The paper had a story about it when the owner died. Some international tycoon."

"The cellar works perfectly," Sonia said.

Victor needed confirmation before he believed her. His general distrust of her obviously showed.

Sonia smiled reassuringly and clasped his hand. "You don't believe that I mean you only good? Let me show you. Let me take you on a journey. Back to Rome. Back to your family. As a gesture of good will."

Victor laughed. "You think I can't conjure up phantoms myself?" Like all of his kind, Victor could summon ghosts of the past. They existed in their own right, appearing as they willed, but they were also subject to conjuring powers. Yet whether they came of their own accord or at his command, apparitions of his father, his mother, and his brother, Justin, ultimately disappointed him. They could speak but never truly communicate with him. They didn't know what was in his heart. Their oblivion left him bitter.

Sonia seemed to read his thoughts. "We're not all alike, Victor. We each have unique gifts. If we rely on one another, everything is possible."

"And what is my unique gift?" Victor said, still cynical.

"We'll know that soon enough. As we compare ourselves. Please let me show you one of my gifts. Let's join hands. Don't resist, Victor." Sonia grasped his hand.

Curious, Victor did not pull away. He closed his eyes but continued to see the torch blazing above the table. The chant grew faint, and noises of the countryside gathered around him—birds, wind in the trees, a braying donkey in the distance. The darkness broke into a bright morning sky. He sat on a brown stallion, the reins in his hand. His father was mounted on a black steed next to him. He appeared as he did before his decline, his carriage upright, his shoulders back, his brown, lined face full of strength and determination. He wore a tunic with his crest embroidered on the sleeves. His boots were laced up his bulging calves. He was a true *paterfamilias*.

His gray eyes fully of gravity, he stared at Victor. Victor knew to prepare himself for the challenge. He tightened the reins. The horse snorted and reared its head. Victor gazed out over the sweep of the open *campagna* ahead. Spring rains had turned the sage and wild grass green. Here and there a tree sprouted. They were outside Ostia, the port city closest to Rome, where they often came to collect goods shipped from a distant part of the empire, Gaul or Egypt. Today they came just to ride. And they had galloped in silence because no words were needed between them. Victor smelled rain in the air. It was the exact scent from the morning on which he had actually taken this trip as a youth of eighteen, only just beginning his military training. He had now returned to that day, so solid, so real. His heart thudded as he anticipated the race. At his father's shout, they charged forward over the terrain, toward a cluster of trees one mile ahead.

Hunched forward, raised in the stirrups, Victor rode the horse hard, gaining on his father. When they were neck and neck, his father glanced at him, whipped his steed, and shot forward. Suddenly his horse lost its footing in a deep rut and buckled, throwing him. Victor sped to his father, dismounted, and cradled the gray head, just as he had cradled it that day, relieved to find, once again, his father's keen eyes open and amused.

"I think I broke a leg," he said in Latin—the same words he had spoken that day. Then came something new. "I know, Victor. I see you now."

"What do you see, Father?"

"The night, all around you. And your power."

"You know what I am?"

The keen gray eyes did not flinch.

"I am *always* your son. *Semper.*" Victor drew a fist to his heart.

"*Semper*," his father repeated.

"The other times, when I saw your apparition. Did you see me, too? Did you hear me when I spoke?"

"I have not heard your voice in an age." His father's own voice was strong and true.

"Where are you? What sphere do you inhabit?"

"The Dark Kingdom."

"How can that be?" Only those with Victor's nature were destined for that place. He thought that he must be dreaming rather than truly encountering his father.

"You are not dreaming," his father said. "Roads lead from realm to realm. You'll see someday."

Victor had many more questions, but his father's face grew hazy and finally faded. Then darkness descended. Wind rushed in Victor's ears and he felt pressure on his hand. A circle of light grew until he beheld Sonia gazing at him.

"What happened?" Paul said. "Who did you see?"

"My father," Victor said, his eyes still on Sonia. "He said he was in the Dark Kingdom. How can that be?"

Sonia shook her head. "I have no access to the visions."

The encounter with his father haunted Victor for the rest of the night. What could it mean? Was it possible that Sonia had simply conjured a vision meant to reassure him of his father's eternal happiness so that he would trust her? Should he trust her? Perhaps. She had disclosed her resting place after all, making herself vulnerable—that is, if she was telling the truth.

Just before dawn, Victor left Paul in the cellar, already asleep. The mounting radiation stung his skin as he approached the gate of Calloway Manor, just four blocks from their home. The dark mansion stood far back from the iron pales surrounding it, a three-story structure with a mansard roof and attic dormers. The two magnolias shielding most of the façade glistened with rain. Heavy clouds lingered after the storm, offering only the allusion of night and no real protection against the approaching rays. Victor rallied his flagging energy, concentrating to stay alert. He followed the circular gravel drive to the covered portico and forced the front door. Inside the dark house, fifteen-foot ceilings, framed in ornate molding, loomed above the empty rooms. The oak floor creaked as he crossed a dining room that would easily seat thirty people under a brass chandelier.

In the pantry off the large kitchen, he found the cellar door. The smell of mildew rose up around him as he descended the dank stairs. A squirrel or a rat scurried in the crawlspace visible from the stairs. In the dark cellar, wiring hung loose from the rafters beneath the kitchen floor. A boiler took up one end of the rectangular room, venting into a crumbling chimney. There was no sign of a modern furnace or hot water heater. But a door led to another large room and he found the modern equipment there. A dozen window-unit air conditioners cluttered the floor. The owners must have replaced them with a central cooling system.

The feral scent of animals and the smell of earth and decaying leaves drifted in from the crawlspace around the area. A door in that room was locked. He considered breaking it. Then words rushed into his thoughts, as though he remembered them from a recent conversation: *use the key*. He found it under the damp cushion of an armchair nearby.

The room inside was even darker than the rest of the cellar. Evidently all of the crawlspaces there had been bricked up. It took Victor's eyes a moment to adjust. Then a casket became visible on the floor. It was mahogany, the lid carved with lilies. Who knew how Sonia had arranged to have it delivered there? Maybe she had created a thrall to assist her—like the thralls that Victor had himself created over the centuries, thralls like Paul had been, though Paul was the only one he'd loved.

He hesitated to open the lid. What if the occupant attacked him? He'd been considering this question since he set out on this task. *He* would certainly strike out at anyone who dared to expose *him* in his resting place. But exactly what kind of injury could a vampire inflict on one of his kind? He had read stories of such attacks in old tomes he'd found in monastic libraries. According to the legends, vampires could mortally wound their kind by paralyzing them and leaving them exposed to the sun. They could also impale them with wooden stakes. In revealing her hiding place, Sonia had seemed to invite him to confirm her words, but what if she was setting a trap for him?

There wasn't time to deliberate. Victor's skin burned now, and his head pounded. Over the centuries, he'd stayed up this long only a dozen times. He opened the lid. Sonia lay peacefully, her freckled hands clasped beneath her heavy breasts, the nipples visible through her red negligee. She had unbraided her hair, and it spread over her shoulders like black silk. Her eyes opened for an instant, took in Victor, and shut again. Satisfied, Victor closed the lid.

Trembling now like an alcoholic with DTs, he left the room, barely managing to lock the door. He lacked the concentration to will himself back to his own cellar. He lacked the strength to run. As he passed the gates of Oak Hill Cemetery, his chest suddenly tightened. He gasped for breath, falling on the iron bars, and then sinking to the ground in pain. Was this paralysis caused by the rising sun? Was the aura of light discernible beyond the head-stones enough to reduce him to this?

No, this seizure was nothing like the stinging enervation caused by the imminent sunrise. It was as though a vise squeezed his chest so tightly that his lungs could not take in air. Gasping, he clung to the iron pales. Within minutes everything would be over. Immobilized and suffocating, he would endure the burning rays of the sun for only a moment before the torture ended forever.

All right, I acknowledge your power! He willed himself to cry out, but the words sounded in his mind only.

Suddenly the pressure eased. His chest heaved as he inhaled the sticky air.

He rose and walked as fast as he could, occasionally stopping to steady himself on a lamppost or iron fence. The birds seemed to twitter hysterically.

He fumbled with the key at his house, and dragged himself to the cellar. As he struggled to lift the lid of the sarcophagus, he thought he'd have to leave it and risk the partial exposure. Then a strange vision of Sonia's alabaster face came to his muddled brain, and he found the strength to seal his tomb.

As September approached, early sunsets extended Victor and Paul's day. They rose at seven and walked to Dupont Circle, less than a mile away. They liked to work out at a new gay gym near the Circle, the Olympic. Their bodies needed no maintenance—they'd remained exactly as they had been before their transformation—Paul's lanky and toned, Victor's as buff and well defined as a suit of armor. But exercise exhilarated them. So did the pretty flesh around them. Sometimes they flirted with a customer, drew him into a shower, and fed on him under the steamy water. The risks of a public setting held their appetite for blood in check. But the taste of it often aroused them so much that they made love in the shower or the sauna after releasing their prey.

Victor's desire for Paul grew every time they made love, like an addict's need for higher and higher concentrations of a drug. He'd never experienced such an intense mixture of lust and love. For him lust had always meant domination, and he could not love a slave. Joshu had aroused both sensations, but Joshu had never given him his body—a denial that only increased Victor's desire. Michael had made him feel both, but his moment with

Michael was brief as a spark. This prolonged ecstasy with Paul must be the product of their shared nature. They could pour their souls into each other because they were identical receptacles. Victor had the advantage of experience, if you could call centuries of lonely killing an advantage. But they were equals, guaranteed a shared immortality.

Unless the Dark Kingdom robbed them of it.

Victor had told Paul nothing about the attack outside the gates of Oak Hill. No need to stir his fears. But he now sanctioned Sonia's presence. He had no choice.

One evening, Victor and Paul walked to a gay bookstore after their gym workout. They had time to kill before joining Sonia for an organ concert, which she insisted that they attend.

The bookstore was packed, mostly with men. Many customers wore suits—the uniform of their government jobs. They all milled around tables and shelves, some of them heading to the porn in back.

"Look," Paul said. He held up a book entitled *Vampire of Washington*. "Listen to this: 'Roderick had tasted the blood of Andrew Jackson and Abraham Lincoln. He had preyed in the corridors of the Old Executive Office Building. But the hustler he found in Senator Deghand's Watergate apartment reminded him that flavor did not depend upon power and position."

"Very brilliant, Roderick," Victor said.

"I guess people never get tired of vampire fantasies." Paul replaced the book on the shelf. "You should write a book and set everyone straight. I could illustrate it."

"It's been done."

"You mean the dusty books you found in monasteries? Like the one at San Benedetto."

Victor had discovered a medieval volume about vampires at San Benedetto, although the writer referred to vampires as *incubi*. Victor translated a few Latin passages for Paul who was thirsty for facts before his transformation. Victor had lacked the patience to educate Paul himself.

"They've taught me a thing or two," Victor said.

"Any books by other violators?"

"No."

They left the bookstore and walked to the Dupont Circle Metro stop. They rode down the long, steep escalator, purchased fare cards, and boarded a Red Line train going in the direction of Catholic University. Rush hour was over, and their car was less than half full. The bright lights in the car made Paul's pale face look white as milk, but no less beautiful for it. His hazel eyes inspected an advertisement for the vampire-slayer movie *Van Helsing, The Sequel*.

"We should go," he said. "We might get some pointers in self-defense."

Victor smiled and squeezed Paul's thigh.

A pack of noisy teenagers exited at Union Station, where a food court and movie theaters attracted youths. Three stops later, Victor and Paul got off at the Brookland Station and crossed the nondescript campus of Catholic University to the Basilica of the Immaculate Conception. The imposing structure with a blue dome and carillon spire presided at the west end of the campus. People labored up the long stone stairway to the entrance.

Sonia was waiting for them in the narthex. Silver studs glittered in her ears and silver bangles on her wrists. Victor could smell a trace of blood on her breath when she kissed them.

They entered the cavernous church with walls of pink travertine marble and soaring arches. Far ahead in the elevated sanctuary rose a marble canopy above the altar, and beyond that, in the high arch of the apse, frowned an image of a muscular Christ in a bright red tunic. Victor liked this rendition much better than the pious depictions abounding in churches. This Joshu—like the real Joshu—had some mettle.

A small crowd of a hundred or so had distributed themselves in pews throughout the nave in readiness for the concert. Sonia, Victor, and Paul slid into a pew near the center of the church. Everyone turned around as the master of ceremonies introduced the bald, bespectacled guest organist. Following the applause, the audience settled back and the organist launched into a Bach prelude.

Victor endured the ninety-minute concert, his gaze wandering over the inviting necks of people around him. He was happy when the trumpet and reed pipes resounded in the final passage of the last baroque fugue.

As the crowd dispersed, the vampires walked around the church, peering in at mosaics and altars in the side chapels. Paul was fascinated by the stylized religious art, completed around 1960, just after the church was built. They climbed the sanctuary stairs and toured the massive apse. Sonia unlatched a rope guarding the altar area and stepped in. Victor and Paul followed her.

"Perfect," she said, peering at the altar.

"For what?" Victor said, suspicious.

"For your wedding." She glanced gravely from him to Paul. "Vows will strengthen your bond. That's important. Do you object?"

Victor laughed. He kissed Paul on the mouth, hoping to scandalize one of the suited ushers collecting programs left in the pews. "What do you think, lover? Would you like a church wedding?"

"It will be perfectly sacrilegious," Sonia said. "I can preside. I was a nun. That's close enough to a holy office."

"Why not at Dies Irae?" Paul said nervously. "It's a church."

"But this is better," Sonia said, her dark eyes sparkling with pleasure. "This is bold. It will be like my wedding with Regina. We exchanged our vows at the cathedral in Milan. A heretic priest married us. Then we fed on him. It was his wedding gift."

An usher hurried up the steps and announced that the church was closing. He angrily reconnected the rope behind them as they clattered down the steps.

Outside the basilica, Victor declined Sonia's invitation to join her in a stroll across the campus of Catholic University with an eye to feeding. He'd had enough of her company for the evening. He and Paul took the Metro back to Dupont Circle and walked home.

In front of Dies Irae, they found Horatio arguing with his new young lover. Victor smiled at the juxtaposition of the seasoned bleached-blond manager in tight jeans and black leather vest and the naïve true-blond protégé in a polo shirt and khaki pants. Paul motioned for Victor to leave them alone, but Victor couldn't pass up the opportunity to interfere. As he and Paul climbed the steps, the pair got quiet.

"Lovers' spat?" Victor said, taking in the young priest's athletic body.

"Just a difference of opinion," Horatio said. He was clearly unhappy about the intrusion, but knew his place. He lit a cigarette and leaned against the brick wall.

"We don't want that. Is he treating you badly, Father Kyle?" Victor patted the priest's shoulder.

"It's none of your business," Kyle said softly.

"Be careful now, Father. I might have to call your superior to come and rescue you."

Kyle absorbed the blow as though he deserved it. Victor smiled at his sense of shame. "What do you think of my club, now, Father? Do you agree with Gimello—that was his name, wasn't it?"

"Let's go, Victor," Paul said.

The young priest cast an appreciative glance at Paul and turned back to Victor. "I know I'm a hypocrite. If you want to report me to Father Gimello, go ahead."

"That's tempting. It'd be quite a scene. The young saint getting reamed for getting reamed."

"Leave him alone," Paul said impatiently.

"I never said I was a saint." Kyle looked at Paul.

"Too bad. You'd be in good company from what I hear. Some

holy popes indulged in sodomy, didn't they? Maybe a few of the twelve apostles did, too." Victor laughed. "Don't be so hard on yourself, Father. Take care of him, Horatio."

Horatio blew out a stream of smoke and flicked his cigarette toward the sidewalk.

As they walked back home, Victor took Paul's hand. "You like the young priest."

"Why torment him?"

"I was having fun. Do you want him?"

"No."

"You never get tired of *me*?"

"You know I don't," Paul snapped. "I don't need anyone else. Do you?"

Victor stopped, pulled Paul to himself, and kissed him.

In one short week, Sonia efficiently handled all the details of the wedding, employing the services of Horatio and Mark to execute daytime errands. She was secretive, answering Victor's questions about the preparations with a sly smile. Just as well, as far as he was concerned. What did he care about such matters? If Paul had not been so excited about the ritual, he would have refused to participate in it. Besides, his attention was focused on the antics of the Dark Kingdom. His experience at the cemetery had not recurred, but he found himself constantly on the alert—however much good his watchfulness might do.

The night of the wedding, a full moon hovered above the

basilica's dome. A strong wind rushed through the oaks around the church, toppled waste cans on Catholic U's campus, and sent trash scudding across the concrete walks. A Jeep full of frat boys honked at Victor and Paul as they crossed the grassy quad. A large boy in a backward ball cap lobbed a full can of beer at them. It struck a tree with a thud.

As instructed, Victor and Paul entered through the narthex. Sonia had assured them that the church's security system would be disabled and the security guard taken care of. He assumed she'd used conventional means rather than risky malice—a large, discreet donation in exchange for use of the church in the dark hours. No electric lights illumined the narthex. Instead, candles flickered on pedestals flanking the heavy doors. Following Sonia's directions they undressed and donned the black satin capes she had left there. Paul chuckled at the capes' high, Count Dracula collars.

The doors to the church opened, by Sonia's power no doubt, and by the same power the organ launched into Bach's "Prelude in G Minor." The ringing pipes reverberated in the marble chamber. Candles in tall stands burned along the aisle in the dark church, and far ahead flames outlined the altar. Barefoot and naked under their capes, Victor and Paul marched toward Sonia, whose robed silhouette was discernible under the marble canopy.

When they climbed the sanctuary steps, she greeted both of them with a kiss on the lips. Her lips and fingernails were painted red as an apple. A white wimple and black veil covered her long hair and made her eyes seem enormous.

The organ faded. Now Bach's fugue echoed quietly around them. Her speech more like that of a Russian diva than a nun, Sonia announced the purpose of their meeting.

"The night brings you here. The moon pours its power upon you. Blood nourishes your immortality. Your passion defies the authorities of the Dark Kingdom. Your passion defies your own limitations."

Sonia cupped their bare testicles in her hands, amazingly warm for someone with her nature, and their penises stiffened with blood. Victor glanced at Paul. He thought he could mount him here and now.

Continuing to hold their testicles as if she weighed them, she initiated their vows. "Do you, Victor, pledge your eternity to Paul, your consort in the night?"

"I pledge myself," Victor said, staring unabashedly into Paul's lovely eyes.

"Do you, Paul, pledge your eternity to Victor, your consort in the night?"

"I pledge myself."

"Then, I announce that you belong to one another for an eternity of cruel nights and unlived days."

When Victor kissed Paul, he thought he could swallow him whole. Paul's cool body trembled in his arms. Victor recalled Paul's epilepsy and had a strange presentiment of losing Paul to the old disease. But he knew it was nonsense. Disease could not touch a vampire's flesh, which offered no nourishment to bacteria or carcinogens. All the same, he clung to Paul with tenderness, wanting to protect him.

Sonia disappeared into the Blessed Sacrament chapel off the sanctuary. She emerged with a naked boy who looked like the performer from Dies Irae, though Victor could not be sure. He'd only seen him washed in floodlight, from the distance of the balcony office. But the bleached hair was the same, and gashes streaked his torso. As Sonia escorted the boy to the altar, he stumbled and stared vacantly, evidently on drugs. He was probably a hustler with a habit, though maybe he'd had some extra help tonight.

At the altar, Sonia cleared the candles from one edge of the altar, placed a chair by the marble slab, and nodded to the boy, who used the chair to crawl onto the massive surface and spread himself in cruciform.

Sonia removed their capes. "Feed," she whispered.

They mounted the altar, lying on either side of the boy within the ring of flames. As Victor caressed the boy's tender pectoral muscles, the boy moaned. With a quick jab, Victor pierced the jugular and sucked. The young, marred body stiffened. The young heart raced audibly in Victor's ears. Victor pulled himself away after a few swallows of blood. Then Paul drank.

"Finish," Sonia said.

Victor looked up. "Too risky."

"I'll take care of the body."

"We don't have to kill him," Paul said, though he eyed the boy hungrily.

Victor nosed the boy's neck, licking the bloody wound. Sonia's offer was too good to pass up. He drank more, then pulled Paul's face to the wound. When the boy's heartbeat slowed to five-second intervals, Victor raised the pretty head and twisted it hard. Over the corpse he kissed Paul.

"I love you," he whispered. He was woozy from the blood, but he meant the words.

Full of passion, they left Sonia to dispose of their victim and hurried home to their bed. Their lovemaking was the sweetest Victor had ever known. His tongue explored Paul's body, finding the spots that brought his lover the most pleasure. He kissed Paul's long fingers and his beautifully sculpted feet.

Holding hands, they descended to the cellar. As Victor drifted off in his casket, the wedding scene replayed in his mind. Then suddenly from nowhere an image of Gimello replaced the sweet vision. The priest knelt on the basilica altar over the body of the dead hustler. He glanced up and glared, as though he could see Victor watching him.

At first the intrusive image annoyed Victor. Then he chuckled triumphantly at the priest's dismay and fell deeply asleep.

UNRAVELING

And ere a man hath power to say "Behold!"
The jaws of darkness do devour it up.
So quick bright things come to confusion.

—*A Midsummer Night's Dream I, 1,149–151*

5

"I just talked to her yesterday," Paul said into the cell phone. He stood at the window of his studio, staring down at a yellow taxi stopped on the dark street. His chest tightened with apprehension.

"She's bad, Paul," his sister said, choking back tears. "They don't know if she'll make it."

"Jesus. I'm on my way. Just keep her alive, Beck."

So, Paul brooded, Victor's boost to Alice the year before hadn't cured her fucked-up heart after all. Maybe a second dose of Victor's blood—or his own blood—could revive her. If he just got there fast enough. He could fly by his own power if he broke up the trip at the halfway point, taking refuge before sunrise in the mausoleum of a cemetery and then resuming his journey after sunset. Victor had taught him the trick. Mausoleums were unguarded and usually neglected. And no one would disturb a grave. He would find a similar resting place in Kansas.

His nocturnal schedule would raise questions in Kansas. But if he tended his mother all night, he could explain his daily absence.

Becky would wonder why he needed to sleep the whole day, but he could do nothing about that. It didn't much matter what she thought at this point. Maybe someday, someday he could tell her about her brother's changed nature.

Right, Paul thought, imagining a conversation that started, "Beck, I have something to tell you. Don't freak out. I'm a vampire."

The words seemed so ludicrous that he laughed. He raising his hands in a menacing way, and made a monster face at the window, where his reflection would be if he had one. "I am a vampire," he announced in his best Bela Lugosi voice.

He apprised Victor of the emergency and shared his idea about curing Alice.

Victor shook his head. In a black shirt, he sat at his desk. "It can happen only once."

"How the fuck do you know that?" Paul snapped.

"You can try if you want. I'm only telling you what I know."

"I know, I know. I just wish . . ."

"We can't all be immortal." Victor's black eyes were devoid of sentiment.

Paul glanced down at the club, where a dozen guests entertained themselves. Most were dining near the stage. A few sat at the bar, where Horatio chatted with the bartender.

Victor got up and embraced Paul. The dark stubble on his face was heavy. "Do you want me to go with you?"

"Yes. But you can't. It'll be hard enough dealing with everything else. I can't deal with *us* and my family. Not now."

Paul's family believed that Victor had abandoned the monastery for him. Alice had invited them both to come and visit, but Paul knew she mistrusted Victor. He had a feeling Becky would, too.

At nine o'clock the next night, his brother Al approached him at the arrival gate at Kansas City International. Al had insisted on picking him up the airport, and Paul had conceded to the conventional arrival point for the sake of appearance, purchasing a canvas bag and some clothes at an airport shop.

Al hadn't changed much in two years. Maybe his paunch had expanded a bit, and the flap of hair combed over his bald head had grown a bit thinner. But his expressionless, puffy face—with no traces of his high school good looks—was the same. So was his awkwardness. If he noticed anything different about Paul, he didn't show it. Without hugging Paul or even shaking his hand, he grabbed his bag and led his brother to his pickup truck in the short-term parking lot.

As they headed to the I-70 turnpike to Topeka, the windshield wipers cleared drizzle from the glass. The rural sky fell like a dark velvet cloth around them.

"Flight okay?" Al said. He lit a cigarette and cracked his window.

"Yeah."

Just to shake Al from his oblivion, Paul wanted to yell, *Do you know you're sitting next to a vampire?* Instead, he asked for a cigarette. Al gave him one without showing the least surprise that he smoked now.

"So the doctors say it doesn't look good?" Paul said.

Al shrugged. "Becky talked to them."

Paul saw that trying to get any information from him was useless. "How are Peggy and the kids?" he said.

"Good." Al seemed almost ready to elaborate, but he stopped himself, drawing on his cigarette. Then he glanced at Paul. "You look different. Pale or something. You sick?"

Maybe Al was thinking of his epilepsy. Maybe he thought he had AIDS. His altered appearance could work to his advantage. "I've had mono or something," he said. "I need a lot of sleep."

Al nodded. "You staying at Mom's house?"

"Yeah." His mother's little rambler sat back from a country road on two acres of wooded land. He could come and go there without any notice. And Rochester Cemetery was only a mile up the road.

"You can feed Emilio then."

Alice loved her yappy Chihuahua. Paul wondered what would happen to him if she didn't pull through.

Al pulled into the parking lot closest to the ICU of St. Francis Hospital. Two orderlies in scrubs were smoking under the covered entrance. Inside, he and Al crossed the glossy linoleum floor to the elevators and rode up to the second floor. Alice's room was at the end of a corridor glaring with fluorescent light.

When he stepped in, Becky got up and hugged him. She started to cry. "God, Paul. I'm so glad you're here."

Her eyes were red from crying, and dark circles shadowed them. Her unkempt short hair was dyed jet black now. In addition to her nose and ear studs, which she'd had for years, a new stud on her tongue flashed when she talked, and two new rings pierced her eyebrow. Exhausted and upset, she didn't seem to notice the change in him.

Alice lay at a slight incline on the hospital bed. The color had drained from her face. Her short, salt-and-pepper hair looked like a mop. Without her dentures, her mouth had caved in. Her horsy features loomed larger than ever on her drawn face. An oxygen tube trailed from her nose, and wires ran from her wrist and under the sheets to a machine with a monitor.

Paul kissed her doughy cheek, and touched her hand. He'd inherited her long, knobby fingers.

"She was just fine after bingo on Monday night," Becky said, standing by him. "She stopped by, happy as a clam because she won the blackout. She made two hundred fifty dollars." Becky half-laughed. "God, what if she doesn't make it?"

"What did the doctor say today?"

Becky shook her head. "It just doesn't look good. He said her heart is too damaged. Maybe there's a chance. Maybe he just doesn't want to get our hopes up."

"She's never regained consciousness?"

"She groaned a couple of times, like she was in pain."

Al's cell phone rang. Sitting in the chair on the other side of the bed, he pulled the phone out of his pocket. "Yeah, I picked him up," he said. He glanced at Alice. "No, just the same. I don't know." He glanced at Becky and Paul. "You guys want me to stay tonight?"

"No. Go home," Paul said.

"I don't think we should leave," Becky said. "What if something happens during the night?"

"Come on. You both need some sleep. Let me stay with her tonight. I'll call you if anything happens."

Becky sighed and wrote down her cell phone number and Al's. She kissed Alice before she left. Al followed her, throwing an abashed glance toward the bed.

All night, Paul sat by his mother in the dimly lit, quiet room, memory after memory flooding his mind, many from the distant past—Alice making him breakfast in her white cafeteria uniform, beaming at his first awful painting, kneeling over him with horror in her eyes when he came to after his first epileptic seizure on the floor of a grocery store.

But here were recent memories, too. One came to him after he had sat by Alice for nearly three hours. It was the moment in Rome when Alice dauntlessly confronted Victor. "What do you want with my son?" she'd demanded, ready to lunge at the man who threatened to break her son's heart. Her boldness had brought a smile of amused admiration to Victor's lips.

He was losing his protector. His tough, unpretentious Alice.

That thought, so late in the night, filled Paul's eyes with tears. He rested his face on his mother's hand. "You don't have a thing to be afraid of, Alice," he whispered. "I'm all right. Becky and Al and I are all right. You do what you have to do. If you have to go, it's okay."

Then a horrible fear rose in him. If Alice did go, maybe she would see him in his separate eternity. Maybe she would see him emerging from a coffin, feeding on human blood. Maybe she would try to call out to him and find herself behind a sheet of soundproof glass. *Whatever you see, Alice, try to understand. There's mystery in the universe. What seems like horror, isn't always. Think of animals that prey.*

When a nurse came in for the third time to take Alice's vital signs, he realized dawn was just two hours away. He had no choice but to leave Alice. He needed to take his bag to her house and call Victor. Then he had to feed quickly before finding a safe resting place. Victor had assured him that with time he would be able to go two or three days without feeding. But in the early years, the cravings would be too strong to resist.

His new clumsy bag precluded traveling by his own power so he took a cab to his mother's house. It passed through the quiet downtown area. Between office buildings, the illumined capitol dome flashed, skinny as a missile. As they crossed the bridge over the Kansas River, he glanced back at the shadowy twin spires of St. Joseph church, built by Germans from Russia.

In the still of the night, the ride north of town took less than twenty minutes. The area was rural, with patches of housing development encroaching on the open country. Scraggly Russian olive trees and elms stretched along the dark country road to Alice's house, and clunky mailboxes appeared like commas along the way.

Inside the house, Emilio barked as Paul approached the dark front door. When he stepped in and switched on a lamp, the dog drew back his ears, growled, and trembled. Then he darted off into the kitchen. Paul hoped that his two-year absence explained this response, but he suspected that the dog sensed his new nature.

The low-ceilinged, paneled living room hadn't changed. It held a big-screen TV, a recliner, and plaid Herculon furniture. There were framed high school graduation photos of Al, Becky, and him on the wall and photos of the grandchildren on the end tables. A tacky painting of a Chihuahua on velvet hung above the TV. The smell of nicotine lingered in the air. Had Alice gone back to smoking after finally quitting?

His old room disappointed him at first. Grocery bags of clothes for Good Will cluttered the floor. A sewing machine and a stack of patterns covered his old desk. But he brightened when he saw the familiar ribcord bedspread on his twin mattress. His mother had bought it when he was in high school. And his old LPs were still stacked in his bookcase—Simon and Garfunkel; Cat Stevens; Peter, Paul and Mary. He'd been a sucker for the folk scene of the sixties and seventies, a hippie born too late. He dropped his bag on the bed, returned to the living room, and called Victor.

"How is she?" Victor said.

"She won't make it. I can tell. It's like I can feel death in the air."

"You'll always know, now."

"I wish I didn't. Sometimes it's better just to hope."

"And your sister and brother?"

"Becky's torn up. Al—who knows? He doesn't talk about things." Paul noticed a pack of Misty cigarettes under a magazine on the end table. He flung it at the floor. "I miss you."

"We haven't been apart since your transformation," Victor said. "Not even one day."

Paul suddenly laughed.

"What?"

"It's surreal. I'm a vampire. I'm a vampire sitting in my mother's recliner, talking on the phone to another vampire."

"I love you," Victor said.

In the warehouse area near the Santa Fe railroad shops, he fed on a worker taking a smoke break outside a dog food factory. Sated, he rose into the night, riding a strong current to Rochester Cemetery.

Growing up near the cemetery, Paul had heard stories of the albino woman who haunted the tombs. Kids at school offered a number of variations of her story. She'd been a beautiful woman who killed herself when her lover left her, turning into a blanched old ghost who pined at his grave. Others said she was the ghost of an elderly woman, drowned in the Kansas River by her son. His classmates reported seeing the ghoul at their bedroom windows, weeping and clawing at the screens. How bizarre that even now, as a ghoul himself, Paul felt goose bumps rising on his arms at the thought of entering her domain. *You're a vampire, man. Undead. What fucking spirit is going to mess with you?*

Light rain fell. He crossed the spongy ground, tramping over unkempt graves and weaving through headstones and stone crosses, toward the mausoleums. The city lights were far away. In the darkness, only the silhouettes of dripping trees rose around him. A train whistle howled in the distance.

Ten marble mausoleums sat in a block at the edge of the cemetery. Rich farm families had built them during the First World War, for sons killed in combat. Now whole families rested together. Each structure contained six berths, three stacked on each side. He might find empty berths. Taking one of them would be preferable to sharing space with remains. He peered through the gates of one mausoleum after another. In the fourth structure, the name BEN-NETT engraved above the iron gate, he discovered a tomb with no inscription. Finding the lock still secure, he jerked the door hard. It snapped open. Stepping in, he closed the gate behind him in case anyone happened to visit the mausoleum. The unmarked tomb was in the top position on the right side. He pried off the marble tablet. A coffin rested in the niche. Evidently no survivors cared enough about this family member to identify the grave.

"Shit," he muttered. He considered continuing his search, but dawn was coming and he decided to make do. Drawing out the cheap pine coffin in the cramped quarters took some maneuvering, but he managed to get it to the floor and break open the lid. Inside lay a mummified infant—like a doll wrapped in a blanket. The scent of embalming fluid, acrid to his senses, made his eyes water. Apparently the tiny corpse was fresh, probably a painful reminder quickly and cheaply disposed of in an old family vault.

Paul removed the casket and slid it into the space above the opposite stack of tombs. Apparently the space allowed another berth if necessary. He crawled in the empty tomb and hoisted the slab backward, using the iron hooks that projected from the smooth face. Who would notice a reversed slab?

In the dark, secure niche he relaxed. To him, the smell of death around him rose like the scent of a newly tilled garden in the rain. Alice would lie in a place like this. But unlike him, she would never leave her tomb. Suddenly, the thought of *her* confined in a casket like his own disturbed him. In a casket, buried in the ground next to his goddamned father. Forever. But her soul would rise, wouldn't it?

In Rome, while he had illustrated the Gospels, he found himself fascinated by the Jesus who preached eternal life. His illustrations captured the forceful, unyielding prophet he envisioned—so different from the pious, frail renditions of artists over the centuries. And then he'd had an extraordinary experience in the monastery chapel—a vision of the crucified, bleeding Jesus. He'd written it off as an hallucination brought on by an epileptic seizure. But later, when Victor told him about Joshu, he wasn't so sure. Maybe the real Joshu had been speaking to him. *Let her live, Joshu. Let her live! Or if you can't, take her to someplace good. And explain everything about me.*

At dusk Paul awoke. For a moment he felt refreshed, and then his tranquility evaporated as he remembered where he was and why. He went out to feed and hurried back to the hospital and his mother's bedside.

Becky was waiting for him in the room. Angry, she immediately confronted him for leaving Alice by herself. Paul invented a story about seizures brought on by fatigue. Becky agreed to relieve him at four and have Al come at noon.

On his third night there, he sat in the hospital room, sketching Alice from an old photograph. Finally, she looked right—her big features, her broad smile, and sharp, mischievous eyes. No trace of fear ruined the image.

Alice moaned in the bed. Her head moved toward him. He put down the sketch pad and pulled the chair closer to her.

"I'm here, Mom. I'm right here." He clasped her hand, careful not to tug on the IV in her wrist.

She squeezed his hand, took in a labored breath, and released it. She didn't inhale again.

He kissed her cheek and continued holding her hand, knowing that soon its warmth would fade forever. But he finally forced himself to release it and call Al and Becky. They both arrived within fifteen minutes. Wild-eyed, Becky rushed to the bed and hugged Alice, sobbing inconsolably. "I should have been here," she blurted. "I just knew I should have come tonight!"

Paul did his best to reassure her, and she eventually calmed, sitting on the bed, stroking Alice's hair. For a while Al stood awkwardly over his mother, finally touching her hand tentatively before sitting in a chair, pale and speechless. Paul sat next to him and described Alice's final moments. When two orderlies came to remove the body, Becky broke into sobs again. Paul took her by the hand and gently led her from the room, Al trailing behind them.

They drove to Al's house and gathered in the kitchen. Becky sat listlessly at the table while Paul and Al discussed funeral plans and Al's wife, Peggy, kept everyone's mug filled with coffee. Of course, Paul did not touch his, but Peggy never prodded him in his grief. Exhausted, they all parted an hour later, as dawn approached.

Paul drove his rented car to the cemetery. He followed the gravel road to the rear of the grounds and parked. He walked through the warm, humid air to the mausoleum where he'd taken refuge before. Locusts buzzed in the wooded area adjacent to the cemetery. At the tomb's iron bars, he jumped. Someone moved inside. At first, the figure who approached the door looked the way he had imagined the fabled Albino Lady to look. A white gown, gathered under her breasts, flowed to the ground. Her long white hair fanned over her shoulders. But her eyes were not the pink eyes of an eerie stranger. They belonged to his mother.

"Alice!" He strained toward the bars.

"Danger," she whispered.

"What danger?" He struggled to take in what he was seeing and hearing.

"They . . . killed me." The apparition spoke haltingly. "You . . ."

"What, Alice? What are you trying to say?"

"You . . . danger. Don't disobey."

"Disobey who?"

Her only response was to mouth his name without emitting a sound. Then she raised her hand to the bars. But when he reached for her, she drew away from the door and backed into the shadows. When he opened the gate and stepped inside, Alice was gone.

Despite his agitation, Paul climbed into the cramped niche in the mausoleum and lay replaying the strange scene again and again in his mind. When he finally drifted off, he dreamed of his mother standing behind the iron bars like a prisoner. He woke himself calling her name, listening for her footsteps inside the mausoleum. *She can't mean it. She can't.* But in his exhaustion, the rationalization failed. The Dark Kingdom had taken her life. As a warning to him? As a warning that he must obey the powers?

"Goddamn you," he muttered, as he drifted off to sleep. "What did she do to you?"

Becky arranged for a morning funeral with visitation on the previous night. When Paul told her he would attend the visitation only, she stared at him in disbelief from across her kitchen table.

"Why are you doing this?" she said. "It's not easy for anybody." Her black T-shirt accentuated the dark circles under her eyes. She suddenly looked much older than she was, her pretty face contorted by desperation. "Please, tell me what is going on."

"I can't, Beck. Not now."

"Are the seizures back? Do you have AIDS or something? Why won't you tell me what's wrong?"

Her questions baffled him. Why would sickness keep him from a funeral? But he didn't try to follow her logic. She was exhausted, and now he'd hurt her. He was at a loss. Any response other than the truth would be bullshit. And the truth wouldn't do.

When he didn't open his mouth, she looked helplessly around the paneled room. On the wall ticked a loud clock shaped like

Elvis holding a microphone, his legs—knees together and feet splayed in the uniquely Elvis style—swinging like a pendulum.

"You're scaring me, Paul. You've changed. I can't lose you, too." She broke down, sobbing.

Paul grabbed her arm. "You're not going to lose me."

"Remember when I got pregnant with Jolinda?" she finally said. "I was so scared about telling Mom. Eighteen, unmarried, and pregnant. And the father was black. I could just hear Mom. 'Mixed children are not accepted, Becky. Whites don't want them, and neither do blacks.' Then she'd tell me that lame story that Doreen at the cafeteria had told her about the boy she'd forbidden her daughter to see. Remember?"

Paul smiled and rolled his eyes. He remembered the story well. The boy allegedly had come pleading with Doreen. "What am I supposed to do? Whites don't accept me. Blacks don't accept me." And then came Doreen's profound reply: that's your problem. "Doreen probably made the story up to justify her fucking racism," he said.

"Or Mom did."

Paul hated the thought. He liked to believe that under Alice's crusty exterior beat a heart that said live and let live.

"I was worried out of my mind," Becky continued. "I thought about having an abortion. I thought about running away. I had no one to talk to. Mom saw something was wrong but she didn't say a word to me. Of course Al didn't either. But you did. You kept pushing until I told you."

"Did you think I'd feel like Mom?"

"I don't know what I thought. I was just scared. And so fuck-ing depressed. When I told you, it was like a pile of cinder blocks was lifted off me." Becky's eyes welled up again.

He touched her hand.

"So what's the deal? What could you ever say that would make me stop loving you? It's something about Victor, isn't it? He's some kind of drug dealer, right? Or, I don't know, maybe some-thing worse?"

She couldn't even put her first fears into words, Paul thought. What was worse than a drug dealer in her mind? A pedophile? A Mafia boss? A serial killer?

"It's late, Beck. Let's talk about this later."

"Tell me."

What should he say? There was no good way to reassure Becky that his kind of existence was just an alternative lifestyle. That, true, he might feed on people, but he didn't kill them. Not usu-ally. And even if he did kill people, he would never hurt her or Dean or the kids or anyone in his family. So he gave up waiting for the perfect words.

"All right. You want to know. I'll tell you."

Becky looked relieved, settling back, preparing herself.

"You said I've changed. Well, I have. When I explain why, you'll either think I'm fucking with you or I'm crazy. Well, maybe I'm crazy to have gotten into this life, but I'm not fucking with you. There's no easy way to say it. So let me say the words and you can roll your eyes or hit me or do whatever you want. Only just hear me out."

"I'm listening."

"Okay. Here goes." Paul lit a cigarette. "I've become the kind of ghoul that Hollywood loves to make movies about. A vampire. I'm not talking figure of speech. I've really become one of those beings."

"Paul," Becky said impatiently.

Paul raised his hand. "Stay with me. When I met Victor in Rome, I fell in love with him. He fell in love with me even though he was a monk—I thought. I knew it seemed like another dead-end relationship. The kind I always seem to find. But he was hot, and I thought, what the hell. Monk or no monk. Guilty or not. You know me. Pretty reckless. He liked my paintings, which were quite daring—it turns out—for monks. He had a mind of his own."

Becky smirked. Alice must have told her all about Victor.

"Okay, he's downright arrogant, something that sticks in *your* craw, but I'm a sucker for. Anyway, I eventually found out why he was so rebellious. He wasn't really a monk. The monastery was a cover for him. He was a vampire. His story is pretty long, so I'll save it for someday after all this info registers in your mind."

Becky shook her head, her eyes tearing as though she thought he was losing his mind, or worse, purposefully trying to hurt her. She stood up. "I'm going to bed."

Paul grabbed her hand. "Please, just listen."

She sat down again, reluctantly.

"I know you're thinking this is all a joke and wondering what in the hell I'm joking for. There's no point in telling you all the gory details. I became what Victor is. That's why I can't come to the funeral. You know the vampire drill—no sunlight. The transformation explains why I'm so pale. And why my eyes probably have a different look in them. I've never seen them in a mirror— you know from the movies that mirrors aren't cool in the vampire world. Again, I'll spare you the details of this life. You know what it involves. The good thing is that when we feed, we don't have to harm anyone. They can walk away without a scratch."

Becky had buried her face in her hands. Paul touched her arm.

"You haven't absorbed a thing I've said, have you? Not beyond the word *vampire*. You're thinking, '*Vampire?* Does he mean *vampire?* Like on Halloween? Like Dracula in the Gary Oldman movie we watched on TV? Come on! Jesus, Paul, when is the punch line coming?' There isn't one, Beck. Look at me. Look at my face. Look my eyes. You can see it."

Becky lowered her hands. Crying, she looked at him, as though she considered taking him seriously.

"I'll be happy to stand in front of a mirror for you. I'll be happy to demonstrate the kind of strength I have now. But whether you think I'm joking or on something, I've said it. I miss you, Beck. I love you liked I've always loved you. You are the only family I've got now. You're the only one who will ever know me. The truth about me. I don't even care if you don't believe me. I only want to hear one thing from you. 'I love you.'"

"I do love you, Paul," Becky whispered. "I want to help you. I just don't know how." She shook her head sadly, got up, and went to bed, leaving him at the table.

The funeral home reeked of blood. Paul smelled it before he even stepped foot into the colonial-style mansion. Salivating, he glanced up the carpeted corridor to a door leading to the stairway. The bodies were probably prepared on the lower level of the building. The funeral director, a middle-aged man with a pink, scrubbed face, greeted him and Al and Becky in the foyer, where a huge vase of gladiolas sat on a mahogany table. Becky wore a short black dress and fishnet stockings. Paul and Al wore dark blazers without ties. The rest of the family would join them in half an hour, after they'd had a moment alone with their mother.

The walk from the foyer to the viewing room seemed to take forever. Paul's heart thudded the way it had on the same long trip after his father's death almost twenty years before. Even though he now slept among corpses, even though he'd killed people, this trip seemed unnatural, even cruel. The cool civility of the funeral director only made it worse. At the viewing room, the man stood aside respectfully, letting the family pass through.

Becky clung to his arm and Al's arm as they approached the casket, which was loaded with white and pink carnations and surrounded by sprays of flowers. The lamplit room smelled like a florist shop. Five rows of chairs faced the gleaming metal container.

Becky faltered.

"It's okay, Beck," Paul whispered. "We're with you."

Alice looked younger, her skin practically wrinkle-free. Makeup made her seem slightly tanned. *This isn't Alice*, Paul told himself. *It's just a shell.*

Becky touched the sleeve of Alice's lavender dress and broke into sobs. Al stood at the casket for several minutes, never unclasping his hands to touch his mother.

As people filled the room, everything felt unreal to Paul, like an out-of-body experience. The recorded violin strains of Handel's "Water Music" melded with the quiet chatter and occasional laughter in the room. Faces of relatives, who welcomed him back home, rose like beige balloons before his eyes, their words flying away unabsorbed, like sounds in space. Time seemed frozen, but it must have passed because Paul suddenly noticed that many people had left. Then he heard a familiar voice. He turned to see his lover gazing at him.

Victor was stunningly handsome in a white silk shirt and black jacket. His dark eyes, boring into Paul's pain-filled soul, were the most welcome sight he could imagine in the oppressive room. When they embraced, Paul felt everyone staring, but he didn't care. Death awaited everyone there, except for him and Victor.

"This is Victor," Paul said to Becky.

"I'm sorry about your mother," Victor said perfunctorily.

As Becky gazed up at him, her despair gave way to hostility. She stood up and glared at him. "God damn you."

"Becky!" Paul touched her shoulder to calm her, but she jerked away from him.

Victor barely repressed a smile.

Becky slapped him. Her whole body began trembling, and she sank to the chair.

Victor eyed her with contempt and withdrew from the room.

After the visitation, Paul left the funeral home with Victor. He described his conversation with Becky as they drove to Alice's house.

"Foolish," Victor said, without taking his eyes off the road. "What did you expect her to say?"

"You want me to just cut her off?" Paul blurted. "She's my god-damned sister. I know she doesn't hold a candle to anyone in your patrician family, but I love her."

Victor threw him an icy glance. "My patrician family is dust. Fifty years from now your family will be dust, too. And you'll be your same eternal self. Let them go."

It was the truth, but Paul almost hated Victor for saying it.

As they pulled into Alice's drive, Paul watched for Victor's reaction to the humble house. If Victor felt disdain, he hid it well, simply eyeing the rambler with curiosity. But when they entered Alice's modest living room, Victor moved like someone from a European royal family visiting a trailer park. With contemptuous amusement, he examined the graduation photographs on the wall, his hands clasped behind his back. Beneath the couch, Emilio snarled at him.

The dog expressed Paul's feelings well. But when Victor kissed him, his anger melted. For the first time during his visit, he pulled back the ribcord bedspread on his old twin mattress, and he and Victor climbed under it. The sheets smelled of the detergent Alice had used since Paul was a child. Paul lay with his head on Victor's hairy chest, remembering his hirsute father. He could understand why Alice had fallen for the ruggedly handsome laborer, even if he was a drunk.

"Is she in Joshu's heaven?" Paul said.

"How would I know?"

"You believe in it, don't you?"

"The place where people spend their eternity on their knees? Yes, I believe in it."

"So you think Alice's future is pretty desolate."

"I don't speculate. You shouldn't, either. You can't change anything. You have memories to comfort you. So does she."

"Was Joshu's mission just a lie? Was he really that deceived?"

"I don't want to talk about Joshu."

"He saved me in Rome."

"I said I don't want to talk about him."

"I saw her, Victor. At the cemetery."

"Who?"

"Alice. Her ghost—or whatever you call it. She said they killed her. Can they do that—kill?"

When Victor did not respond, Paul raised his head. Victor's expression was solemn.

"They *can* kill, can't they?"

"If you're in danger . . ." Victor said.

"No! You're not leaving me. Why would they hurt *me*? You're the one who broke the rules. It's just another scare tactic."

"We shouldn't take a risk."

Paul shook his head. "There is no risk. Alice had a bad heart. She died. They took credit for it."

Victor did not press him. Instead, he wrapped his arms around Paul and held him in silence.

Paul could feel his own heart pounding. "Say, you'll never leave me," he finally whispered.

Victor remained silent.

"Say it, Victor!"

"I'll never leave you." Victor kissed the back of Paul's neck.

After Victor made love to him tenderly, they dozed. At four in the morning, they went out to feed, then retreated to Paul's borrowed mausoleum, Victor occupying the empty niche opposite Paul's.

Paul slept fitfully, his mother's words of warning echoing through his dreams: *Danger. Don't disobey.* When he awoke at sunset, he was determined to inspect his mother's new grave, as if to do so would somehow assure him that she rested in peace. Victor made no objection, clearly curious himself. So they drove across town to Memorial Cemetery, near a large city park.

They found no signs of a troubled ghost on Alice's grave. The black earth was heaped with carnations. On one half of the headstone his father's name was engraved, along with the dates of his birth and death. The other half awaited an inscription for Alice.

You in heaven, Alice? What's it like? As much as Victor badmouthed Joshu's static, frozen eternity, he wondered about the scene Victor liked to conjure: a kingdom of pale souls with no wills of their own in a fixed state of genuflection to the "Lamb of God" ensconced on a golden throne. What if people in heaven laughed and played? What if they got to continue doing the stuff that made life wonderful, the creative stuff? Like painting. What if all the fucking abuse in families stopped?

What about that, Dad?

Back in Washington, Sonia comforted Paul, taking his arm as they strolled among the quaint Georgetown homes in the early hours of the morning. In her low, Slavic voice, she called him *Tesoro*, Italian for *treasure*. She listened to him talk about his confession to Becky.

"The truth was inevitable," she said, removing the silk shawl from her shoulders. "She had to hear it. She'll believe it with time." She paused, adding wistfully, "They always do."

"How did you tell Regina?"

"I didn't have to." The subject of Regina seemed to pain her. "She caught me feeding on one of the nuns in the convent. To silence her I made her a thrall. Then it was too late to go back. She needed me to survive."

"Something like that happened with Victor and me." Paul told her about the night he walked in on Victor hovering over the dead body of a monk at San Benedetto. Victor's only recourse was to transform his witness into a thrall.

"But you loved him before the transformation, didn't you?"

"Yes." The remark surprised him. "How did you know?"

"You show no traces of bitterness."

"Regina was bitter?"

Sonia nodded. "Even though I loved her deeply and wanted her to have all the happiness in the world. When I couldn't stand

VAMPIRE TRANSGRESSION

the guilt anymore for forcing her to live in a half-existence, I transformed her again. Then I couldn't bear to leave her. The Dark Kingdom seemed like a hell to me, instead of a heaven. And I'd already known hell in my life. As a girl, I was sent to a nobleman's house to work. I was just an ignorant peasant girl. He beat me. Raped me. I ran away. The nuns at a German convent took me in. Eventually, one of the nuns transformed me. I lived in convents for two centuries before I met Regina. I had never loved anyone. I couldn't leave her once I transformed her."

So Sonia came from common stock, like him. No wonder she understood him. "So you both became fugitives."

Sonia chuckled. "Fugitives. How dramatic."

"But that's what we are."

"You are right." Sonia was serious now. "The Dark Kingdom will never give up its claim on all of us."

"What can the Dark Kingdom do to us?"

"The powers destroyed Regina. My love made us vulnerable."

Paul didn't like what he was hearing. "But you said association makes us strong."

"Association with detachment, yes. Not association with love. Love always creates vulnerability."

Paul stared at her, confused.

"My obsession weakened my powers," Sonia explained. "I know now that my detachment would have saved her life."

"How in the hell did you *know* that?" Paul suddenly snapped.

"I just know it."

"I can't stop loving Victor."

"Then you will always be vulnerable."

They walked back to Dies Irae in silence, Paul brooding over Sonia's cruel pronouncement.

Inside the club, they found Victor amusing himself with a new guest, a pretty young editor of a glossy S and M magazine. She wore a miniskirt and a lacy top over a push-up bra. She sat with her long, silky legs crossed. Victor finally escorted her to the guest house. Paul did not look at Sonia, who undoubtedly tried to convey her approval of Victor's tryst. He reminded himself that whatever sexual fantasy of the woman's that Victor acted out, what he really wanted was her blood only.

Victor was gone just a few minutes when the sullen Jesuit, Gimello, entered the club, along with the young associate pastor.

"Mr. Lewis?" Gimello said.

"Who let you in?" Paul said.

Gimello shrugged. "The door was open. I just want one word with you."

"Look, it won't do any good. You better leave before Victor gets back."

"Just one word. Then we'll leave."

Paul glanced at Kyle, who was obviously uncomfortable. Paul felt sorry for him. Horatio had treated him like shit, and now the priest regretted the futile tryst. He'd violated his vows for nothing. Maybe Gimello had discovered the affair and was here to scold. For Kyle's sake he stepped into the vestibule with the two priests.

"Mr. Lewis, I'm here to appeal to you. It's my obligation." Gimello's chocolate eyes flashed with the clarity of someone who knows he's on a righteous mission, someone with every confidence in each moral decision that he makes. "You're crucifying him again, every day that you conduct your business in this holy place. I'm begging you to take your club somewhere else. I believe in the Gospel's command to give a private check to an offending brother. I've done that. I've waited and I've prayed for you and your—friend. I've appealed to you independently of him. The next step will be to bring in help. You'll find protestors outside your front door. You may find the police. They pursue allegations of illegal activity. I know the kinds of habits that flourish in a place like this."

Paul found himself staring at Gimello's thick neck. If he pounced on him, feeding until his heartbeat faded, this talk would end and Gimello would go away. He could break into the priest's room tonight as he slept.

The temptation scared him. How easily he slipped into the role of killer. How ready he was to assert his power over the mere mortals around him.

"It won't do any good, Father. Victor likes a good fight. You'll just make him dig in all the more."

"Do you believe in Christ?" Gimello said.

"Your Christ?"

"There is only one. He is abundant in mercy. But on the last day, he will stand as judge."

Paul grinned. "The dude sounds mean."

Gimello ignored the irreverence. "He is a lover. Infidelity to him brings its own punishment. Infidelity is the worst sin."

The aptness of Gimello's analogy struck Paul. Victor did once think of Joshu as his lover, though their love was never consummated. In Victor's eyes, Joshu had betrayed him, not the other way around.

"I'll be right back," Gimello said to Kyle. He walked back into the club and approached Sonia's table.

Paul let him go. Let Sonia put up with his fire and brimstone.

"He doesn't know anything about me and Horatio," Kyle said.

"Don't worry. I won't tell him."

"I appreciate it." Kyle hesitated. "It was wrong. I sinned—getting involved with him. I broke my vow of celibacy. I sinned against nature."

"You don't need to confess to me."

Kyle dropped his gaze, and then turned his gray eyes back to Paul. "Horatio told me your mother died. I'm sorry. You've been in my prayers." He took hold of Paul's arm.

Paul had a sudden urge to kiss his plump lips.

Kyle reached into the pocket of his trousers. "I brought this for you." He handed Paul a small silver crucifix inlaid with dark wood.

Paul thanked him.

When Gimello and Kyle left, Paul watched them retreat down the dark street, still clutching Kyle's gift.

6

The e-mail message was brief: *I know what you are. A. Gimello.*

It was midnight when Victor read it. At 12:05 he stood before St. Ignatius Church. Between two stone spires, the rose window of the façade softly glowed, and as Victor approached the double doors he detected the scent of blood. The first door he tried was unlocked. When he entered the dark vestibule, the acrid smell of embalming fluid rushed at him. Through the open doors of the nave he located the source of the smell: at the end of the long aisle, a coffin rested below the elevated sanctuary. On a prie-dieu, Gimello knelt before the coffin, his back to Victor. He did not turn as Victor traveled down the aisle, nor when Victor finally loomed over his shoulder.

"I was expecting you," Gimello said without lifting his head from a missal.

For an instant, Victor considered falling on Gimello's sturdy neck and making short work for himself. But his curiosity won over his anger. He walked around the small coffin, a child's casket, and faced Gimello, his elbows on the metal lid.

"Guarding the child's soul from the devil?" Victor said.

Gimello glanced up. "The child's innocent soul is in heaven."

"So why are you here?"

"Christians are not Docetists. You must be familiar with their heresy. You were a priest."

"Yes, I recall." Victor studied the calm figure before him, his dark head inclined, his strong hands on the missal. "Christ was not simply a spiritual being who appeared to have a body. He took on real flesh. And in doing so, he blessed all human flesh. On the last day, the body will rise from the grave and join the soul once again."

"And you believe that or are you mocking the dogma?" Gimello glanced up, his coal eyes riveted on Victor.

Victor laughed. "Oh, I believe that Christ was flesh, very delectable flesh, from what I hear. I believe his followers still like to eat it."

Gimello glared at him. His goatee gave him an enticing, Satanic look.

"Who told you I was a priest?" Victor said.

"You brag about it to all of your guests. Why should they keep it secret?"

"Ah, I see." Victor moved to the head of the coffin and lifted the lid. A girl of five or six lay inside, dressed in pink, her blond hair in pigtails. "How did she die?"

Gimello hastily rose to his feet and stood by the coffin, as though prepared to protect the dead child. "She fell and struck her head."

"That's a pity. She's lovely." Victor fingered the ruffles on the girl's collar. "You know, Father, you are becoming very annoying."

"Annoying?" Gimello smiled disdainfully. "I should be frightening."

"Oh?" Victor chuckled.

"I know what you are."

"Yes. You know I am a defrocked priest. You know my soul is in danger."

"It's not *your* soul I'm worried about," Gimello whispered. "I know what you are."

Victor peered into Gimello's eyes, searching for the knowledge he possessed. Unable to penetrate the priest's sanctimonious thoughts, he grabbed the dead girl by the arm and lifted her from the casket, as though she were a rag doll. A patent leather shoe fell from her foot. When Gimello tried to wrench the girl from his grip, Victor gripped his throat and shoved him to the slate floor. Before Gimello could rise, Victor stood over him, his foot planted on his barrel chest. "Tell me what I am."

Gimello's horrified glance moved from the lifeless child in Victor's grip to Victor's face. "You are evil incarnate," he muttered.

Victor once again scrutinized Gimello, who strained to breathe beneath the force of Victor's weight pressing on him. And once again the effort to read the priest's thoughts failed. It was this frustration of his own power that enraged him, more than any kind of baiting from the likes of Gimello. What was Gimello after all but a petty cleric? Yet a petty cleric bestowed with knowledge beyond his scope, knowledge of the existence of beings outside the human sphere. And was he also bestowed with the even more dangerous knowledge of the vulnerabilities of such beings?

Determined to destroy Gimello, Victor tossed the child aside and fell on the priest, piercing his throat. But with the first swallow of the priest's blood, he recoiled, crying in pain. It was as though he had swallowed fire. It burned all the way to his stomach and then shot through his veins until his whole body blazed. He rolled on the cool floor to extinguish the flames blazing within him. At first the pain only grew worse, as though the movement actually fanned the fire. But he could not resist the instinctive reaction. And he knew that even if the pain finally destroyed him, he must continue to thrash. Then just as suddenly as the intense pain had flared, it subsided. And he lay panting but still.

When he rose, the priest had not yet regained consciousness. He lay with his arm around the dead child. If he were like all victims, he should remember nothing of the encounter. But was he like all victims?

Until three in the morning, Victor walked the streets of Georgetown, his head spinning. Who was protecting Gimello? And what exactly did Gimello know about him? If the priest really knew what kind of being he was, what was to stop him from hunting down his resting place, a stake in his hand?

As dawn approached, Victor's energy dwindled. He returned home, climbing down to the cellar, where Paul was already safe within his own resting place. He slept fitfully. When he awoke and found Paul gone, he climbed up to his studio, where he found him at the easel, shirtless, a cigarette in his mouth.

"What did Gimello say to you the other night?" he demanded.

"Good evening to you, too," Paul said, through clenched teeth.

"What did he say?"

Paul removed the cigarette. "I told you what he said. What in the fuck is the matter with you?"

"Tell me again," he said, kicking at Paul's new calico cat as it brushed against his legs.

Paul scowled. "He tried to convert me. You've heard the spiel. Accept Christ. Change your ways."

"How about his protégé? Did he say anything?"

"No." Paul turned his attention back to a chalk drawing.

"Sonia said you spoke to him. Alone."

"So? Is there a law against that?"

"You like his ass, don't you?"

Paul waved his middle finger at Victor.

Victor snatched the canvas from the easel and flung it across the room. It struck the wall above the sofa. Then he picked up the easel and ripped it apart, hurling the broken pieces to the floor.

Paul stared at him in disbelief. When he finally registered the offense, his hazel eyes widened in rage. He jumped to his feet and lunged at Victor, grabbing his throat. His face inches from Victor's, he glared at him, the pupils of his eyes scintillating with rage, his teeth gritted as though he was determined to tear off Victor's head. Paul's incredible strength caught Victor off guard. For the second time in twenty-four hours, he found himself threatened by a superhuman force. But the origin of Paul's strength he knew. He shared it, and he would be damned if he would succumb to one of his own kind. Concentrating his effort, he pried Paul's hand from his throat and heaved Paul against the mantel. The painting of the little boy fell from the wall. The crash seemed to bring Paul back to his senses. He picked up the painting as though it were an infant that had fallen from his arms. He inspected it for damage. His frown suggested that his fears were confirmed. He threw a wounded glance at Victor, as if they had both lost something precious.

The gaze did nothing to placate Victor. But he resisted his impulse to strike out again. Glaring at Paul, he left the room and hurried out of the house.

As he trudged through the dark neighborhood, his anger did not dissipate. Paul's irritability and black moods had been trying his patience since his mother's death. The woman was a working-class nonentity. In his own mother's household, servants had more grace and skill than Alice Lewis had. Any comparison between Alice Lewis and Lydia, wife of Severus, would be ludicrous, and that great woman's death he'd accepted stoically, in Roman fashion—anything less would have been an insult to her memory. Humble, homely Alice had outlived her allotted years, thanks to Victor's own blood, drizzled into her mouth in Rome. Maybe he shouldn't have extended her life. Maybe her renewed strength after her heart attack had created unrealistic hopes in Paul. Hopes dashed by the powers of the Dark Kingdom. At least that's what Paul believed. And maybe Paul blamed him for inciting those powers.

Deciding to confer with Sonia about the danger lurking around them, Victor walked to Calloway Manor. The windows on the first floor glowed. He rang the bell, gazing out over the dark lawn where the two magnolias stood motionless in the still, humid air.

Sonia opened the door. She was barefoot, in a peasant blouse that showed off her white shoulders and cleavage. As usual her hair was pulled back into a single, long plait. "Victor! Come in. How good to see you."

In the foyer, two lamps burned on a lacquered ebony table. A heavy mirror hung above it, the frame carved with gargoyles. Sonia led Victor into an enormous sitting room, apparently once used as a ballroom. Victor had not entered the room the night he searched the dark mansion, having traveled through the dining room on the other side of the foyer. The ballroom was furnished with plush chairs and sofas upholstered in jewel-toned damask. A grand piano stretched like a sleek black leopard in one corner of the room. Handwritten sheets of music covered the music stand. Paul had mentioned that Sonia was a composer.

A caramel-colored shitzu bounced over to Victor, sniffing his trousers and jumping on his leg.

"Down, GiGi," Sonia said. "She's used to our kind of scent. It doesn't frighten her anymore. Please, have a seat. Could I get you a glass of this?" She picked up a wineglass half filled with blood, more brown than red. Victor accepted a glass, which Sonia poured from a decanter before seating herself in an armchair, her legs tucked beneath her. "Cheers." She raised her glass in a toast.

Victor sipped from his glass. A trace of freezer burn lingered in the blood. "Why do you jeopardize us with this?" He said.

"You've not a thing to fear," Sonia said, dismissing his concern with a wave of her hand. "The victims are not from here."

"I still don't like it."

Sonia shrugged, indifferent to his opinions.

"I received an interesting message from the priest who's been hounding us," Victor said. "Gimello."

"I know who you mean. He spoke to me at the club. Something about changing my ways. If he only knew." Sonia laughed and sipped from her glass.

"Maybe he does know."

"What do you mean?"

"In the message he claimed to know what I am."

"A vampire, you mean?" Sonia looked skeptical. "How could he know that?"

"I had my own doubts. I went to find out for myself."

"And?" Sonia stopped petting GiGi, who had jumped up on her lap, and strained toward him.

VAMPIRE TRANSGRESSION

"When I tried to feed on him, his blood burned me. I thought it would kill me."

Sonia frowned. She scanned the room as though trying to process the information.

"If he knows," Victor said, "Paul and I are in danger."

"If he knows, we're all in danger," Sonia snapped. "Maybe one of your employees has loose lips."

"My employees know nothing. Why would I tell them?" Victor drained the last of his wine. "I don't believe he does know. Or else he would have used the word. He would have threatened me the only way he can. But what is the source of his power? Is it the Dark Kingdom?"

"It's possible," Sonia mused, petting the dog once more.

"For what end?"

"Religious zealots make perfect instruments. The Dark Kingdom uses them to put us in danger. To make us submit. I saw it happen after I transformed Regina. The mother superior from my old convent discovered our coffins when she came to demand our return to the order. She would have killed me had I not allied myself with others like us."

"We should kill him."

"Of course. If we can. But then, why anger the powers? If we band together, he can't harm us. Our own power is too concentrated."

"How can you be so sure?"

"Fine. Kill him." Sonia pulled her braid over her shoulder and

117

began to unravel it. "How is Paul doing? He seems very with-drawn since his mother's death."

"He was close to her." Victor settled back in his chair, watching Sonia throw back her lovely head and shake out her hair.

"He's still new to the life. The old attachments die hard. He needs some diversion. You both do. The worse thing you can do is act out the forbidden love story. That will precipitate the end."

"What do you mean?"

"I mean that love creates vulnerability," Sonia said gravely. "Detachment is the key to survival. Detachment allows you to consolidate power. Love depletes it."

"I want him."

"Fine, if you mean lust . . ."

"I mean love."

Sonia shook her head. "I promise, it will bring you down. You can have his body. But if your souls become entwined, you are doomed. I've told him the same. Find other lovers. Amuse your-self." Sonia yawned, stretching. "Besides, you'll grow to resent him for forcing you to break the rules. I'm telling you, if you don't want a life of bitterness, expand your horizons, as they say here in the States."

"I fuck whomever I want when the urge strikes me." Victor leaned back in the chair and crossed his legs. "Why do you think I created Dies Irae? Blood and sex at my disposal."

"But you love Paul."

"So?"

"Maybe you're right. You're the one with centuries of experience. Perhaps you can avoid obsession. But what about Paul? You are his world. That's dangerous for him. He needs independence. Otherwise, when things go wrong, he'll start to hate you."

"What will go wrong?"

"*You* know," Sonia said, bitterly. "You've lived this life for centuries. You've seen the costs of feeding on infants and old women—skulking in the night, hiding from weaklings who could end your existence with a quick jab of a shaft of wood." She tapped her bosom to indicate the target. "You depend on yourself. You trust only yourself. You're deluded if you think that you've found an eternal lover. The rules exist for a reason. It's the way we're made. We can't help it." Sonia got up and walked behind his chair. She laid her hands on his shoulders and whispered in his ear, "We're lusty creatures, aren't we?"

Victor rose and pushed her to the floor, burying his face in her breasts, reaching beneath her skirt. She moaned with pleasure under his touch. He stripped off her clothes and tore at her breasts with his teeth. As though she were demon possessed she writhed and shrieked, clutching at his hair. Rolling her over on her stomach, he secured her arms to the floor and entered her from behind, spending himself in five quick thrusts. But she commanded him to continue his motion, until she cried out in ecstasy. Then, he collapsed on the floor next to her.

Sonia nestled her naked body against his hairy flesh. "I like this world, Victor," she said, kissing his lips. "I enjoy the power I have in it. What kind of power does the Dark Kingdom offer? You love the power, too. Never give it up for love."

Calmed by the sex, he strolled the streets east of the Capitol dome, considering Sonia's advice. He wasn't one to stew over the hypothetical. If his love for Paul did, indeed, fade—well, he had no control over that. Here and now, he loved Paul. That's all that mattered. He'd risk anything for him. And with Paul at his side, Joshu's hold on him loosened.

He had always blamed the never-ceasing force of Joshu's presence on his own impatience with human lovers. If Joshu had dwindled to a memory, there might have been the chance to replace him with a real flesh-and-blood lover. But as a constant presence—competitors couldn't stand a chance against him.

Yet, perhaps, it was his own fault that Joshu haunted him. He'd planted himself in the midst of the Christ cult, Roman Catholic monasteries, where bloody images of Joshu above every altar kept him alive. He may have taunted Joshu in all the monasteries where he'd posed as a monk—defying him with every victim he created—but Joshu taunted him back, in ghostly apparitions, pleading for Victor's conversion to his god, and in memories so vivid Victor could smell Joshu's perspiration and the wool of his homespun tunic. He had no control over the apparitions. But the memories were fading now, for the first time. Now that he had escaped monastic chants and rituals. With Paul. Maybe now he could jump out of the ring with Joshu.

But what if Sonia was right? Was love worth annihilation by the powers?

As a tall woman in an evening gown climbed out of a taxi, Victor stepped behind a tree. His hand was clapped over her mouth and his fangs were in her throat before the taxi reached the corner.

The next day, a group of twenty arrived at Dies Irae. They belonged to a San Francisco club of Satan worshippers who included rough sex in their rituals. They called themselves the Fallen Angels. Victor snorted at the name. Obviously, originality held little value with them. They heard about Dies Irae from a New Yorker who recently joined the club. He'd apparently spent a week at Dies Irae. After taking the reservation by phone from the coven's high priest, as he called himself, Victor inspected the group's Web site. The homepage displayed an upside-down crucifix overlaying a shadowy skull. Beside it in gothic script was the club's credo: *We answer the tyranny of religion with defiance. Long live the darkest powers of the human soul.* A disclaimer warned that the site contained sexually explicit graphics and asked the visitor to acknowledge the warning before clicking the entry icon. Links took him to a series of photos. In one, a ring of nude men and women joined hands around a bonfire. In another, an overhead camera zoomed in on a naked woman spread-eagled on an altar. In a gesture apparently inspired by the film *The Exorcist*, she held a crucifix to her crotch, as though she'd just drawn it from her vagina. Blood, real or fake, streamed down her legs. Several photos featured a robed man with a goatee suspending an upside-down crucifix over a copulating couple and over a group sex scene of tangled limbs.

From his office, Victor watched the club members mingle downstairs. Two stunning men with tattooed bare arms sat at the bar on either side of a woman in a spandex top with an abundance of teased hair. A large group of young men and women, many in form-fitting black clothing, were gathered in the lounge area. Moving gracefully in his monk's robe, Mark Seepay was helping a robed kitchen boy clear the dinner plates from the tables near the stage. The aroma of grilled steak lingered in the air. Victor had overcome his cravings for food very early in his nocturnal life, after violently vomiting meals he'd been unable to resist. But blood from the rarer steaks made him salivate. Seepay's pretty Asian features and wide, slopping shoulders made him a tempting meal. Perhaps later he could call Seepay up to the office and take what he needed.

At eleven, the lights dimmed to signal the evening's entertainment and the guests made their way toward the stage. Seepay had booked a local band called the Defilers. The three male band members soon gyrated and shrieked under strobe lights. They wore leather vests, thongs, and chaps. Crosses dangled on their bare chests. All that Victor could make out of their lyrics over the heavy metal discord was the refrain "Fuck you, God." Not surprisingly, the Fallen Angels ate it all up. They waved their arms and joined in the refrain. Some of the women stripped off their tops and flung them at the stage.

The act soon bored Victor. He went home, led Paul to their bedroom, and stripped him. In the midst of rough foreplay, he reached for their latest toy. Inside the drawer of Paul's bed table, he found a silver crucifix inlaid with wood.

"What is this?"

"The priest gave it to me," Paul said guiltily.

"You mean the young priest."

"Yes. The night he came to the club with Gimello."

Sonia had mentioned nothing about an exchange between the protégé and Paul. The crucifix was the last straw. He'd tolerated Paul's perusal of *The Imitation of Christ*, a volume introduced to him by the monks in Rome. He'd tolerated Paul's interrogation about Joshu's heaven, his morose longing for his mother's salvation. This he could not allow.

"How can you keep a crucifix in your possession?" he demanded.

Paul propped himself on his elbows, his face flushed from their wrestling. "What about the fucking crucifix in the club, staring everybody in the face?"

"Defiance is one thing. Secret piety is another."

"Defiance, my ass," Paul had said. "I think all this vampire shit is true. Hide all the crucifixes. Hide the garlic." He sat up in bed and lit a cigarette.

Victor got up and threw on a robe. "You make no sense. You've made your choice. You are what you are. Praying to Christ won't change that."

"It's about Alice."

"No. Your mother is dead. What happens to her soul is out of your hands. This religious rot is for you, not her. And you know it."

"Will you ever be over him? Ever? Will it ever be just you and me—without Joshu crowding into our lives?"

Without thinking, Victor backhanded Paul. Like a wild ani-mal, Paul bared his fangs and sprang at Victor, ripping into his throat. Blood spurted on the sheets. Victor clasped his hand on the wound, his own fangs descending. He forced Paul onto his back and sliced into his naked belly with his own fangs. Paul cried out in pain.

"You fucker!" Paul yelled in pain.

Victor rolled off Paul's body. Paul lay back on a bloody pillow, his eyes filled with tears.

Victor's heart pounded in his throat when he lighted in front of St. Ignatius Church. A sign on the lawn next door identified a square brick building as the parish rectory. A light burned on the covered porch, but all the windows were dark.

Slipping around to the back, he found two cars parked on a patch of concrete, an old model Buick, most likely Gimello's car, and a small SUV that suited Kyle. Both priests were home. A sense of caution rose in him as he thought of Gimello, armed perhaps with an implement that could kill him if he were taken by surprise. But he was determined to have his revenge.

No exterior lights glowed at the rear of the building, and all the windows were dark. The door to the screened-in back porch opened with a firm jerk. Inside, plastic lawn chairs were stacked and a ragged, upholstered armchair held a container of alu-minum cans. The solid door to the house was bolted. Breaking through the frame could be noisy. Two windows looked out on the porch, and he found one unlocked. Sliding it open, he moved aside a table covered with plants, and crawled in. A large dining room table sat in the room, and in the corner a grandfather clock quietly beat the time. The aroma of garlic lingered in the air.

A set of French doors opened into a large living room, full of heavy furniture. Crossing the thick, oriental carpet, he moved into a narrow central hallway. Through another set of French doors, he found a room with a desk and armchairs at the foot of a staircase. On a cabinet behind the desk stood a large statue of the Virgin Mary, her hands outstretched. The room was probably Gimello's study.

He tested the first step of the staircase. Finding that it creaked, he kept to the edge as he climbed, stopping whenever a board moaned under his weight. The upstairs hallway had four doors, one on each wall. Sniffing the middle doors, he detected no trace of blood. The priests apparently occupied the two rooms at either end of the hallway. The first door he tried was locked. The second doorknob turned easily. In the darkness, his keen gaze fell on Kyle, asleep on his back, his muscular arms on the comforter. A crucifix hung on the wall above the headboard. Victor stepped in, locking the door behind him. The room smelled close and stale, but the scent of Kyle's blood absorbed his attention. He inhaled deeply, his fangs descending as he eyed the beautiful boy, whose face was turned toward him on the pillow.

In that moment, a strange, new alertness filled Victor's mind like a bright, clear light.

Up to this moment he had moved automatically, urged on by the sort of compulsion that sometimes led him to siphon a victim's blood to the danger point or ravish the lovely flesh he fed upon. Unlike his self-protective instincts—to feed, to flee the dawn—this compulsion jeopardized him. He had carried the compulsion from mortal life into supernatural life. It was born of deep fury against every force that threatened his control. But he, more often than his opponents, paid the price for it.

What good would come of killing the priest? His death would make him a martyr in Paul's eyes, maybe even drive Paul more deeply into religiosity. And taking his life would undoubtedly mean fleeing from the law. No, there was a better way to cure Paul.

He clamped his hand over Kyle's mouth. The priest's eyes flashed open. He tried to push away Victor's hand, but his own strength was no match for Victor's. Panic-stricken, he thrashed, determined to get free.

"Calm down, Kyle," Victor said. "You know me. Victor Boudreaux." Victor pierced Kyle's throat, willing his submission. Instantly, Kyle relaxed. Victor stretched his body over the warm body of the priest. Redoubling his concentration, he forced his own thoughts into Kyle's confused thoughts—a kaleidoscope of bright, stormy colors. He willed more than a moment's submission. Moving his lips from the wound, he kissed Kyle's lips and caressed his hair. *You know what you need*, he said with his thoughts. *You know what you need and you know where you have to go to find it. You have no choice. Your body wants it too much. Even your soul wants it. You can't resist.*

So aroused by his own act of seduction that he was in danger of ruining it by taking what he wanted, Victor let himself swallow very little of Kyle's blood before pulling away from his throat.

As he pulled Kyle's bedroom door shut, he sensed movement in Gimello's room, though he heard nothing. Perhaps Gimello had gotten out of bed. Or perhaps he simply lay awake on his pillow. Victor crept down the stairs, keeping close to the wall. A step creaked at the bottom of the staircase, but he was out the back door within seconds.

The next night just before ten, Kyle appeared downstairs, dressed in blue jeans and a polo shirt. He looked awkward and desperate. The Defilers had started to scream above chaotic electric strings. As stobe lights pulsed on stage, last night's audience once again imitated the spasmodic movements of the performers. Kyle watched from the rear of the church. Perversely, a Gospel story came to Victor's mind—the parable of the unworthy man beating his breast at the back of the temple while the self-righteous Pharisee sang his own praises in the front. Victor felt a twinge of pity for the priest. But it passed. He went downstairs.

During a lull in the music, he approached Kyle. "Looking for Horatio?" he said.

Sheepish, Kyle shrugged. "I guess."

"He told me he's through with you. In fact, he's out with someone." This was true. Horatio had left with a marine on leave from Parris Island. "So unless you want something else."

7

From his studio, Paul watched twenty protestors march on the sidewalk in front of Dies Irae. It was early evening. The air was balmy. Many of the men, women, and children wore shorts and T-shirts. A streetlamp flashed on their poster messages: DON'T CRUCIFY CHRIST AGAIN. LEAVE THIS HOLY PLACE; DIES IRAE BELONGS TO GOD ALONE. WELCOME DAY OF WRATH!; HOMOSEXUALS ARE AN ABOMINATION BEFORE GOD; GOD WILL DESTROY THOSE WHO DESECRATE HIS HOLY TEMPLE. Gimello's long black ponytail and goatee made it easy to spot him. In a clerical shirt, he led the little parade, a rosary dangling from his folded hands. His assistant marched in the middle of the file, his face down, his mop of blond hair ruffled by the wind. He carried no sign. His hands hung awkwardly at his side.

What a fucking hypocrite. Paul lit a cigarette, and exhaled a stream of smoke in disgust at the sight of Father Kyle. For the past three days, he'd watched Kyle slink into the club every night at ten o'clock. The first time he saw him enter, he figured that he was coming to proselytize Victor the way he'd proselytized him. He waited for Kyle to emerge looking distraught. But when he emerged with Victor an hour later, Victor kissed him long and hard, and Kyle stumbled off, glancing around the street. That night, Paul hadn't bothered confronting Victor. He figured Kyle was Victor's way of striking back at him. Kyle was a pathetic pawn, struggling for purity.

Paul's pity had evaporated when Kyle showed up the next night, and the next. Then he seemed no better than every other religious hypocrite. *God damn him and every fucking priest!*

But tonight as Paul stewed at the window, he suddenly saw how ludicrous the moral indignation of a vampire was—and how ridiculous to blame Kyle for succumbing to Victor's irresistible power. A power exercised under Paul's nose instead of discreetly with deference to his pathetic but insurmountable jealousy. Why did Victor have to flaunt his conquests?

When the protestors disbanded, he went over to confront Victor in his office.

"Since when do you care who I fuck?" Victor said, looking up from his computer monitor. "You know it means nothing."

"Every single night?"

"It means nothing. What is he compared to you? What have you got to worry about?"

"I don't know."

"Nothing. Nothing. Maybe you need your own toy."

The words twisted like a knife in Paul's stomach.

Paul met Sonia at Calloway Manor that night, and they took a cab to the Kennedy Center to see a performance of *Turandot*. Sonia loved Puccini, and Paul had never been to an opera.

The red carpets of the Kennedy Center's halls reminded Paul of blood. Most everything red did. Out of the sea of red rose an elaborate stage set. A round moon loomed over the façade of the palace of Princess Turandot. The satin costumes of townspeople shimmered as they cheered for the executioner commissioned with the killing of the Persian prince.

The elegant auditorium was packed with spectators dressed up and down—in gowns, tuxes, short sleeves, and jeans. He inhaled the rich mixture of blood in the air, scanning the necks of people in the row in front of them. Sonia playfully slapped his hand as though he were a mischievous child.

During intermission, they stood outside among the smokers, gazing over the Potomac. The moonlight revealed a shadowy forest of trees on Roosevelt Island.

"So, you like the opera," Sonia said, accepting a cigarette from Paul. She wore a silk shawl over a flowing lavender gown and had swept her dark braid into a bun at the nape of her neck.

Paul nodded, lighting Sonia's cigarette and then his own.

"You're quiet. What is on your mind?"

Paul described the attack in the bedroom and Victor's appropriation of Kyle.

"Jealousy," she said pensively. "It's inevitable."

"The fucker does this to me, and I love him."

"That's dangerous. You mustn't love him."

"Then what's the point?" Paul blurted, astounded at Sonia's flippant attitude.

"The point is survival," Sonia snapped. "I have told you." She paused, collecting herself. "Trysts are normal. And men like variety. It's very true."

"What if it's more than a tryst?" Paul tugged at his collar, which suddenly felt tight.

Sonia smiled at him indulgently. "You've read Stoker's novel, haven't you?"

"You're kidding. *Dracula*?"

"Don't scoff. The fantasies of fiction writers often touch the truth. For example, the girl seduced by Dracula. She was under his power."

"Like a thrall."

"Less free than a thrall. But yes. Seduction is the first step."

"Victor didn't seduce me before I became a thrall. I fell in love with *him*. You said so yourself. Remember? He pushed me away. I was the pursuer."

Another indulgent smile.

"I can't believe anything else, Sonia. I freely chose Victor."

"What does it matter how love begins? It is ultimately enthrallment of some kind or another, right? You are choosing him now, every day. And all for nothing. He cannot be true to you."

A sense of betrayal welled up inside of Paul like a great, sorrowful wave. *Victor was planning to make Kyle a thrall.* Paul had been naïve to hope for love eternal. What wasn't possible before his transformation wasn't possible now.

"You're taking this too hard," Sonia said, touching his arm. "It's best to let go of unrealistic ideas about fidelity. Vampires are not faithful. Take care of your own needs. Find yourself a lover. If you don't, you'll hate him. You can stay with each other forever. But you must be realistic."

A soft chime signaled the end of intermission, and Paul and Sonia returned to their seats. But when the performance resumed, Paul was too distracted to enjoy it. For the rest of the opera, images of Kyle and Victor played through his mind. They touched hands, kissed, and then stripped and wrestled on Victor and Paul's own bed. His chest tightened with panic.

Several times during the performance, Sonia cast him a reassuring glance, clearly aware of his consternation. But he took little comfort in her efforts. By the time the final curtain fell, he was beside himself with rage. Although Sonia tried to reason with him on the drive home, he hardly heard what she was saying. He bid her good night at the front door of the guest house and headed toward Dies Irae.

"Confronting him will do no good, Paul," Sonia called after him.

But he ignored her and entered the club. When he climbed to Victor's office, he found the door locked. No light shined beneath it. He went to their house. The living room showed no signs of recent company. No glasses on the tables. No cushions out of place.

Upstairs in their bedroom, he found the bed just as he had left it, neatly covered by a plum comforter with deep green and cream stripes, the pillows in their shams. He smelled no hints of sex. He checked the playroom on the third floor. The table of toys—handcuffs, rope, nipple clamps, dildos, and chains—was in order. The black velvet spread lay smoothly on the mattress.

The silence in the house was maddening. Paul changed into jeans. He looked up the address of St. Ignatius Church and stepped out into the little patio behind the townhouse. On the wrought-iron table there he found a glass that smelled of bourbon. He flung it against the brick wall enclosing the patio, and rose up into the night, in the direction of Northeast Washington.

The twin spires of the church made it an easy landmark. He lighted on the street in front of it. The square brick rectory next door was clearly marked. All the windows were dark. But then why would Victor come here where he'd have to deal with Gimello? Maybe he and Kyle had gone to a nightclub. Maybe they were strolling along the Mall, with the illuminated Washington Monument and Capitol Dome rising like the structures of Victor's Roman Empire. Paul thought of the ruins in the forum where Victor had transformed him. Pathetic rubble that Victor had left behind for the vigorous, stunning capital of the New World.

Driven to find Victor, Paul walked up Q Street to the Georgetown commercial district and searched several pubs. From the tables and the bar, patrons glanced up at him with curiosity as he marched purposefully through their midst, like a Gestapo officer seeking an enemy of the state. He went to Dupont Circle and beat the pavement past sidewalk cafés and then on to the late night spots on Capitol Hill before flying eastward to Congressional Cemetery, where Victor sometimes prowled.

As usual, the cemetery's iron gates were wide open, even at this late hour. Paul passed the little stone house used for storing the cemetery's archives and the brick chapel with its steep roof. He crossed over the oldest graves of the dark, disheveled cemetery that abutted the concrete hulks of the city jail complex. Broken angels, their features dissolved with time, knelt over earth-encrusted bones, which infused the air with pungent mustiness. Here and there, lozenge-shaped headstones, their engravings worn away, had collapsed on the ground, as though they themselves had finally succumbed to death. The bricks of the early nineteenth-century mausoleums still emitted the sweet scent of decay.

He found Victor leaning against one of the brick mausoleums. He wore jeans and a tank top. He smelled of fresh blood. His lips tasted of it, when he kissed Paul.

"Where is he?" Paul said.

"Don't do this. I love *you*. I was wrong to hurt you. I lost my head."

Paul's eyes welled with tears. "I just want to know . . ."

"What? Don't you believe I love you?"

"I can't do this."

"What can't you do?"

Paul wasn't sure how to answer. Was it that he couldn't keep hunting Victor, mad with jealousy—couldn't live with tormenting doubts about Victor's love? Or was it more? Maybe he could no longer bear living only in the night, feeding on people, fighting to control his urge for blood.

"You have to keep your wits about you," Victor said firmly. "This is all new. I went through it. When I realized that the darkness I woke up to every night wouldn't pass the way it had before, I flew into a rage. And I was alone. If I'd had you then . . ."

"It's not the dark," Paul said, suddenly glimpsing the source of his nearly primal desperation. "It's that nothing matters to me but you. Not my art. Not my family. No cause. No mission. You are my whole world."

Victor stared at him, his pupils so dilated in the darkness that they were undifferentiated from the black irises. With his own vision weirdly refined in the night, Paul perceived a glimmer of anger in Victor's eyes, a diffuse anger, aimed not at him but at the world. "We can't cling to each other," he said. "We'll destroy ourselves."

Paul was too exhausted to question Victor's logic. And the radiation of the coming dawn stung his skin like a mild sunburn. He wanted to take off his clothes to keep them from chafing. The monuments in the cemetery were growing more discernible as the sky lightened.

"We better go," Paul said, turning away.

Victor pulled him back, kissing him. Their tongues probed each other's bloody mouths. Their embrace at once hurt Paul's stinging skin and excited him. He imagined clinging to Victor until the rays of the rising sun set them on fire, fusing their flesh forever. Suddenly, a frantic screeching rose around them, as though thousands of birds had lighted on the branches of every tree in the cemetery. They glanced around at the trees. They did not spot a single bird. But the high-pitched sound grew so intense they had to cover their ears. Victor nodded and they both lifted into the air, moving on their thoughts to Georgetown.

Paul's watch said five-thirty when he locked the front door behind them and followed Victor down to the cellar. Victor unlocked the steel door to their place of rest and they stepped in.

Paul's sarcophagus was gone.

"Jesus!" Paul said.

Alarmed, Victor inspected the rows between the empty shelves where wine had once been stored. He checked the anterior room.

"Where the hell is it?" Paul said.

"We'll both use mine," Victor said, unruffled. He locked the door, testing it, as though he could keep out whoever had already managed to get through it, take the casket, and lock the door again.

He removed the lid of his sarcophagus, and they both climbed in, hoisting the lid back in place. They had to lie on their sides in the narrow container. Paul felt Victor's solid chest against his back. With Victor's arm around him, he quickly dismissed the breech of security. He thought once again about dying in Victor's arms—should the intruder return during the day to finish his job.

Victor replaced Paul's sarcophagus with a Moroccan chest, the lid inlaid with ivory filigree and Arabic keyhole designs. The import shop where he found it specialized in politically incorrect goods decorated with ivory from endangered elephants or diamonds mined by laborers subject to questionable demands.

Sonia shook her head solemnly when Paul told her about the stolen coffin. She sat on his studio couch in a strapless cotton dress, her hair up.

"You don't need to remind me," Paul said, standing by the fireplace, the cat in his arms. "I can't just turn off my feelings for him—like a television."

"No?" she said, lighting a cigarette. "What happens when both coffins disappear?"

"How do I let go of him?"

"Discipline. I learned it in the convent."

"I'm lost, then. I don't have an ounce of fucking discipline."

Sonia stood and came to him. "You'll find it," she whispered, caressing his cheek.

Paul and Victor walked along the river the following night. When the strains of the Marine Band wafted across the Tidal Basin, they followed the reservoir around to the Jefferson Memorial. In red uniforms with gold braiding the thirty musicians played a Sousa march on the promenade along the water. A casual audience of tourists and families with children sat on the steps of the Memorial. Here and there cameras futilely flashed in the dark.

Paul's spirits soared. At his request, Victor had left a pile of paperwork to accompany him. Sonia, a constant reminder of his dangerous love, had flown to New York for the weekend. It was just the two of them, in this beautiful city of manicured parks, marble monuments, and wide avenues.

Victor held Paul's hand as they stood behind the crowd, just yards away from Jefferson's statue. When Victor kissed him, Paul's heart pounded. Even in the dark, people could see them. A man and a woman on the top step hustled their three children away from the area. Paul pulled away from Victor.

Victor looked surprised. But when he followed Paul's gaze to the fleeing family, he understood the reason for his discomfort and laughed. "What do you care what people think? What can they do to us?" He wore a new linen shirt. He hadn't shaved and his blue-black beard accentuated his square jaw and broad, high cheekbones.

"It's habit," Paul said. "Men don't kiss men on the street in Topeka. From what I've seen, they don't do it in Washington, either."

"Cowards," Victor said.

"It's easy for you to say." Paul touched Victor's cheek.

"It should be easy for you to say, too."

"So what would I do if someone gives me a hard time? Destroy him? Rip his throat open in front of everyone? Suck every last drop of blood out of him?"

Victor patted Paul's crotch. "Just pull that out and you'll send the bastard running."

They held hands all the way back to Georgetown. When a car

blasted its horn at them at a well-lit intersection, Paul waved his middle finger at the driver.

Victor eyed shoppers on M Street, but he didn't say a thing about feeding. Paul was glad. Victor's arousal as he sucked the throat of a college boy might ruin the romance of the night.

When they got home, Victor led Paul up to their bedroom, undressed him, and shoved him on the bed. They pierced each other's bodies with their teeth and fangs. Wounds, like bloody mouths, flamed on their undead flesh and instantly healed. With every thrust or squeeze or slap, Paul's sense of hot euphoria swelled. He felt high. In the heat of his surrender to Victor, every doubt fell away, like meat boiling off a bone.

Content and exhausted, Paul slept well past sunset the next night. When he climbed out of his casket, he sensed that Victor's casket was empty. On the mantel in the living room he found a note. "I'll leave you to your painting."

Paul had told Victor that he wanted to spend the evening working, but he intended to shop for Victor's birthday gift. From Victor's calculations his Julian calendar date of birth corresponded to September 18. Victor already knew about one gift, a portrait of the two of them that Paul had nearly finished. The store-bought gift was a surprise. It would demonstrate Paul's financial independence. Two of his paintings had just sold at a little art shop near the university. After giving the owner his cut, Paul had five hundred dollars in his pocket. If Victor worried about the dangers of clinging, then this was one way to put that fear to rest. There was no need for Kyle or any other lover.

In the gray marble bath off their bedroom, he showered and shaved, cutting himself twice—the frequent result of shaving without benefit of a mirror. Then he left the house and headed for the shops around Dupont Circle.

Saturday night traffic was heavy on Connecticut Avenue. Pedestrians on the sidewalks entered restaurants and coffee shops. Paul entered an import shop on the avenue and perused African tribal masks and bright textiles woven in Peru. He saw nothing Victor would want. A shop two doors down displayed Irish sweaters. He strolled through the rows of wool, but the September warmth made the heavy garments especially unappealing. He crossed the street and entered a jewelry shop. When none of the watches or rings or chains struck his fancy, he gave up on shopping for the night.

On his way out the door, an attractive bearded man passed the shop window in the direction of the circle. He decided to follow him there to relax and people watch on a bench near the fountain. He walked up Connecticut and wove his way through a traffic jam around the circle.

As he cut across the circle, he saw Victor and Kyle standing near the fountain in the center amid kids on skateboards and people on the benches.

His stomach fell. Why were they here, ruining his night, making him feel like a chump for wanting to please Victor with the perfect gift? He couldn't take the sight. But just as he started to turn back and escape the pain, Victor pulled Kyle toward him and kissed him and Paul found his gaze frozen on them. He couldn't bring himself to move. The sound of traffic swelled in his ears. Laughter and voices bounced around him. But he stood as rigid as the statue at the base of the fountain, a nude Neptune, towering over a ship, whose sail hid his crotch.

Nearby two college boys were passing a soccer ball back and forth. When one of them bumped into Paul, the spell snapped. Adrenalin rushed through him, and he jolted toward the fountain, stopping in front of the Victor and Kyle. "You're a fucker!" he yelled at Victor.

A cluster of drag queens on the benches applauded. One yelled, "You go, girl!"

"Go home," Victor said calmly.

Kyle glanced around, uncomfortable.

"I want the world to know what a fucker you are," Paul said, shoving Victor so hard he nearly tripped into the fountain. "He's a vampire!" Paul screamed, facing the crowd.

"Mr. Vampire can suck me," a drag queen cried.

Furious, Victor steadied himself and lunged at Paul, knocking him to the ground. Kyle heroically pushed past Victor and offered Paul his hand.

Paul pushed it away. "Leave me the hell alone." His heart thumping, he climbed to his feet, and glaring at Victor, turned and retraced his steps, leaving the pair in the middle of the circle.

His rage made him oblivious to everything and everyone he passed on the sidewalks back to Dies Irae. When he reached the club, he unlocked the front door, crossed the empty, echoing church, and descended the stairs to the basement. He didn't bother turning on the light in the dark kitchen. Pots and pans dangled from a ceiling rack. The Formica countertops and stainless steel sinks were spotless. On a butcher block, sat an oak knife caddy. Paul found a knife with a six-inch blade and took it to his studio. Then he placed the finished portrait of him and Victor on the easel. Victor's handsome face transfixed him. He almost felt the solid hands that the painted Victor placed on his own painted shoulders. He raised the knife, willing himself to slash the canvas. *It's a fucking obsession*, he told himself. *Cut yourself loose.* It was no good. He couldn't ruin the painting.

But in that moment, a plan came to him.

When he rose the next night, he didn't confront Victor. He was quiet, but Victor was accustomed to his reflective moods, especially since Alice's death. In his studio he phoned St. Ignatius. A message recorded by Gimello announced a Sunday benediction service at eight-thirty, following a meal for the homeless served in the basement soup kitchen.

At the church, Paul followed two scraggly men down concrete stairs at the side of the building. In the basement, thirty or forty disheveled men at long tables ate roast beef and mashed potatoes. Most of the diners sat in silence, oblivious to the people around them. A dozen more men stood in a line, waiting to be served. Two men in their sixties filled the plates, along with Kyle, who wore a white chef's apron over his clerical shirt and Roman collar. His blond hair was wet and his face flushed, as though he'd just showered after jogging or working out. He reminded Paul of the sweet-faced jocks in his college classes, fresh from the locker room.

Paul exited before Kyle could see him, entered the church, and sat in a back pew. Over the next hour, worshippers wandered in, genuflecting and kneeling. Some lit votive candles at side altars. As eight-thirty approached, the organ played a chantlike melody. Two acolytes in surplices lit the candles near the altar, and finally the acolytes and Kyle processed down the aisle, led by a cross bearer. Kyle wore a gold chasuble and folded his large hands with perfect piety, his fingertips pressed together.

Throughout the service, Paul positioned himself directly behind an old couple, out of Kyle's line of vision but able to peer around them. Desire for the priest flared in Paul's crotch and belly as Kyle led the prayers and raised the gold monstrance containing the consecrated wafer.

As worshippers dispersed, Paul slipped into the dark confessional until everyone was gone and the lights extinguished. Behind the confessional's heavy drapes, he watched Kyle kneel before the dark altar, his head bowed. Paul approached the altar with the stealth of a cat.

He hovered over Kyle's beautiful neck, waiting for him to notice his presence. He finally did, scrambling to his feet.

"You scared me."

"Sorry. I stayed after the service."

"I didn't see you."

Paul shrugged. "I was here." Paul studied Kyle's gray eyes. Did he love Victor, or was he simply overcome by Victor's power? If under Victor's power, how far gone was he? "You're a hypocrite, you know."

"I know."

"You're fucking my lover."

"He said . . ."

"What? That I don't care? That we have an agreement?"

Kyle swallowed and stared helplessly at him.

Paul focused his thoughts until they became like a beam of light that penetrated Kyle's mind. And he saw lurking there, in Kyle's own confused ideas, the shadow of Victor. The discovery jarred him, but he intensified his own concentration, determined to drive the shadow away. It worked. The gloom evaporated. Kyle winced and then relaxed. He gazed expectantly at Paul, as though he wanted to say something. He kissed Paul, at first tentatively, then in an act of surrender. Paul kissed him back, holding him close, a promise sounding in his mind. *I'll protect you. I'll protect us all.*

Every night for a week, Kyle gave himself to Paul. At first, like a fire fed with fuel, Paul's passion burned brighter with every touch of Kyle's flesh. And every lustful thrust into Kyle was a slap in Victor's face. Of course, Victor would laugh at the displaced vindication. What was Paul's fucking to him? And because Paul's heart and mind were nothing like Victor's, he quickly began to regret using Kyle to vent his anger. His rage-driven lust began to mix with tenderness for the pawn that once existed for Victor's pleasure, but now existed for his own. So he resolved to cut Kyle loose and spend his evenings working. When he tried to do that, however, he stared at a blank canvas for an hour without sketching one stroke. It was no use. He couldn't concentrate. He called Kyle and arranged to meet him at a bookstore café near Dupont Circle.

Kyle showed up looking tired. They sat in the café's crowded addition, a steel and glass structure like a greenhouse. Kyle unzipped his windbreaker and ordered a sandwich and a beer. Paul ordered one of the Chinese beers on the menu. He swished it around in his mouth, enjoying the flavor, and then spit it back in the glass when Kyle wasn't looking.

Between big bites of his sandwich, Kyle talked about a boy's basketball team he coached at the parish school. He bragged about the team's first win of the season. The boys probably worshipped their dedicated young coach.

You must let him go, Paul thought to himself as Kyle spoke. *Leave him to his holy vocation.* Maybe Paul was trying to protect himself by holding onto Kyle. Maybe he really believed Sonia. *You can never have a truly mutual relationship with Victor. For a vampire, mutuality is impossible. Protect yourself from unrealistic expectations. Take a lover to maintain the proper perspective.*

Kyle wore a V-neck T-shirt under his windbreaker. Paul's eyes kept falling on his sinewy throat and the Adam's apple that bobbed whenever Kyle chugged his beer. He would feed on Kyle tonight while they made love—something Kyle was always eager to do, like an adolescent at the mercy of exploding hormones.

Kyle seemed to read his thoughts. "Look, tonight I don't want to do it. I just went to confession."

"To Gimello?" Paul had a hard time imagining anyone baring their soul to the severe priest.

Kyle shook his head. "At the basilica. Visiting priests hear daily confessions. Priests I'll never run into. I go every time we have sex."

"Jesus."

"It's a mortal sin," Kyle said adamantly. "If you're in the state of mortal sin you can't receive communion. I have to receive it every day when I say mass."

"So, if I left you alone . . ."

Kyle sighed. "It wouldn't matter. I can't control myself."

Paul imagined him humping a scraggly hustler in a dark car.

"Do you want to?"

"I don't know." Kyle looked away.

They exited through the crowded bookstore and strolled along the shops on Connecticut Avenue. When they turned down a dark street, Kyle suddenly pulled Paul to him and kissed him, his hand roaming down to Paul's crotch.

"Let's go to the rectory," he whispered.

"What about confession?" Paul said.

"I don't care."

"What about Gimello?"

"He's on chaplain duty at the hospital. He doesn't get back until ten."

They went to the Metro station and boarded a Red Line train. By the time they hiked to the rectory, it was late, but they could still manage a quick session in bed. They entered the back door, and climbed the stairs. Kyle suddenly stopped as he reached the second-floor hallway. The light glowed under Gimello's door. Kyle approached it gingerly and pressed his ear against it, nodding to Paul who waited at the top of the stairs. When Paul made a motion to leave, Kyle panicked. He rushed to Paul, grabbed the sleeve of his shirt, and pulled him toward his room. Inside, he locked the door without turning on the lights. He kissed Paul hard and stripped him, as though he hadn't had sex in years instead of days.

Just as Kyle shuddered in orgasm, Paul pierced his throat and sucked deeply. Unconscious, Kyle lay on him, still and heavy as a statue.

Why not do it? he thought as Kyle's warm blood filled him. *Why not turn him into a thrall and save him from his fucking religious scruples? From that bastard Gimello? Why not give myself what Victor has now? Maybe I can't have Victor forever. Maybe not even for another year. What will I be left with?*

The thought of a lonely life of prowling by night horrified him. An image flashed in his mind of a gaunt Hollywood vampire—pathetic, tormented, and lonely—creeping through a cemetery, stooping over a corpse, and racing to his grave as the sun rimmed the horizon. With an act of will and a little of his own bloodletting he could guarantee that he would never be such a figure. He had no power to tame Victor, to remold what centuries of cruelty and solitude had created. The forces of the Dark Kingdom knew the heart of a vampire would never permit lovers to cling faithfully to each other throughout the eons. Maybe those powers had even designed their ghouls with this incapacity.

Paul pulled his wrist to his mouth. He closed his eyes and inhaled deeply. The moment his fangs touched his flesh, footsteps sounded in the hallway. Gimello knocked on the door.

"Are you asleep, Kyle?" he called.

Kyle did not stir. His unconscious state would last as long as Paul willed it.

After a second knock, the floor creaked as Gimello returned to his room.

Paul rolled Kyle onto his back, got up, and drew the sheets over his chest, leaving the sheet crumpled at the foot of the bed. Quickly throwing on his clothes, he opened the window, removed the screen, and crawled onto the window ledge. Scanning the empty street below, he rose into the night.

8

Joshu directed the two shaggy boys to hold the ram's legs, front and hind. The boys, in homespun tunics, relished the job, gazing at the ram's walnut-sized testicles and then at each other on either side of the animal. In a white tunic that exposed his sinewy arms and throat, Joshu rubbed his thumb along the blade of his knife, its handle tied in place with coiled rope. The Jerusalem sun beat down on his long hair and broad back. His brown skin, further darkened by the summer sun, glistened with perspiration. The craggy hillside radiated heat around him. Joshu squatted, raised his eyes to heaven, and with a steady swipe, sliced the skin over the left testicle. Then he bent down and removed the bloody node with his teeth, spitting it on the scraggly grass. A tawny dog, his skin dull and patchy, suddenly appeared and lapped up the testicle. He had barely finished swallowing it when Joshu spit out the second testicle for him. He and the two boys laughed as the dog snatched it up. With one swift motion, Joshu docked the ram's tail, to keep it from collecting brambles. With the job com-

MICHAEL SCHIEFELBEIN

plete, the boys released the ram. For the first time, it bleated, having lain silent and docile through the procedure.

Joshu glanced up at Victor, shading the sun from his eyes. "Like a lamb," he said, "he did not open his mouth. Like a lamb."

"What kind of heroics do you call that?" Victor said. "It's weakness. You let them defeat you. You walked into their trap. They castrated you."

Joshu grinned, his chestnut eyes clear as a baby's. "Love is the only power."

"Love? For who?"

Joshu nodded toward the boys.

"For filthy shepherds? They're too ignorant to scrape the lice out of their hair."

Worried, the boys ran their hands through their nappy locks.

"Sedition charges, Joshu. What for? Leading a mob of mangy shepherds and fishermen and rotting lepers?"

Joshu's expression turned serious. "You're in danger, Victor."

"You had your chance. Don't pretend to love me."

"You're in danger." Joshu stood and raised the bloody knife toward Victor's throat.

Victor's eyes snapped open in the dark sarcophagus. The warmth of the sunlight, so real in his dream, gave way to cool cellar air. But the dream seemed just as real as it had in his sleep. He almost expected to find Joshu waiting for him when he raised the heavy lid, to hear Joshu's warning once again and feel Joshu's cold blade against his throat.

But he knew Joshu was not really present. Only twilight awaited him outside this tomb. It lingered beyond the cellar's walls—every cell of his body registered it—though he could rise now with little risk. He climbed out of the casket and caressed the ivory ornamentation on Paul's Moroccan chest. He lifted the lid. Pale and tranquil, Paul slept, his long hands clasped together on a red shirt, the tapered nails nearly two inches longer now than when he had climbed into his resting place. Victor kissed Paul's full, pale lips. Immediately a sense of apprehension arose in him.

The feeling, which he'd noted periodically after Paul's transformation, had grown more intense lately. He'd begun testing himself for it, the way a hypochondriac tests himself for fever, touching Paul or kissing him to register the response. What was the source of the apprehension? Perhaps he felt threatened by the mere presence of another vampire. Even one he loved, one who would never harm him. Not willingly. But then a natural predator might have no choice, striking out instinctively against a competitor. If that was true, then maybe he feared as much his own potential to harm Paul as he did Paul's potential to harm him.

But perhaps a much more human fear explained the apprehension. Perhaps he feared losing the one he loved. Again. Perhaps the primal sense of despair that had enveloped him when he lost Joshu, a loss that brought him to this life, so defined him that he could never trust an equal lover. In that case, this life with Paul was futile, absurd. In that case, Sonia was right. He could not invest in this love. He needed diversion.

And apparently their lives depended on it.

Victor quietly lowered the lid, and went to find Horatio. He needed a quick, easy feed. He found him carrying towels to the guest rooms. Members of a German S and M club were due in from Berlin at nine o'clock. With his white-blond hair and eyebrows, Horatio looked German himself. Victor told him that he'd get along well with the guests, caressed his firm pectoral muscles, and sank his teeth into his neck. Horatio's blood had a strange, fishy aftertaste. He'd probably been taking fish oil or some other supplement—at the prompting of one of his men's health magazines. Victor withdrew his lips after swallowing just enough to dull his hunger pain. He cleaned the wound with his tongue, kissed Horatio on the lips, and lowered him to the guest bed where he would regain consciousness in a few moments.

Victor returned to his house, showered, and dressed before going out into the night. He hiked to a stretch of 17th Street crowded with gay establishments—a video store, a restaurant with sidewalk dining, and two bars. They surrounded a Safeway popular for cruising. He stepped into the bar where he'd arranged to meet Kyle for a happy hour drink. In the dimly lit room, men in suits gathered at tall cocktail tables near the window. The seats at the bar were all filled. Two bald men in trench coats chatted at one end. Victor willed them to relinquish their seats. They immediately got up and took their drinks to a back room where a music video played. Victor climbed on the stool and ordered a beer to avoid attracting the bartender's attention. As he waited, a man with horn-rimmed glasses and a flat top eyed him from the opposite end of the bar. If he hadn't been expecting Kyle, Victor might have led him into the shadows somewhere and pierced his throat. Now, he glared at the man, who smirked and turned his attention to a stocky man with a mustache.

Thirty minutes after the appointed time, Kyle still hadn't arrived. Maybe Gimello had cornered Kyle to run an errand. Victor pulled his cell phone from the pocket of his trousers and punched in Kyle's number. After five rings, Kyle's recorded message played. Victor went outside, away from the noise of the bar, and trained his thoughts on Kyle's face. He focused on Kyle's gray eyes, which granted him access to Kyle's mind. But the image vanished. When Victor tried to summon it again, it would not appear intact. Only pieces of his face—an eye, his brow, his full lips—floated before him on a canvas the color of the sky above him, awash with city lights.

What did it mean? Gimello came to mind. Perhaps he'd discovered that Kyle was breaking his vows. Could the powers give the priest the ability to protect his protégé's mind from interference? Was this a show of strength?

He walked to a dark side street, where he rose above the trees and fought a strong wind all the way to Kyle's church, lighting across the street from the rectory. Gazing at Kyle's bright window, he once again tried to summon the priest, but the energy he emitted dispersed into the air. When a light appeared in what must have been Gimello's room, Victor instinctively stepped back into a shadowy yard. The curtain moved aside. Gimello's face appeared. His long hair hung loose on his shoulders. His barrel chest was bare, but its dark hair looked like a shirt. He seemed to peer directly at Victor, though he could not possibly discern Victor in the darkness. When he disappeared and the light vanished, Victor remained motionless for some time in case he continued to peek through the curtains. The front door of the rectory opened. Gimello emerged, in an unbuttoned clerical shirt. He walked to the church, unlocked the front door, and entered.

Crossing the street, Victor climbed the stairs to the church and eased the door open. Inside, the aroma of incense lingered in the large nave. The only light came from the sanctuary candle, which glowed on the bronze doors of the tabernacle in the high altar. Gimello knelt at the marble communion rail. He prayed quietly at first, then stretched his arms as though he mimicked the crucified corpus at the peak of the soaring reredos and called out, "O Christ, Savior, keep us from evil," repeating the cry like a mantra.

The performance felt like a dare to Victor. At the speed of thought, he transported himself to the sanctuary steps. Bending to Gimello's ear, he whispered, "Let's see how mighty your Christ is."

The priest scrambled to his feet and backed against the communion rail, facing Victor. His eyes were wide with fear. With his long, loose hair and open shirt, he looked like a madman.

"In the name of Christ, I command you to leave this place," Gimello said, his voice shaky.

Victor laughed. "You're a lunatic. You think you can exorcise me? Like an evil spirit?" Victor approached him, his fangs in view.

"Dear God, dear God, dear God," Gimello repeated. He dropped to his knees.

It struck Victor that the priest was emotionally unstable, a pathetic problem for his religious order. Victor lifted him to his feet and sliced into his throat. Gimello went limp. Victor did not drink, however. He wouldn't risk burning himself again. Better to simply kill the priest and dispose of the body. But when he tried to twist Gimello's head, it became in his grip as solid as the marble head of a statue in the hands of a mortal. He grabbed a candlestick from the altar and raised it over the priest's head. Pain suddenly shot through his chest as though someone squeezed his heart. He dropped the candlestick and clutched his chest. Gasping for air, he backed away from Gimello. When the pain finally subsided, Gimello lay quiet and untouchable.

Angry, Victor climbed to the tabernacle. In his frenzied thoughts, the powers of the Dark Kingdom and of the Christian God merged. Yanking open the locked bronze door, he removed the ciborium cover and shoved the consecrated wafers into his mouth. When he swallowed the last one, he hurled the gold-plated container across the nave. It struck a stone column with a clank.

He left the church and turned down a dark street. Occasionally, he stopped and took deep breaths to keep himself from vomiting, for now. When the door of a corner liquor store opened, he watched a fat woman waddle up the block with a bag under her arm. He followed her until she was well out of the light cast by the store's plate glass. Then he rushed forward, flung her to the sidewalk, and sank his fangs into her fleshy throat. He swallowed until he felt her heartbeat slow to the danger point, beyond which he would put his own life in jeopardy—*she* was already lost. When he got up, his face smeared with her blood, he retched. White fragments appeared in the shower of brown bile.

"Body of Christ," he whispered, his throat raw. He knelt and wiped his face on the woman's skirt.

The mound on the sidewalk was still. The smell of urine rose from it. Victor glanced around. No one stirred on the street. Boards covered the windows of several of the brick rowhouses. He got up, rallied his strength, and lifted into the night, in search of the nourishment he had just deprived himself of.

The next day was his birthday. Brooding over the scene at St. Ignatius, Victor slipped on a ring studded with amethysts that had once belonged to his brother Justin. It was the last birthday gift his father had given him, and he wore it every year on this day. His father had twisted the ring from his brother's finger as Justin lay dying of venereal disease contracted in Gaul where he was an officer. Despite the protests of Victor's mother, Lydia, her husband had suffocated Justin to end his misery. It was a way to preserve dignity.

Justin had been awarded three metals of valor by Emperor Tiberius before his early death. The glorious funeral ceremonies were still vivid in Victor's mind. They began with the *conclamatio*, when the family gathered around the body and called out the dead son's name three times, while a servant blew a horn. Then came the magnificent procession through the streets, accompanied by musicians, wailing female *praeficae*, jesters, and torch-bearers. At the forum, Justin's body was displayed upright, while Victor delivered the funeral oration, without once choking up. The funeral rites ended with a roaring funeral pyre and a feast of roasted meat, bright fruits, and choice wine.

The ring revived Victor's spirits. It reminded him of his noble family, of the legacy of power carried on in him.

Paul gave him an expensive smoking jacket, emphasizing that he'd made the purchase with his own money. Victor saw through Paul's attempt to prove his independence, but he refrained from smiling. Paul also gave him the portrait he'd been painting. In it, Paul sat in his studio armchair, his legs propped on the coffee table. Victor stood behind him, his hands on Paul's shoulders. Victor admired his own handsome image. He'd seen no likeness of himself since commissioning a bad portrait in 1748. The inept painter had paid with his life. By the feel of his face and by the attention of men and women, he knew his dark, intense looks hadn't changed over the centuries, but the portrait was proof of it.

Victor praised Paul's work in the portrait and they walked around the house considering where to display it. After selecting a wall in their bedroom, they hung it and descended to the living room to watch a DVD. At Paul's suggestion they chose *Gladiator*. This Hollywood version of the Roman Empire amused Victor. It caught well the majesty of the Eternal City but left out the pockets of squalor. And Russell Crowe's noble character was far-fetched, but he was pretty to look at. After the movie, they strolled through the neighborhood, holding hands, stopping to kiss in the moonlight. Paul was quiet. But Victor didn't probe, lest he open the floodgates of Paul's grief over Alice, which would have irritated him. Their lovemaking back at the house was tender.

Afterward, Victor worked in his office while Paul painted. Long after midnight he showered, relishing the hot spray on his cool flesh. Refreshed, he slipped on the smoking jacket and went up to find Paul. As he approached the studio door, he heard Paul talking on the phone. He entered without knocking and found Paul seated on the green sofa in a T-shirt and jeans. A canvas stood on the easel, sketched with the façade of Dies Irae. A low table nearby held a container of brushes, tubes of oil paint, and an ashtray made of coral. Paul looked up at him.

"I'll talk to you later," he said. He laid the phone on the coffee table. He lit a cigarette, sat back and crossed his legs.

"What's this?" Victor nodded toward the canvas.

"Something to dabble at until I'm more inspired."

"I was just admiring our portrait." Victor sat in an armless, upholstered chair near the sofa.

Pleased, Paul grinned. "Really? What do you like about it?"

"I like seeing my face."

"Figures."

"Who was on the phone?"

Paul hesitated. "Becky," he said, tapping his cigarette on the ashtray. "Checking up on me. Hoping I'm sane again."

The cat suddenly slipped out from under the sofa, climbed onto Paul's lap, and kneaded his crotch before settling down.

Paul petted the cat thoughtfully. He seemed to avoid looking at Victor.

"And what did you tell her?" Victor said.

Paul shrugged, without answering.

Victor sized him up. "Who were you talking to on the phone?"

"I told you. Becky."

The truth suddenly became clear to Victor. "You were talking to *him*."

Paul looked up. He gazed directly at Victor now, his hazel eyes full of a surprising determination.

"You've been fucking him."

"What if I have?"

"Why can't you find your own lover?" Victor said.

"You're my lover."

"You know what I mean."

"He's not your lover," Paul retorted. "You were controlling him."

So Paul was responsible for his inability to make contact with the young priest. Now as Victor gazed at his lover, he saw an adversary. "I do what I choose to do," Victor said.

Eyeing him angrily, Paul took a last drag on his cigarette and stubbed it out.

Victor got up and walked to the window. Down the street a motorcycle idled. The rider waited while a hefty woman in jeans locked her front door. Victor turned back to Paul. "You think you're a match for me?"

"We have the same nature," Paul said defiantly.

Adrenaline like hot, churning water rushed through Victor. "You cannot begin to comprehend the kind of strength that develops over two thousand years. You're pampered. What do you know about foraging for blood during a plague? What do you know about surviving when the monks discover your tomb? When they hover over you with a spike in their hand."

He'd survived worse things—centuries of lonely preying, with no family or lover, centuries of feeding on babies, of killing his own companions, centuries of being haunted by memories of the old Joshu, and the reality of the transformed Joshu, who prompted his loathing and violence. These things came to mind, but he was not about to bare his soul to an opponent—and a betrayer, as Paul had just revealed himself to be.

Paul glared at him. "Everything's a power game with you, isn't it? Why did I ever expect something different? You couldn't love before you entered this fucking life, and you sure as hell can't love now."

Victor wanted to tear off the look of contempt on Paul's face. His anger alerted Paul. He stiffened as Victor approached him, and the cat jumped to the floor. Before Paul could stand, Victor leaned over and grabbed him by the throat. Paul clutched Victor's wrist with both of his hands and applied force that felt like a vise. Victor thought his bones would snap. Paul shoved him with so much power that he flew across the coffee table. Automatically, he sprang to his feet ready to lunge at Paul. But now Paul seemed confused by what had happened and repentant. He started to reach for Victor, but Victor pushed him away and left the room.

He rushed out of the house. As he crossed the street, a white SUV nearly hit him. When the bearded driver slammed on his brakes and laid on the horn, Victor lifted the vehicle with one hand and tipped it on its side.

Victor observed Paul's moves the next night without taking action. He must be on his guard. He knew Paul had no desire to harm him directly, but perhaps he couldn't help himself. He loved Victor in the imperfect, maybe futile way that Victor loved him. But Paul's tenderness could not undo centuries of witnessing the darkest of motives.

After rising, Paul disappeared into his studio, where he stayed until eleven. Then he appeared at Victor's office and invited him to go feed. Victor declined. Early in the morning, Paul returned home and watched television in their bedroom. Victor watched with him. Whenever he lifted his eyes, he found Paul's innocent face irresistible. Nearly.

Was it possible that Paul was right about Victor's inability to love? Was he simply a predator through and through? Had he always been so, even during his days as a Roman officer who took whatever he wanted from woman or man? The impulse had an elemental intensity. It always had. Joshu was the first man who left this impulse unsatisfied. Joshu could not be taken. And the result? Restlessness. Emptiness. Until he could find someone to replace Joshu—replace the one who could not be possessed—the void could not be filled. But a paradox stared him in the face: despite his impulse to possess, he longed for an equal companion, one who could not be possessed.

Impatient with self-scrutiny, Victor dismissed such thoughts and turned to his familiar concern. Self-preservation—for him, the same thing as dominance. No doubt, Paul, in his new existence as a vampire, operated from the same concern. His acquisition of Kyle was his way of asserting his power. Victor realized he should feel relieved to see things as they were. But relief eluded him. Paul wanted more than independence. Like any vampire, he wanted mastery.

That would not do.

When Victor awoke at sunset, a clear plan of action lay before him. He rose and tended to business in his office until nearly nine. Then he left Dies Irae and headed up the street to Georgetown University. When he reached the campus, he found the modern athletics building. The main door was locked. Near it was a slot for inserting ID cards, which served as keys. With one quick yank, Victor broke the door's latch and entered. Inside, he heard voices in the gym and the squeak of sneakers on the floor. He poked his head in and saw two college boys shooting baskets. Leaving them to their game, he followed signs to the pool, which was in a separate building connected by a corridor.

Inside the cavernous pool room, underwater lights revealed the sloping floor and lap lanes of the Olympic-size pool. The room itself remained in shadows. Victor stood on the concrete deck, watching Kyle's substantial body plow through the water. As Kyle switched from the crawl to the breaststroke, his muscular deltoids bunched and released rhythmically. His powerful arms swept back the water as though it had no more mass than gauze.

Tuesday night laps all alone. Victor imagined that Kyle lived for the quiet, vigorous swim, a privilege allowed him as a Jesuit in a Jesuit university. No doubt, the workout exorcised the frustrations of his repressed life.

Victor sat on the end of the diving board, directly over Kyle's lane. As Kyle splashed toward him, he suddenly stopped, raising his head. He stared at Victor through swimming goggles.

"What are you doing here?" he said, panting.

"I miss you."

"I want you to leave me alone." Kyle resumed swimming, flipping over as he touched the wall beneath Victor and moving back down the lane.

When he reached the center of the pool, Victor focused his gaze on him. Kyle stopped in midstroke and struggled in the water. Victor stripped off his clothes and sliced into the pool, speeding like a missile, propelled only by his volition.

He stopped short of Kyle, who splashed desperately, his head bobbing.

"Do you want help?" Victor said, treading water with ease.

"I have a cramp," Kyle muttered, reaching out for Victor.

Victor grabbed him and dunked his head. Kyle thrashed violently. Victor finally pulled him up by the hair, towed him to the side, and hoisted him to the deck, where he stood over him, naked and dripping until Kyle recovered.

"Why did you betray me?" he finally said.

Kyle opened his mouth to speak but could only cough.

"I scare you. That means I can give you what you want. Can he do that?"

"You don't even know him," Kyle blurted.

"Oh? Tell me about him." Victor crouched on his haunches and snatched off Kyle's goggles.

"His heart's not made of stone, for one thing," Kyle finally said. "He's human."

Victor laughed. The sound of his voice echoed through the room.

"He's not a bastard like you," Kyle snapped. "He's good."

"I doubt that your superior agrees," Victor said. "He thinks every sodomite is a bastard. Wait until he hears about your own perverse nature."

"He doesn't have to tell me about you. I can see it for myself."

"And yet you found your way into my arms."

"Like you said. I'm afraid of you."

"Why is that?" Victor pressed him. What did the young priest know about his nature? What had Gimello told him?

Kyle shook his head. "I don't know why. Some kind of phobia. I don't know. You say something and I do it without thinking. It's like a compulsion."

"And with Paul?"

"I do what I want." He eyed Victor belligerently. "I'm in love with him."

"I suppose you think he loves you."

"I hope he does. God help me."

"You're a confused boy."

"*I'm* confused?" Kyle propped himself on his elbows, his jaw set in anger. "Look at you. You think you can control me. But you can't make me love you. You can't make Paul love you, either. So how much power do you really have?"

"I'll show you," Victor shouted. Pouncing on Kyle, he held him down with one hand and stripped off his trunks with the other. All the while Kyle writhed to free himself, beating Victor with his fists. Victor barely felt Kyle's puny efforts. He forced apart Kyle's legs with his own knee and fell on him, clamping his arms to the concrete deck. Kyle gritted his teeth and thrust his hips in a futile attempt to push Victor away. Victor laughed and thrust himself into Kyle. Kyle winced and groaned in pain. Desperate, he spat in Victor's face.

Angered, Victor raised his hips to drive himself into the defiant boy. But just as he lifted his body, he felt powerful hands clamp his throat. He felt himself being wrenched away from Kyle and forced into the water. When he broke through the surface, his assailant stood over him on the deck. It was Paul, of course. He glared at Victor, his hands making fists at his side. When Victor opened his mouth to taunt him, Paul suddenly leaped into the water, clutched him by the arm, and dragged him to the bottom of the deep end of the pool. There, Paul pinned him down. Paul's hair rose in the water like the tentacles of an anemone. His face, frighteningly pallid against a blood-red shirt, was contorted in anger. His lips uttered words incomprehensible in the water, but discernible to Victor. *I hate you.*

For the first time in Victor's nocturnal existence, he had lost the upper hand in a contest of physical strength. The shock of his defeat was intense, but it quickly gave way to panic. How long could he survive without air? In the whole course of his existence, he never had been forced to test his endurance this way. Paul remained tenaciously clamped to him. Was he willing to die for the satisfaction of killing his creator?

Clenching his teeth, Victor thrust his arms forward. Paul lost his grip and Victor was free. Now he pressed Paul to the floor.

"I'll kill you." The water bubbled around Victor's words.

Looking defeated, Paul stared at him, communicating his thoughts to Victor's mind. *Then kill me. And get it over with.*

By now, Kyle had come to Paul's rescue. Applying a headlock, he futilely tried to pry Victor loose. Victor could have drowned him in an instant. But he needed air himself. He rose to the surface and, gasping, treaded water as he waited for Kyle and Paul.

When they emerged, he prepared himself to attack. *Why not kill them both now?*

But Paul's wounded glance struck a nerve. It was madness to want to let Paul go. But he couldn't help himself. He swam to the edge, climbed out of the pool, snatched up his clothes, and crossed the deck to the door.

In a sour mood the next night, Victor sat with a table of guests visiting Dies Irae for the second time. They dabbled in the occult, inserting a bit of S and M into their rituals. Karen, the woman with the crucifix tattoo on her buttock, was part of the group. When Victor sat next to her, she immediately laid her hand on his thigh. The other two women in the group were obviously impressed with him. The two men, bruisers whose biceps stretched their short sleeves, eyed him guardedly over the drinks that Mark Seepay supplied. The sound system churned out New Age music with a heavy drum beat and tremulous panpipe.

"Tell me about your Black Mass," Victor said to the group in general.

"We use the Roman Catholic ritual," Karen said. "We just substitute Satan's name for God's."

"There are other changes, too, baby." The fortyish, blond woman who spoke had introduced herself as Maureen. She wore a low-cut, lacey black top, exposing ample cleavage. One breast was tattooed with a skull and crossbones. She fanned her fingers on the table. The long scarlet nails lay like drops of blood on the white tablecloth.

"Like what?" Victor said, returning her obvious flirt.

Maureen smiled wickedly. "We fuck."

"All of you?" The vision of the little coven engaged in an orgy was pleasurable.

"The women draw straws," said Deborah, a petite woman with delicate features and dyed black hair, short and spiked.

"And is there a crucifix involved?" Victor said.

They all laughed, even the men, evidently getting his allusion to the scene in *The Exorcist*, in which the possessed girl masturbates with a crucifix.

"No," said Eric, the bruiser with the tiny mouth and chest hair that escaped the neck of his red shirt. "Gary and I do the job." He glanced across the table at a heavy-lidded man with a goatee.

"Not very politically correct," Victor said.

"Believe me," Karen said, patting his crotch, "the women call the shots in our coven. We are the high priestesses. They are the acolytes. The powers of Darkness are female, after all. The women represent them. We choose which man has the honor of entering the night. Would you like a turn?"

"I'm never an acolyte. But I'll watch."

After another hour of drinking, the group went to their rooms and changed into robes made of sheer black fabric that fell like shadows over their naked bodies. They paraded by Victor, who sat a table near the stage. Eric produced a box of candles. He and Gary lined the tapers up on the high altar, lighting them with cigarette lighters. They instructed Mark Seepay to turn off all the lights and play a CD they had brought, a strident, unaccompanied chant of bass voices that sounded like the grunts of men thrusting. Serving as high priestess, Karen intoned prayers to the powers of darkness and led a litany of "saints," including the Marquis de Sade and the Whore of Babylon in all her manifestations. Then she circled the group standing around the altar. Stopping at Eric, she untied his silky robe and it slipped from his wide shoulders. She led him to the altar, directed him to spread his legs, and brace himself. Then everyone in the group moved counterclockwise around the altar, lashing his body with cords they had tied around their necks, and chanting the words "Dies Irae." When red lash marks streaked his back, legs, and buttocks, Karen directed him to crawl up onto the altar. He lay on his back, his purple erection jerking with each breath he took. Then Gary lifted Karen up on the altar and she mounted Eric.

The scene aroused Victor's thirst for blood as much as it did his lust. But the one he suddenly wanted was not among the group before him. He had to have the young priest. Paul had blocked his power to summon Kyle, but there was another way to take what he wanted. Another, fiercer way to strike back at Paul.

Leaving the group to their amusement, Victor exited the building and lifted into the night, finally lighting before the rectory of St. Ignatius Church. But he sensed that Kyle was not in his room. He walked to the church. Trying the door, he found it unlocked. Stepping into the dark nave, he spotted Kyle's silhouette, fifty yards away, kneeling before the tabernacle in the alcovelike apse. His hands were extended at his sides, mimicking the crucified Christ at the peak of the reredos. He wore a cassock now, instead of a clerical shirt, as though he wanted greater protection from the world's lustful temptations. A large sanctuary lamp glowed softly in the apse, and votive candles burned before a statue of the Virgin Mary on one side of the sanctuary and of St. Joseph on the other.

With the speed of thought, Victor transported himself to him.

But Kyle remained frozen in his cruciform position, oblivious to the presence behind his shoulder.

"Kyle," he whispered.

Kyle's head turned slightly, but his arms stayed in place.

"I'm here for you."

"Please leave," Kyle said.

"I'm afraid I can't. I want you too much."

Kyle lowered his arms and got up, facing him. His cassock accentuated his stocky, muscular figure. The Roman collar fit tight around his broad throat. Victor felt a tingling in his fangs.

"Let's go to the rectory," Kyle said.

Victor laughed. "Worried I'll defile the holy sanctuary?"

Kyle looked horrified now. He made the sign of the cross.

Victor touched Kyle's warm cheek. "How does it feel to meet someone who can overpower such a brawny boy as you?"

"You can hurt me physically. But you can't touch my soul."

"Can't I?" Victor nuzzled Kyle's throat. Kyle's body stiffened, as though he prepared for the worst. "I remember you begging for me."

"I strayed, but Christ has forgiven me. I've recommitted myself."

"You don't sound happy."

"I don't want happiness. That's the way of the world. Christ teaches us to reject the world. He gives us life in the spirit."

Victor kissed his cheek. "I want you, Kyle."

"The spirit is willing, but the flesh is weak. That's what Christ said to the disciples when he found them asleep the night he was arrested. They couldn't stay awake and watch with him."

Victor pressed himself against Kyle, smiling when he felt Kyle's erection.

"I made a promise. My eternity depends on it."

Despite Kyle's half-hearted attempt to defend himself, Victor flung him to the slate floor. Pouncing on him, he pinned back his arms and fell on his throat.

Kyle softly groaned when he pierced it. Victor willed him to remain conscious, and when he began siphoning his blood, Kyle tensed in alarm, trying to push him away. But Victor sucked until Kyle's heartbeat quickened drastically. Whenever he had drunk to this point, the illogic of a victim's adrenaline struck him: the chemical was supposed to help a victim flee, but it only shot more blood into his mouth, hastening death.

Victor ripped the tender skin of his wrist and forced the wound into Kyle's mouth. Kyle tried to turn his head away.

"Drink it." Victor clutched a handful of Kyle's thick blond hair to immobilize his head. Kyle swallowed. When his gray eyes registered the beginning of the transformation, Victor released him. Now Kyle willingly lapped his wrist. Victor closed his eyes and moaned in pleasure. The erotic sensation was fuller and more prolonged than an orgasm. By sheer effort of will, he retracted his wrist.

Kyle's whole body shuddered in spasms—like the spasms that had overtaken the dozen thralls that Victor had created in his lifetime, Paul included. Kyle panted wildly, as though he struggled for air in his move from one kind of existence to another. Finally, his body relaxed. Sweat beaded on his face. He opened his eyes and gazed listlessly at nothing. Victor helped him to his feet, led him to his room, and got him out of the cassock. He moved soundlessly to avoid waking Gimello.

"You won't need this anymore," Victor said, tossing the sweaty garment on the bed. He pulled a pair of jeans and a T-shirt from a chest of drawers, and helped Kyle into them. Like a child awakened from sleep, the groggy young priest let himself be dressed and transported through the night sky to Georgetown.

They lighted in front of Victor's townhouse. On the third floor, the windows of Paul's studio glowed. Victor smiled with satisfaction. He unlocked the front door, and led Kyle in and up the stairs to the bedroom.

The thrall needed an initiatory ride by the master to obliterate any lingering inclinations for rebellion.

Victor laid Kyle on the mattress and stripped him. He bent him over the side of the mattress, stroking Kyle's full, muscular buttocks. As he penetrated Kyle, he let him feed once again from his wrist. Kyle lapped the blood excitedly, until both of them shuddered in orgasm.

The door opened. Just as Victor knew it would.

"Jesus Christ!" Paul lunged at Victor, pulling him off Kyle. When he rolled Kyle over, Kyle smiled up at him drowsily, his erect penis throbbing on his belly and blood trickling from his mouth. Paul stared at Victor, incredulous. "Why did you do it?"

"Why do you think?"

"You bastard." Paul came at Victor, grabbing his throat with both hands.

Victor pushed Paul onto the bed. They struggled, Paul's long nails tearing into Victor's bare back and his fangs slicing his shoulders. Finally mustering his superior will, Victor clamped Paul's arms to the mattress and bore down on him with his body. He could feel Paul's own body responding to him despite his fury.

"You can't help wanting me, can you?" Filled with a sense of mastery, Victor laughed and released his defeated lover.

9

Paul woke up, aware that twilight lingered outside his dark casket. He waited for the night, wanting a cigarette. As the grogginess left him, he sensed an unfamiliar presence in the wine cellar. At first he thought a cat had found its way through a hole in the foundation of the house. But the presence seemed larger, distinctly human. A quiet presence, not someone waiting to attack, which would have accelerated his heart and stimulated the growth of his fangs. Then he remembered. When the last traces of radiation dissolved, he opened the lid of the chest. Kyle lay on the earthen floor by Victor's sarcophagus, his back to Paul. His pale, muscular body was naked.

What Paul felt was worse than abandonment. If Victor had failed to return in the night, leaving him without a word, his pain would have a sense of purity. He could name the wrong that seared him like a flame. He could cry, he could scream, he could seek comfort. But he knew Victor still lay beneath the stone lid. Instead of choosing to leave him, he had chosen against loving him—or being vulnerable, which was the same thing. Isn't that what this thrall meant? Whether Victor had created him to get revenge or to assert his power, the result would be an inevitable, chilling distance between them.

Paul went to their bedroom, smoked a cigarette, and climbed into the shower. As he massaged shampoo into his long hair, the bathroom door opened. Victor's silhouette appeared through the frosted glass door. The shower door opened, and Victor stepped in. He stared at Paul, the dark hair on his chest flattening under the water's pressure. His black eyes hinted of triumph, even cruelty. Despite himself, Paul wanted him. He closed his eyes and let Victor kiss him. He dropped to his knees and let Victor guide him in every way he chose. When they finished making love, they both dried themselves silently in the bathroom.

"Where is he?" Paul said.

"The guest house. Resting. Horatio's given him a room."

"What about Gimello?" Paul realized how stupid the words sounded even as he spoke them. Why should Victor care about a fanatical Jesuit, robbed of his protégé?

But Victor did not laugh. "What about him?"

"You're putting us at risk."

The mean glint returned to Victor's eyes. "Make your own thrall if you're jealous."

"I don't want my own thrall."

"No, you want something worse. A lover."

"Now who's jealous?" Paul knew he was saying all the wrong things. But he couldn't keep himself from lashing out. "You wanted Kyle. But I got him. You couldn't stand it, could you?" He wadded up his towel and threw it on the tile floor.

Victor followed him into the bedroom, where they both dressed in silence.

"What are your plans for him?" Paul finally said.

"What do you think?"

Paul's chest tightened. He lit a cigarette to quiet the rising panic. Victor could always turn Kyle into a vampire. The rules forbade it, but the rules meant nothing now. And if Kyle were a vampire, he would share their powers. *Please, Victor*, he wanted to say, just *get rid of him*. But how could that happen, without killing Kyle? That was the last thing he wanted. If he could save Kyle, he would. But it was too late now.

Victor seemed to read his thoughts. He cast Paul a triumphant glance as he buttoned his shirt.

Paul needed air. He finished dressing and started down the stairs, where he met Kyle coming up. He wore a T-shirt and jeans. His face was livid. By now he must have experienced some of the other changes that came with his transformation into a thrall. Fingernails that grow faster than you can cut them. A keen new sensitivity to sounds and smells. Sweet foods that now taste sour and sour foods that now taste sweet. Paul had experienced it all. He felt sorry for Kyle, forced to need a creature he feared. Forced into a life that would deprive him of his cherished soul.

"I'm hungry for him," Kyle whispered, desperation in his eyes.

"I know." Paul started down the stairs, but Kyle gripped his arm.

"Can you save me?"

"No." Why lie and give Kyle false hope? His fate was sealed.

Upstairs, the door opened and Victor appeared on the landing. He glanced at Paul, then Kyle. "Up here, thrall. Now."

Paul's walk through the dark streets of Georgetown did little to relieve him. When he returned, he sat on the living room sofa, his eyes falling on one of the abstract paintings, a maze of red and black strokes. Discordant voices seemed to shout from the canvas, as though each brushstroke was really a tortured soul longing to escape the confines of the frame. He finally climbed up to his studio and sat at the easel before a canvas sketched with an impressionistic profile of a victim he'd fed on the night before, an old woman who'd fallen near her front steps as she carried her garbage to the curb. She must have been ninety and weighed all of ninety pounds in her cotton housedress. He'd helped her up, dropped the full plastic bag into the garbage bin at the side of her house, and wheeled it to the curb. Grateful, she had invited him in for a cup of herbal tea. As he sat at her expansive dining room table, surveying the ornately framed landscapes on the walls, listening to her describe her great granddaughter's ballet performance, he knew he should take advantage of the privacy to feed. Taking the teapot from her unsteady hand as she poured him a second cup, he clutched her throat. Her skin was so thin he thought it would tear. Her rheumy blue eyes gazed at him in horror. But she fell limp under his grip, and he comforted himself with the thought that she would remember nothing. He drank and returned her to her seat. He didn't have the stomach to wait until she recovered, gazing at the wrinkled face of an old woman he'd attacked. So he left her there, slumped in her chair.

The sketch before him captured that pathetic image of the shriveled, crumpled woman. Sometimes he thought he chose subjects just to torture himself for being what he was. But deep down, he felt a more important motive. He wanted to retain his humanity. He wanted to remember the costs of his nourishment so that he would never take for granted the lives he depended upon.

While he worked, he heard Victor descend the stairs alone and go out into the night. Kyle was still upstairs.

He tried to resist the temptation to go to him. It could only get Kyle hurt. Is that what he wanted? Or did he want to strike out at Victor?

Whatever his motive, he found himself in his bedroom. Kyle's naked body was splayed on the bed, his wrists and ankles cuffed to the bedposts. Bite marks covered his neck and chest. The sheet under his crotch was bloody.

Paul broke the steel bands. He washed the wounds. Kyle was alert, but docile. *Like a lamb led to the slaughter.* The fucking Bible words just popped into Paul's head. He'd spent too much time at the monastery.

"You'll be all right," he said.

"I wish he would kill me. Maybe my soul would have a chance then."

"Shut the fuck up." Paul was in no mood for martyr talk.

"I drink his blood."

"You need it. That's the way it is."

Paul brought him a glass of water.

Kyle gulped it down. "He's says I'm his thrall. He's my host. What does it mean? What will happen to me?"

Paul told him about a thrall's existence, halfway between that of a mortal and a vampire. The thrall's mortal qualities allowed him to operate in daylight, tending to the needs of his vampire creator, especially the need for someone to guard his resting place from intruders—should such a danger arise. The thrall's supernatural qualities included a strength derived from his creator, as well as heightened senses. These changes took some getting used to, of course. Paul assured Kyle that the body acclimates.

However, in his explanation of a thrall's nature, Paul left much unsaid. A thrall's utter dependency on his vampire host rendered him unable to draw fully from his own previous strengths or from the strengths of the vampire. And while the thrall maintained all of the hopes and longings he had experienced as a mortal, he did not possess the means to satisfy them. Worst of all, the moment the vampire ceased to require the services of this slave, the thrall's very existence was threatened. The vampire had the ability to destroy his creation, and he did so by default if he left his own nocturnal existence behind to enter the Dark Kingdom. The thrall never became a vampire unless his host chose to make him one, and with his own consent—something very difficult for an insecure and frightened thrall to give because it meant separation from his creator for at least two hundred years.

Paul knew this predicament too well. Even now as a vampire, he could not endure the thought of separation from Victor.

Kyle listened with keen interest to Paul's description. When Paul finished, the thrall reflected quietly for a moment. "You're what he is now?" he finally said.

"Yes."

"You kill people?"

"Sometimes."

Kyle squeezed his eyes shut and heaved a shaky breath. When he looked at Paul again, his pupils had dilated. They flickered strangely, as the pupils of thralls do. "Will I become what you are?"

The words cut into Paul. What *were* Victor's plans? How far would he go to hurt him? "No," he finally said to soothe Kyle.

"I still love you," Kyle said. "I prayed. I fasted." He shook his head. "My flesh won. Maybe that's why."

Paul smiled ruefully. *You're not the one being punished*, he thought.

"If I have to be like this, can't I be yours?"

"It doesn't work that way. I can't take you away. He made you. You'll do whatever he wants."

"God help me then."

Paul shut himself in his studio that night and finished sketching the old woman. As dawn approached, he smoked a cigarette and fed the cat, who'd sat on his lap while he worked. He climbed down to the basement. When he clicked on the light in the wine cellar, he found only his casket there.

Victor's stone sarcophagus was gone.

Had Victor moved it to another location, where he and Kyle could be alone? Before he had the chance to go confront Victor, Victor's footsteps sounded on the stairs. Entering the room, he glanced at Paul and then at the empty spot.

Alarmed, he searched the aisles between the empty wine shelves in the lateral alcoves.

A sense of dread filled Paul. *The powers won't relent. They'll win in the end.*

Victor folded his arms and brooded. He wore a white linen shirt, turned up at the sleeves, and tight black jeans.

"We'll have to sleep in mine," Paul said.

Victor seemed to resist the idea, but he finally acquiesced. "It's too late to do anything else." He locked the door and clicked off the light.

Paul climbed in first, rolling on his side. Victor crawled in after him, pulling the lid over them. Pressed against Paul's back, he drew his arm around him. He kissed Paul's neck.

Paul squeezed his eyes shut, savoring the sensation, wishing they could remain entwined like this forever.

As soon as they climbed to the living room the next evening, Victor looked up the number of a Georgetown funeral home.

"What are you doing?" Paul said.

Standing near the bay window, Victor glared at Paul.

After lying in Victor's embrace all day, the look made Paul's stomach fall. "What about the goddamned neighbors?" he said.

"To hell with them."

Paul sat on the sofa, incredulous, as Victor tried to order a coffin and have it delivered that night, blowing up when the funeral director questioned him about the strange purchase. Apparently the director wanted to check the legalities of such a sale. He also wanted Victor to make the purchase in person, with all the proper ID. Victor hurled the cell phone across the living room. Then he stormed out of the house.

The casket came two hours later. The two men who delivered it wore tailored suits and wingtip shoes. Apparently they were the funeral directors themselves, unable to get delivery men on such short notice or unwilling to involve workers in the transaction. Paul suspected that Victor had paid an enormous sum—probably in cash—for both the coffin and the immediate delivery. Victor had them carry the coffin into the living room, where he'd cleared a space for it. Paul stood by the window, watching for any suspicious neighbors. The directors had transported the coffin in a hearse, which was double-parked in front of their house. No one appeared in the windows across the street, and the only pedestrian was a man lugging a bag of groceries. He didn't even glance at the hearse.

When the men had gone, Paul helped Victor carry the coffin to the basement. With their strength, the weight of the solid oak container was easy to manage, but the narrow stairs took some negotiating before they safely deposited it on the earthen floor of the wine cellar.

Paul tried to talk to Victor, but it was useless. Frustrated, Paul worked in his studio until he heard Kyle's cries rising from their bedroom. He opened the bedroom door to find Kyle kneeling on the floor, with bloody lash marks across his bare back. Victor stood over him, stripped to the waist, a flagelium in his hand. The whip with knotted cords was an invention of sadistic monks intent on disciplining their sinful flesh. Victor kept them in Dies Irae's stock of toys.

Paul wrestled the flagelium from Victor. When Victor lunged at him, Paul snapped the cords across Victor's face. Blood oozed up on his cheek. His eyes were wild. He turned to Kyle and grasped his blond head between his hands.

Kyle's eyes widened in fear. Though he knew the futility of any effort to free himself, he instinctively clutched at Victor's hands.

"One little twist is all it takes," Victor said, glaring at Paul. "How would you like that ending for your boy?"

"Let him go," Paul blurted, his heart racing. He took a menacing step toward Victor, but kept his hands to himself, afraid to provoke him.

"No," Kyle suddenly blurted. "Do it. Get it over with." He dropped his hands to his side and shut his eyes, as though resigning himself to martyrdom.

The request took Victor by surprise. He glanced from Kyle to Paul, and then withdrew his hands from Kyle's head. "A quick death would be too easy," he said with calm contempt. "For both of you." He smiled arrogantly at Paul, crouched down over Kyle and began lapping the blood on his back, glancing up triumphantly.

Hot tears filled Paul's eyes. He thought he could kill Victor in that moment. But to destroy Victor—if that was possible—was to destroy Kyle. With nothing to do but admit defeat, at least for now, he left the room.

He was barely out the door when the crack of the flagelium against Kyle's bare back resumed.

Paul had never felt so much rage as he looked for prey that night. It was wrong to proceed like this, but he didn't give a fuck. If a vampire's nature was to take, then so be it.

The small bar where he ended up was in the warehouse section of Southeast Washington. A haze of tobacco smoke filled the dark front room, where a dance beat pounded the windows. The twenty patrons were young, in their twenties and early thirties, most standing in clusters around cocktail tables, laughing and shouting at one another with no self-consciousness. But a short, meaty man leaned against a wall plastered with flyers. He'd pushed up the sleeves of his shirt and crossed his hairy arms. One of his black boots rested against the baseboard. He stared unabashedly at Paul. Paul approached him.

The man smiled, his dark eyes bright. His nose was prominent and his hair thinning, but his swarthy self-possession made him sexy.

"Hi," Paul said.

The man raised his beer. "You want one?"

"No, thanks. I like to get down to business."

"A man after my own heart."

Paul let him lead him by the hand out of the smoky bar. Outside, he turned to Paul. "My place or yours?"

Paul shook his head. "No. Over here." He pulled the man toward the alley that ran along the side of the club. Stepping behind a parked car, he kissed him.

The man responded with plenty of tongue and groping, finally dropping to his knees and fumbling with Paul's zipper. Just for a moment, Paul enjoyed the man's well-honed technique, but he raised him to his feet before he climaxed. He kissed the man tenderly and pierced his jugular, lowering him to the pavement while he drank from his inert body. The warm blood seemed to rush through every vein in Paul's body. He kept drinking past the usual amount. The blood was like a hearty Chianti. Finally, he tried to pull away, but the blood was so good, and the man's solid body so comforting next to him that he allowed himself a little more. Then a little more. Before he knew it, he'd reached the danger point. The man's heart thumped at three-second intervals. Paul stared into the bright eyes that gazed without seeing.

"I'm sorry," he said. He shut the man's eyes, and taking hold of his head, twisted it until the spine snapped.

Paul stood up and gazed around the alley. When he was sure he was alone, he left the body and hurried to South Capitol Street just two blocks away. Then he trudged all the way to the Mall.

As he sat brooding on the grass, he thought of the overgrown field in Rome where the Circus Maximus once stood. The stadium had held three hundred thousand fans cheering for the chariots racing around bronze dolphins in the center of the elliptical track. He thought of all the blood the arena had absorbed while the Roman Empire flourished—the blood of gladiator contests, assassinations, and Barbarian invasions. No wonder Victor could kill so ruthlessly. He was a product of such a world. But Paul Lewis was just a boy from Kansas. *Fucking Kansas!* He couldn't just snap someone's neck and sleep like the dead. His was the sleep of the undead.

The illuminated Capitol dome rose like St. Peter's Basilica. He remembered the moon shining on the colonnades and stark obelisk—erected there in the sixteenth century, with the help of a hundred fifty horses, according to Victor, who lived in Rome at the time and heard about the daytime feat from the monks in his monastery. "Never underestimate the hubris of puny mortals," he'd said to Paul.

Paul closed his eyes and imagined himself on the square stones of the piazza, under the gaze of stone saints along the colonnade. He silently called Victor's name. As if in response, a current ruffled his hair. Would his love for Victor ever die, even if Victor's love for him vanished? Maybe—since even if Victor left him and he grieved for decades, decades formed only a fraction of his existence. If you could divide eternity into fractions. *Jesus. Eternity!* Who really wanted to live for an eternity?

Dawn was still an hour away when he got back home. He entered Dies Irae, now empty, and gazed up at the twisted corpus on the reredos. He remembered the crucifix at San Benedetto. He remembered the apparition: the naked, bloody corpus had turned to flesh. Then, he had thought that his epilepsy had caused the vision. Now, he believed that Joshu was trying to save him from Victor's kind of existence. *You failed, man!*

He'd been a different person then. A different being. He'd arrived at the monastery a thirty-two-year-old man commissioned to illustrate a vellum manuscript of the Gospels. In one year, he'd created 123 illuminations, fallen in love with "Brother" Victor, and joined him in an existence he was still trying to fathom. And despite the seizurelike experience the night he killed the boy at Georgetown University, his epilepsy had vanished forever. Along with his mortality.

Exhausted, he climbed down to the cellar. In his dark coffin, his thoughts drifted to the place where Victor had transformed him, the Forum, sprawling with ruins of temples and markets and public buildings, all within sight of the jagged Colosseum, stripped of its marble mantle, like an impotent monarch. Amid the rubble of the Basilica Julia, he had nursed at Victor's breast, like an infant, but sucking blood from his nipple instead of milk. With the sensation of fire rushing through his veins, his mind had spun, a kaleidoscope of bright images, until he couldn't stand the heat or brightness another moment. Then darkness had come. When he opened his eyes, he had seen the world as Victor saw it, forever shadowed by night, but forever his to wander.

With Victor as an eternal lover. *Please bring him back to me!* He whispered the words to no one in particular and fell asleep.

Two nights later, Kyle's canvas bag was open on Victor and Paul's bed, where Paul stretched his lanky body. In the bag, Kyle's breviary lay on top of a pair of jeans. So Kyle planned to pray tonight as well as screw.

The sad contradictions of the priest-turned-thrall might have made Paul laugh, if he hadn't felt so guilty for bringing this tragedy on him.

Through the open bathroom door, the scent of Ivory soap wafted from the shower. It was the only soap Kyle used. Paul had suggested a joint post-sex shower. But Kyle's paradoxical modesty would not allow it.

Kyle emerged with a towel around his waist. He pulled a pair of briefs from the bag and, turning his back to Paul, dropped the towel and slipped them on. The lash marks were still vivid on his shoulder blades. He picked up a photo album on Paul's bed table and opened it. It contained pictures of every illumination Paul had painted for the manuscript at San Benedetto. The illuminations mesmerized Kyle. He stared for a long time at the illumination heading the Gospel of Mark. In clear, bright colors, it depicted John the Baptist facing Jesus in the Jordan River. Both bare-chested, the swarthy men gazed intimately at each other, John holding Jesus by the shoulder.

"You like it?" Paul said.

"It's not how I imagined the scene."

"That doesn't surprise me."

"Jesus would never . . . He was the Son of God. I'm surprised they let you do this."

"Maybe the monks' minds aren't as dirty as yours." Paul saw no need to mention how much the illumination had scandalized Father Rossi, the priest in charge of the project. As a new thrall, he had lost control and strangled him for destroying several of his paintings. Paul lit a cigarette. "You're sure you want to do this? It's futile, you know."

"I'm sure." Kyle put down the album and dried his wet hair with the towel. "I have to stand up to him. I don't care what he does to me—as long as he knows that I won't be what he wants me to be. My soul has already been claimed."

"You see the contradiction here, don't you?" Paul said. "Standing up to Victor, but not standing up to the church."

"How can you equate the church and him?" Kyle snapped.

"How? You don't want Victor to violate you, but you spread your legs like a whore for Gimello."

"Father Gimello represents God's law. Submission to God's law isn't weakness. It's strength. It's salvation."

"God's law doesn't bind you anymore. You're in a new dimension with new laws. You can't escape them."

"He's right, Kyle." Victor stood in the doorway, dressed in black. No sound had announced his coming.

"God will send you to hell," Kyle said. "For all eternity."

Victor laughed. "And you'll be in the flames with me."

"I don't give assent. Whatever you make me do, it's against my will."

"What about the sin of sodomy?" He glared at Paul. "Don't you give assent to that? Or is he forcing himself on you?"

The comment gave Kyle pause.

"He loves me," Paul said, adding too late to be effective, "and I love him."

Victor's look turned hateful. "Love him all you want," he said. "He needs what I can give him." Tearing at his wrist with his fangs, he offered the oozing blood to Kyle.

Kyle's face trembled. He fell on his knees, his head bobbing obscenely as he sucked at Victor's wrist.

Victor's eyes gleamed cruelly at Paul.

Paul felt a wave of nausea rise up in him. He looked away until Kyle finished.

Then Victor patted his thrall's head and, without another word, marched out of the room and down the stairs. They heard the front door open and shut.

Still kneeling, Kyle buried his face in Paul's belly. "I'm sorry," he mumbled.

Paul ran his fingers through Kyle's hair. "You can't help it," he whispered.

Chastened, Kyle finished dressing, and they walked to Dupont Circle where they boarded a Metro train to Catholic University. Kyle was scheduled to say a private mass in the basilica's subterranean chapel.

As the train whirred along, Paul's mind was on Victor. He made idle talk, hardly knowing what came out of his own mouth.

Kyle seemed to be talking about his ordination, apparently a recent event.

"When did you know you wanted to be a priest?" Paul asked.

Kyle sighed sadly. "When I was ten."

"Really?"

"I was in Catholic school. Father O'Brien talked to our class about vocations. The church needs priests. That's what he said. We need soldiers for Christ. Hundreds of priests had left the priesthood after the Second Vatican Council."

"The big reform council," Paul said. "No more Latin Mass, no more fish on Friday." He'd heard about all the changes from the monks at San Bendetto.

"Vatican Two meant well. I guess it's good to make religion more relevant. But experimentation can be dangerous. Priests dabbling in this and that. Getting led astray by their own selfish needs." Kyle reflectively gazed out the window as they approached Union Station.

"It's not selfish to want love," Paul said.

Kyle studied him. "Are you talking to me or you?"

"You."

"I made a promise. I broke it. I turned into some kind of sex maniac."

"You were finally sowing your oats."

"It's all about sex, isn't it? The homosexual lifestyle. Bars, parks, public bathrooms."

"Why starve yourself and then beat yourself up for wanting food?"

Kyle threw him a troubled glance. "It started with Victor. The urges got so strong around him. It was like . . . I had no control. Then you came along and . . . I don't know . . . I was in a constant state of mortal sin. And now this hell." He brooded quietly for a moment. "Do you love Victor?" he finally said.

"No."

"You're lying."

Paul did not deny it.

"If you love him, why are you doing this?"

"It's complicated."

"Maybe you're the one who's afraid."

At the Brookland Station, they exited the train and crossed the campus of Catholic University to the basilica. They entered on the ground floor and headed to the chapel there, called the crypt. Paul sat in a pew while Kyle donned his vestments in a small sacristy before approaching the altar. The ritual that he conducted turned out to be surreal. Without a congregation, he proceeded as though the room were full. Aloud, he prayed, read the epistle and gospel, and consecrated the wafer he'd brought with him. He looked so pure and innocent—all his raging lust wrapped up in an alb and a chasuble.

When he lifted the white wafer in an act of consecration, he started to cry. He stood frozen, staring at the wafer, his body wracked with sobs.

As Paul watched him from a dark pew, contemplating the life

ahead of Kyle, a resolution formed in his mind. He had to free Kyle in the only way possible. Then his tortured soul would find rest—in heaven, if there was such a thing as divine mercy.

And if taking Kyle's life was also a way to get back at Victor, so what? It didn't make the act any less merciful.

He would do it. But not tonight. He would give Kyle a last visit with his adoring mother. She believed that her son had taken a leave of absence from the priesthood. The lie was intended to soften the blow when he finally told her that she would never again see him offer the holy sacrifice of the mass, as she called it.

In Kyle's white Saturn, they pulled up in front of Mrs. Durham's house at seven the next night. She lived in a big foursquare house in Cleveland Park, a wealthy neighborhood near the zoo and the National Cathedral, full of hundred-year-old oaks and grand front porches. An idyllic setting for a Norman Rockwell painting. Mrs. Durham lived there alone. Kyle's father, a corporate lawyer, was dead. Kyle's sister and brother had moved away. Mrs. Durham occupied herself with charity events and parish committees, when she wasn't at a church retreat or pilgrimage to Lourdes or Fatima, known for apparitions of the Virgin Mary.

Kyle opened the front door with his key, and they entered an enormous living room with floor-to-ceiling bookshelves, a grand piano, a fireplace, and a wall of photographs. The central photograph, larger than all the others, featured Kyle on ordination day. In his pristine alb, he knelt with his hands folded before the bishop, whose own well-manicured hands rested on Kyle's head. The furniture in the room was sturdy and unpretentious, but tasteful and undoubtedly of the best quality. Paul couldn't help but compare the room to Alice's hole-in-the wall living room in her little rambler. On the wall above the piano hung a painting of the Madonna, probably an antique from Europe, a far cry from the Chihuahua on velvet above Alice's TV.

Mrs. Durham rushed in from the kitchen, a towel in her hand. She was in her midfifties, a slender, fit woman with Kyle's gray eyes. She wore pleated slacks and a dark silk blouse that set off a single strand of pearls around her throat. She kissed Kyle and extended her hand to Paul. As far as she knew, Paul was a friend who provided a room for Kyle. He'd never come out to her, and she'd never voiced suspicions—as inevitable as they had to be. He was her golden son, the family priest. She would not let herself take his leave from the priesthood seriously. She had convinced herself that after a rest from his labors, Kyle would return to the parish with renewed spirits.

Mrs. Durham offered them a drink. Kyle took a beer. Paul accepted a glass of merlot, pretending to sip it as they sat and chatted. When Mrs. Durham went to retrieve a photo album, Kyle drank the wine.

Mrs. Durham sat between them on the sofa. With unabashed pride, she turned the pages of the album, pointing to photos of Kyle the little boy making his first communion, Kyle the teen kicking a soccer ball past a goalie, Kyle the priest offering his first mass. She described how Kyle's father had beamed on that glorious day—exactly one month to the day before his fatal heart attack. Kyle's ordination was surely the last image in his mind, she said.

When it was time to leave, her gray eyes hinted of panic. She tried to keep Kyle there, suddenly asking Paul questions about his art and his family in Kansas. He answered politely. He felt sorry for her. Perhaps he should let Kyle live. Even as a thrall, he remained her son. But if she knew what kind of son, she would wish him dead for the sake of his soul. After a gracious good-bye to Paul at the front door, she turned to Kyle.

"You're sure the doctor said it's nothing?" she said softly, touching his pale, pale face.

"Just a bug. I'll get my color back."

Did she suspect that Kyle had AIDS, as Alice had suspected when she saw Paul's livid face and strangely flickering pupils?

When Kyle kissed her on the cheek, she must have noticed his cold lips, but she said nothing. She simply embraced him. When she drew away, her eyes were filled with tears.

"Don't worry about me, Mom," Kyle said. "I'm in God's hands."

"Give me your blessing before you go."

There in the foyer, she knelt before Kyle. He made the sign of the cross over her. When she stood, she seemed at peace.

Kyle bid his mother good-bye and silently followed Paul to the car. He remained silent as they drove home. They passed Washington Cathedral on Wisconsin Avenue. The illuminated Gothic towers cut into the night sky. Within ten minutes they came to the familiar Georgetown shops.

Finally Paul spoke. "It's not your fault that you are what you are. You didn't do anything to make it happen."

"No." Kyle sounded unconvinced.

"It's not a punishment for being gay if that's what you think."

Kyle turned to him, oddly resigned. "Maybe there is a purpose. I just don't know what it is."

Paul reminded himself of what he had to do. The dark Georgetown Canal would be a good place, wedged between two rows of dimly lit buildings near the river

As they strolled past the canal lock, Paul scanned the pathway on either side of the water. No one was in sight. But suddenly someone stepped out from behind a brick building on the corner and turned toward them. It was Sonia.

She greeted Paul, kissing his cheek. "This must be Father Durham. Victor has told me all about you." She wore a black tunic and pearls. Her dark hair hung loose.

Kyle took the hand she offered him, smiling awkwardly.

Sonia's remark struck Paul as uncharacteristically insensitive. He introduced her without associating her with Dies Irae. No need to make Kyle more uncomfortable.

They sat on a bench near the water. During the course of their conversation, Sonia asked Paul if Alice had ever been to Washington.

"No," Paul said, lighting a cigarette.

"That's too bad." Sonia's tone was oddly insincere.

"What about your family, Father? Do they live here?" she said, laying her hand on Kyle's knee.

"My mother does."

"She must be so proud to have a priest for a son. I know how Catholic families are. I come from one myself." She lit a cigarette and raised her head to exhale a stream of smoke. "But, you know, your new state is all for the best."

"She's one of us," Paul explained.

Kyle stared at her fearfully.

Sonia continued. "The Catholic Church is a decrepit behemoth, crawling to its demise. But as it perishes, it tries to suck the life from virile young men like you. Of course, you know that. You're right to look elsewhere for vitality." She glanced at Paul and patted his leg.

His face white with anger, Kyle stood up. "Let's go, Paul."

"I hope I didn't offend you," Sonia said. "Perhaps I'm too outspoken."

She gave Kyle her hand and then embraced Paul. "Don't kill him," she whispered. "You'll lose Victor. Make your own thrall."

Her voice in Paul's ear was like the voice of death.

10

The noon radiation wrapped the house like a giant electric blanket, roasting every piece of furniture and penetrating all the way to the cellar. Victor's new coffin, like every coffin he had ever inhabited, destroyed the rays because it was a symbol of death, a symbol so potent that it produced the very thing it represented. This was the definition of *sacrament*. Over the centuries, Victor had listened to countless priggish abbots crowing about this mysterious means of grace—*not a mere symbol, but a sign which effects that which it represents, and so baptism is indeed new birth and the Holy Eucharist is indeed communion with Christ, with the very body of Christ.* Thanks to such constant catechizing, a veritable mantra over the centuries, Victor could understand his coffin only in this sacramental way. This container for human remains, this morbid sign, actually extinguished the life force projected by the sun, a limited life force that marked off the years of mortal existence. The force of a vampire's eternal life belonged to the night. Hence the great, dangerous paradox: the limited force of day could destroy the eternal force of night, and so as each dawn approached, the vampire fled to the safety of his tomb.

So at noon, when the daylight reached its deadliest level, Victor struggled to rouse himself as the doorbell rang repeatedly. The visitor threatened him. He sensed this danger in his deep sleep, the same way humans in the deepest moment of their sleep cycles sense the rising heat of a fire just beyond the walls of their room. He rallied his attention the best he could, focusing on the presence outside the house. Was it Gimello? Would he force the door or search for an open window? Even if he did, he'd ultimately face the wine cellar's steel door, with a steel bolt and a steel frame. But assisted by the powers, Gimello could easily break any lock or bolt. Despite this disturbing thought, Victor's undead body, designed to slow its functions drastically in the daylight as it restored itself, summoned him back to sleep.

When he climbed upstairs after sunset, he switched on a lamp in the living room, and played the message on the flashing answering machine.

"You can lock me out," Gimello said. "But you can't avoid God's judgment. I know my assistant has gone to you. His soul is in God's hands now. But you are guilty of the worse evil. 'Better that a millstone be tied around your neck and that you be cast into the sea, than that you should lead the innocent astray.' The Almighty will expose your darkness to the light of the sun. And you will be destroyed."

Only if love weakens you, Sonia would remind him. And hadn't he proven himself above love, severing himself from Paul, taking a thrall to distract himself from jealousy? Then he could fight the powers speaking through Gimello, even if the priest knew the truth about Paul and him. Even if he invaded their resting place.

Still, Victor was uneasy. Perhaps he had not stifled completely his love for Paul. Perhaps he must redouble his efforts to rechannel his attentions.

Erasing the message, he went up to his room, where he found the bed unmade and the sheets bloody thanks to a night of punishing young Kyle. He raised a pillow to his mouth and licked a dried, rust-colored spot. The taste made his nipples and groin tingle. He remembered Kyle's face reddening and his eyes widening as his own powerful hands squeezed the boy's windpipe, and then his sweet body falling into spasms as the dangerous fangs of his master tore into his chest.

He'd given Kyle a list of errands for the day. He wanted new clothes—linen trousers and silk shirts from the Italian designer boutique on M Street, a few new pairs of Italian shoes, and underwear to drive the club's patrons wild—thongs, briefs, and jockstraps—which could be purchased at a specialty store near Dupont Circle. He also wanted him to arrange for the interior of the house to be painted. He was weary of the glaring white living room. Now he wanted dark walls, wine perhaps, or a dusky plum color. Kyle could bring him samples and bids from prospective painters. Expenses meant nothing to him, but he enjoyed seeing men compete for his business.

Possessing a thrall simplified a vampire's life in many ways. Unfortunately, thralls also demanded attention. Their lust for the vampire host could grow tiresome. They would do anything for him, contort their bodies, bare their throats and offer their flesh to the master's fangs, expose themselves to any danger for him. But utter submission quickly lost its appeal for him. A fight excited him more than the ready stretching of throat or spreading of legs. So ultimately, bored and irritated, he'd killed every thrall he'd created over the centuries—between his stays in monasteries, when he needed someone to guard his resting places and take care of practical matters. Every thrall, that is, but Paul Lewis, the thrall he had loved with a tenderness he had experienced only for Joshu. And that thrall, he had transformed into his equal, risking for love the wrath of the Dark Kingdom's forces. He had dared to hope for true, lasting love, and what he discovered was the inability to surrender—his, and now Paul's. For the sake of their survival, this was a happy fact.

Thralls still cast a reflection, and after recovering from the initial comalike state, in which he developed a consciousness of his new nature, Kyle stood before the mirror for long periods. His white skin had grown paler, even translucent. His pupils, now dilated, subtly vibrated. His senses had sharpened. A blaring car horn sounded like a locomotive whistle blasting just yards from his ears. Victor's red shirt made him squint. As a thrall his tastes also had changed, strangely—sweet apples seemed bitter, he'd told him, and rare steak tasted sugary. The food he mainly craved was his blood, which he licked from Victor's wrist. His life depended on it the same way that humans depended upon water. If Victor withdrew his blood, Kyle would die within days. He'd let

Kyle believe that this transitional state would end with time, that he'd eventually join him as a vampire. Kyle himself came to this conclusion in bed that night after drilling him about a vampire's life expectancy.

"All the movies are right then." He drew his hands behind his head, and stared at the ceiling in wonder. Kyle's transformation had heightened his naiveté. It was as though a child lived inside the muscular body, inside the innocent mind perverted by religiosity.

Yet, Kyle had far to go before escaping completely his indoctrination. Victor had never seen a thrall cling so tenaciously to religious scruples irrelevant in the sphere of their existence. Kyle continued to carry his rosary, to light votive candles in his room, to fall on his knees and pray. Twice on rising from his coffin, Victor found him in that position, on the earthen floor of the wine cellar. The first time, he laughed. The second time, he ripped the rosary from Kyle's hands and flung it across the damp room. "Get your loyalties straight," he had said, his finger in Kyle's face.

It was time for the next step in Kyle's education.

"I want you to come with me tonight when I feed," he said.

Kyle looked alarmed. "Why?"

"We'll leave at eleven. Stay in your room until then."

It was time to test his thrall. Sometimes the transformation did not take well. Too much of the thrall's old sensibilities remained and he could not bear watching Victor feed. Such had been a tender thrall named Quirinius, created during the second century. He had tried to run away when Victor ripped into the throat of an old woman sleeping in her bed. Victor forced him to watch, clutching him by the back of the neck. Quirinius sobbed so loudly that Victor finally smashed his head against the wall. Afterward, he had destroyed him by draining his blood.

A thrall unable to guard him, no matter how gruesome or dangerous the circumstances, was of no use to him.

As ordered, Kyle proceeded to his room. Victor dressed and went to his office to work. Kyle appeared punctually at eleven, in jeans and a jersey. Outside, Victor surveyed the streets. His apprehension about the powers never left him. Who knew how they might attack?

He and Kyle walked through quiet residential streets, keeping an eye open for anyone arriving home late or taking the dog out for a last walk. But the streets were empty. On M Street a light still burned in a Vietnamese restaurant although the CLOSED sign was up. Inside, a stocky man checked receipts at the cash register. Victor nodded for Kyle to follow him to the alley behind the restaurant. He listened at the back door. Everything was quiet. They had to wait only five minutes behind a foul-smelling Dumpster before the back door opened and the man stepped out. As he locked the door, Victor quietly advanced, clamped his hand over the man's mouth, and sank his fangs into his throat. He lowered him to the ground, straddling him.

As he fed, Victor looked up at Kyle's blanched face, growing even whiter as his eyes filled with fearful incredulity. Then his new instinct took effect like an injection of a fast-acting drug.

His breathing quickened until he was panting and pulling at the collar of his jersey. His nostrils distended, his innocent eyes grew lascivious, even cruel. He tugged impatiently at Victor's shoulder. Victor moved aside.

On his hands and knees like a hungry dog, Kyle at first lapped the oozing wound and then pressed his lips to it and sucked with relish. Victor let him. The more Kyle filled himself, the more dramatic, and hence effective, the consequences.

Kyle's shoulders suddenly jerked. He raised his head, grimaced, and vomited repeatedly until every drop of the blood he had swallowed had rushed from his body. He lay back on the ground, wiping his mouth with his shirt.

"You crave it," Victor said. "But you can only feed on me." He sliced his wrist with his fang. A thread of blood appeared. He offered it to Kyle. When Kyle shook his head, Victor pressed his wrist to Kyle's mouth. At first Kyle seemed to force himself to drink. Then his eyes rolled in pleasure and he swallowed contentedly until Victor pulled away from him. Victor waited for Kyle to regain his bearings. When he did, it was as if he'd awakened from a dream. He threw a panicked glance from him to the man. Crawling to him, he felt his wrist.

"He's still alive," he said. "We've got to get him to the hospital."

"Move," Victor said. "We need to finish this."

Kyle ignored Victor, tracing the sign of the cross on the man's forehead and mumbling a prayer. Victor yanked him away, clutched the man's head, and twisted it until his spine snapped.

Frozen, Kyle stared at the body. Victor had to pull him to his feet. Docilely, Kyle let Victor lead him from the alley. On the street, Kyle suddenly stopped, listening for something.

"There's no one," Victor said. "Let's go."

"No, listen," Kyle whispered.

Victor inspected the row houses up and down the street. Nothing stirred. But Kyle couldn't be convinced. He stood in front of Victor, as though he shielded him, scanning the alley.

Finally, he relaxed, and they returned home, Kyle walking in bleak silence.

The next evening, Victor sat on the sofa in his office, extending his pierced wrist to Kyle. As Kyle sucked greedily, Victor scrutinized his face. Had his thrall truly begun to understand his desires and their limitations? Had his experience last night taught him the depth of his dependency on his creator, despite any stray, wayward thoughts? Had he learned that his vampire's thirst for all blood was a chimera? That his only source of nourishment was the blood of the one who had transformed him?

Victor smiled. Who knew the answers and who cared? If Kyle failed to learn, he could be disposed of.

Victor dismissed his thrall when he'd finished drinking. Then he examined accounts until midnight, periodically gazing down at the quiet club, where half a dozen guests gathered around a game table, drinking and reading tarot cards. Feeling the need to feed, he went out to the street. As he stood on the sidewalk, considering the best place to stalk, he glanced up at Paul's studio. The light glowed and Kyle stood with his back to the window, gesturing as he spoke.

Determined to investigate, Victor entered the house and quietly climbed the stairs to the third floor. Outside Paul's door, he heard both Kyle and Paul. Despite Paul's own keen senses, he knew he was in no danger of being discovered there since he willed himself to evade detection.

"But he killed a man," Kyle said. "I can't believe I witnessed it. This wasn't a crime drama on TV. It was murder. And I saw it."

"Like I said, Kyle, it doesn't always end that way." Paul's voice was low. He was probably sitting on the sofa next to Kyle. "Usually, we just feed. We take some of their blood. That's all. They don't miss it. And we need it. It's that simple. I don't have a choice. Neither do you."

"God forgive me. I wanted the blood, Paul. I wanted to suck that man dry. I would have, if Victor hadn't pulled me away."

"But he did pull you away. And now you know you can't take anyone else's blood but his. You won't do it again. I promise. I know what it's like. I was a thrall. I wanted blood, too. I even killed a man. A priest." Paul told him about killing Rossi at San Benedetto.

Victor frowned. *Why is he confessing this? Why is he entrusting his sins to* him? *He's a moral inferior who does my bidding now.*

"So, I'll kill, too," Kyle said. "I won't be able to control myself. 'I do what I would not do'—that's what Saint Paul said. But he was talking about everyday sins, not murder. I'm some kind of monster. Look at my skin. Look at my fingernails. They grow faster than I can cut them. I'm messed up. Colors. Smells. They're too intense. It's like God's punishment."

"The intensity subsides," Paul said soothingly. "This is a different universe. Think of it like that. We live by a different set of rules. You can't go on judging yourself by the old rules. The church means nothing in this world. It's irrelevant."

Victor opened the door. Paul sat with his arm around Kyle on the sofa. A half-finished portrait of an ugly woman sat on the easel and open tubes of paint lay on the little table nearby. Kyle had evidently interrupted Paul's work.

"All that matters," Victor said, glaring at Kyle, "is that you obey me. Understood? Every impulse in you commands you to. Fight your impulse, and I kill you." He glanced at Paul. "Your lover wouldn't like that, would he?

Kyle looked frightened. The beautiful, innocent boy, turned monster, as he put it. In his jeans and jersey, he might have been a college youth or a high school coach rather than a ghoul.

Suddenly Victor spied a chain around Kyle's neck. He approached the thrall and yanked off the chain. A large crucifix dangled from it. Enraged, Victor clamped one hand around Kyle's throat and suspended the crucifix before Kyle's eyes. "This goes up your ass the next time I see it." He released Kyle and flung the crucifix to the floor. "Now come here," he said. Grabbing Kyle by the wrist and pulling him to his feet, he led him to the middle of the room. He unzipped his own trousers.

Paul stood up, ready to fight him. "Leave him alone."

"He's my thrall," Victor said, smiling. "You think he doesn't want it? Tell him, boy."

Kyle could not look at Paul. The truth of Victor's words was undeniable. The desperate lust in the thrall's face betrayed him. Not only did he need Victor's blood, but he also longed for union with his host. Though not union as equals. What he longed for was absolute submission, to be overshadowed by a force so potent that not even the God he worshipped could squelch it.

Realizing the uselessness of his presence, Paul left the room.

Victor quickly stripped Kyle and mounted him. The crucifix on the floor became a focus for the rage coursing through him. The rage of rejection that had driven him to violence when Joshu spurned him, requiring him to escape the law and seek the Ethiopian seer, Tiresias, who had given him the means. "You cannot imagine the power you will possess," she'd said, offering him her brown breast. And he'd sucked blood from it, as he mounted her beautiful body. The heat of orgasm extended itself through his whole body, like a fiery chemical, as images of Tiresias flashed before his eyes—Tiresias at table, with lovers, over bloody, gaping throats.

Damn her. Damn Joshu for sending me to her. Damn this existence. He kept his gaze fixed on the crucifix as he rammed his thrall. At the point of climax, he sank his fangs into his back.

He lapped up the blood and whispered, "good boy" in Kyle's ear. Then he got up and left the room. As he descended the stairs, he heard Kyle sobbing. The sound brought a smile to his lips.

In Dies Irae, he found Sonia amusing herself with a handsome guest from Hawaii, destined, no doubt, to appease her appetite. He watched while Sonia read the young man's tarot cards, registering only an occasional word about fortunes or dangers. His mind could take nothing in. Sonia seemed to notice his preoccupation. Several times, she threw a scrutinizing glance across the large table. When the guest went to the bar, she finally spoke to him.

"It's good to see you going about your life as you should, creating a thrall. You're strong. Much stronger than Paul." She took hold of his hand and laid it on her crotch. "Yes," she moaned. "So strong. Love makes our kind impotent. You'll never succumb to it."

Victor avoided Paul the next night. It was better this way. Once they had established their independence, they could safely interact, hardened to the old feelings. But as he lay on their bed, surrounded by their room, he found himself hoping that Paul would walk in.

The deep green walls in the bedroom set off Paul's portrait, which occupied the space between the set of bay windows. A massive nineteenth-century wardrobe that he and Paul had purchased locally took up much of one wall. On the wall opposite the wardrobe hung a Bavarian tapestry that depicted two wolves fighting against a wooded background. One wolf had sunk his fangs into the neck of the other. Victor couldn't resist the tapestry when Paul saw an image of it on the Web site of a German textile dealer.

He heard the front door open at eleven-thirty, followed by footsteps on the stairs. He knew that Paul's senses had told him where Victor was. Victor probed himself for tenderness and discovered that his defenses had satisfactorily squelched all traces of it. But when Paul walked into the room and gazed at him hopefully, his heart responded despite himself. He had to feign cold detachment, and Paul knew it.

"You're home early," Victor said, barely glancing at him over the magazine.

"Am I?" Paul's long hair was windswept. He wore blue jeans and a navy jersey with long sleeves. He looked tired and needed a shave. He sat on the bed. "I can't stand this, Victor. It's killing me."

"Make your own thrall."

"That's what Sonia told me. She thinks it would be for my own good. Two vampires aren't capable of giving each other what they want. She said I needed to take care of myself. It's what she told you, isn't it? Well, I think that's fucked up."

"What do you want from me? Do you expect me to destroy my thrall?" Victor eyed him with suspicion.

"I want you to love me. That's all." He touched Victor's leg.

A fiery ball of anger suddenly flared in Victor. He felt mocked—by fate more than by Paul. He was sick of centuries of wanting what he could never have. He got up and threw himself on Paul, straddling him on the bed and pinning back his arms. "You want me to love you? That's all you want? You know my history? You know what you're asking?"

With irresistible force, Paul heaved Victor off his body. He pounced on him, barring his fangs. Then instead of attacking, he sank to Victor's crotch. Victor was about to kick him away, when

Paul's tongue found his testicles. The pleasure was intense. Within minutes they had both stripped. Clawing and biting each other's neck and arms and belly, they made love with abandon. A mantra pounded in Victor's head as he slid in and out of Paul. *I want you forever. I want you forever.*

In the early morning hours that week, Victor and Paul walked under the cherry trees along the Tidal Basin. The September air was balmy, summer temperatures lingering though Labor Day had come and gone. Victor peered into the water wondering what the powers held in store for Paul and him. But he was determined to be with Paul no matter how vulnerable it made the two of them. They would go where they wanted. Do what they wanted.

During evening thunderstorms, they traipsed the wet streets of Georgetown or sat together in Paul's studio, Paul painting merrily away while Victor pored over favorite classics. Machiavelli's *The Prince*—which he read in the original Italian—stirred him with its honest assessment of the human need for domination. Ruthless rulers were always the most feared and revered. Countries thrived under them. Saddam Hussein, though ultimately a sniggering coward, once demanded order from a country now in chaos. He also read *Paradise Lost*, just to savor his hatred for Joshu's God, a divine prig rather than a lusty, honest god like Jupiter. Joshu's God created flesh and then condemned humans for discovering its pleasures. In many monasteries over the centuries, Victor had discovered the essence of the Christianity institutionalized in Rome and every Reformed sect: a mean, petty, negation of the flesh supposedly inhabited by God, whom Joshu's followers believed him to be. The quintessential rule of this Christianity was don't fuck or think about fucking. Monks scourged their backs to stop themselves from doing it or from thinking about it. Popes, bishops, and abbots, not men enough to rule by a fist, ruled by instilling self-hatred in the masses for their carnal desires.

On some nights, the scorn aroused in him by reading transformed itself into pure lust, and he ravished Paul. In every conceivable position they used their mouths and teeth and hands and implements of pleasure to satisfy one another. On some nights, in the midst of passion, they delayed gratification until they fed together in a dark alley or in a bedroom they had invaded. Then with blood on their lips, they finished their lovemaking as the victim slowly returned to consciousness. It became a game, to see how long they dared to linger, naked and erect, over the body they'd fed upon. When a victim did awaken on the brink of their orgasms, Victor fell upon the wounded throat again, turning to pleasure Paul with his bloody mouth.

The season of our love. The words danced through Victor's head after he crawled into his coffin every night. He thought he'd never loved before. And, indeed, he had never loved before if love required prolonged reciprocation. *The world is ours. Eternity is ours.* He didn't need to say the words to Paul. He thought them, and Paul heard, expressing his happiness in a bold Impressionist painting of a pride of lions. He'd never seen a lion, but Victor had, in his travels over the centuries, and Victor imagined them vividly enough for Paul to see in his mind. Paul seemed to forget about his puny family, as worthless as the dirty peasants Victor used to see in Europe's villages. Victor had become family enough for him.

Kyle took care of them both now. What did his infatuation with Paul matter? It would fade. And if Paul's jealousy threatened their love, the solution was simple. He would destroy the thrall.

Over the course of the week, Victor failed to return several phone calls from Sonia. As he saw it, Sonia had done them a grave disservice, planting unnecessary fears in both of their heads. What did she know about love? What did she know about the powers of the Dark Kingdom? Sonia finally showed up at his office.

"You must not shut me out, Victor." She caressed the obscene sculpture and seated herself on the sofa, lighting a cigarette. She was sheathed in violet silk. "Your safety depends on me. Just as mine depends on you. I know the Dark Kingdom. Don't believe its forces have finished with you. Besides, I've been lonely without you."

"That's a pity," Victor said, sitting back in his desk chair, his hands behind his head. "Because I haven't been lonely."

Sonia flashed him an angry glance. "No, because you've done exactly what I told you not to do. And for what? Are you willing to risk so much for something that can't last?"

Victor laughed. "You're jealous."

"He loves your thrall, not you. He told me so himself."

"Beware the green-eyed monster, Sonia."

"No, you beware."

"Go to hell."

Sonia glared at him and left the room without another word.

Victor continued working until very late. Just before dawn, he finished responding to several reservation requests. The group from Canada wanted to book all of the guest rooms for a week in November. An S and M group from Sydney, Australia, wanted to book four of the rooms the first week of June. *It's our fucking winter, mate,* the e-mail from the group coordinator said. *We're looking for some heat. Can't wait to find it at Dies Irae.* Just as Victor fired off an obscene reply, Paul came to get him and they went to the basement.

As he unlocked the door to the wine cellar, a sense of foreboding crept up in him. He turned and scanned the room.

"What's wrong?" Paul said.

He raised his finger to his lips and listened. The only sound was the dull creak of the house settling.

"It's nothing," he said.

He kissed Paul before climbing into his coffin and fell into an uneasy sleep. Just before dawn, a strange dream paired Sonia and Gimello in a confessional open to his eyes. Wearing a nun's habit, Sonia knelt in one compartment, while in his compartment, the priest inclined to hear her sins. As she confessed, her hands traveled to her breasts and belly and suddenly she was naked. Gimello, his hairy body also suddenly naked, emerged from his compartment. His erection turned into a diamondback snake dripping with blood. Lustily, Sonia swallowed it, and in the next instant it oozed from her vagina and rose in a stiff arch. With her newly acquired erection, she entered him. Over her shoulder, the priest opened his mouth to reveal fangs. When he pierced Sonia's throat, she cried out, "You must obey." Gimello laughed and repeated her words, "You must obey." Then they chanted together, "You must obey. You must obey. You must obey."

Victor's eyes snapped open. Disturbed by the strange dream, he lay pondering its significance for several moments before finally deciding to dismiss it as meaningless. But despite his efforts, a sense of dread lingered. Eager to rise and leave the place where the nightmare had originated, he pushed against the lid of his sarcophagus. It would not give. He suddenly sensed a presence outside the box.

"You must obey," two voices announced. They belonged to Gimello and Sonia.

Redoubling his effort, Victor continued to press the lid, but with no effect. "What are you doing?" he shouted. "Who are you?" He asked the questions, though he knew the answers now. Gimello was not a helpless pawn of the Dark Kingdom, oblivious to the powers working through him. He came from the powers, insinuating himself into the lives of the fugitives as an opponent, just as Sonia, also from the powers, had insinuated herself as an ally.

Gimello and Sonia laughed. The sound echoed and then dwindled to a wisp before vanishing. The air grew cold.

"Paul," Victor shouted. "Are you there?"

There was no reply.

Victor called to him repeatedly. Had they taken Paul's life? Was his corpse lying just three feet away?

He continued trying to force open the lid, but he might as well have been a child trying to break through a brick wall. His attempts to summon Kyle were unsuccessful.

For hours his mind spun with the possibilities of his fate. Perhaps this entombment was the Dark Kingdom's final act, his slow execution. He would lie next to his dead lover without feeding until he lost all strength and finally succumbed after two thousand years of existence. Or maybe they had abducted Paul, holding him for ransom until the rebel vampire submitted to the powers? Why else had Sonia and Gimello reminded him of obedience? *I'll obey if you free him. I'll go to the Dark Kingdom. Let him live!* Victor shouted the words in his mind.

For the entire long night, Victor continued his futile efforts to lift the lid and his futile efforts to summon Paul and Kyle. He also repeated again and again his promise to the powers he now believed must be trapping him. Finally, when dawn came again, he drifted to sleep, exhausted, waking after sunset only to begin a new desperate cycle of struggle and bargaining.

Three days passed this way—three days without nourishment. And his energy was nearly depleted. He could survive another forty hours. Perhaps more. If Paul was alive, he could not last so long. He was too young in his nocturnal life. Over and over, he had called to Paul. He had trained his thoughts on Paul's mind, but without even a glimmer of a response.

Then, in the quiet of the night, he heard Paul call his name. Paul's voice was weak. It came from the cellar. Victor tried the lid and it gave way.

He found Paul in his coffin, staring listlessly, unable to respond. Victor tried to scoop him up, but he was too weak. He must feed and bring blood to Paul.

The bald, muscular Dies Irae guest stirred in his bed when Victor entered the room. But when he saw Victor's brawny form, he lay docilely, letting Victor creep into the bed beside him, losing consciousness with the first jab of Victor's fangs. Victor drained over half of the man's blood. He had no choice. The guest would have to be sacrificed for Victor's existence and Paul's. Revived, Victor returned to the cellar and carried Paul to the guest house, laying him on the victim's bed and directing his mouth to the wounds. Paul sucked, limply at first, but gradually gaining strength and clinging to the victim until withdrawing as he reached the danger point. Victor suffocated the man with a pillow.

Leaving Paul to recover, Victor loaded the body in Horatio's car and transported it to Congressional Cemetery, interring it in a mausoleum tomb that bore the remains of John Anthony Ransom, buried in 1835. Then he returned to find Kyle. He was locked in his room, unconscious. He revived when he tasted Victor's blood.

Dawn was still an hour away when Victor walked up the winding gravel drive of Calloway Manor. Faint lights glowed in the lower part of the house, and as he approached the door, he could discern the dissonant strains of a piano. Before he could touch the latch on the door, it opened.

Gimello met him at the door. But he seemed dazed, like a zombie.

His clerical shirt was open, the collar gone. Black hair crawled over his collarbone. Without a word, he turned and led Victor in.

The foyer gleamed with candlelight. On the hall table, two candelabras cast their light on the gargoyles carved along the frame of the door-sized mirror. A shower of flames flickered in a chandelier hanging by a chain from the soaring wooden truss.

Victor preceded Gimello into the hall that served as a living room. Flames danced on the round newel posts at the base of the staircase rising between the two entrance archways, on the grand piano in the corner, on the mantel of the stone fireplace, and on all the heavy tables in the large, rustic chamber. Without a musician, the piano played a nocturne. Absorbed in her tarot cards, Sonia sat at a game table. She wore a shimmering sari of cobalt blue. A dark window of leaded panes loomed over her.

She looked up at him, a hint of tenderness in her gaze. "I tried everything possible, Victor. Force from without, chaos from within. I tried to turn you against each other. That was my best hope." She raised a goblet to her lips.

"You wanted us to destroy each other?"

"No. I wanted you to separate. There can be no concentration of our kind of power. We cannot associate in this world. The design of the universe precludes it."

"And yet you urged us to band together."

"Only to intensify your jealousy and hatred until you could not stand the sight of each other. Until *you*, the offender, inevitably went your own way. Then, in your loneliness, you would go where you belong. What would keep you here?"

"What about the priest?" Victor nodded toward Gimello, who stood expressionless near the stairs.

"He's a mere human being, protected by me and under my power. As I told you, religious zealots make effective tools." As if to illustrate her point, she nodded at the priest.

Gimello's glassy eyes suddenly became like red lasers, and as fast as a laser beam, he shot through the air, attaching himself to Victor's body, tearing at his throat. Victor grabbed the priest's long hair and pulled until Gimello released him. Then he sliced into Gimello's throat with his fangs. No blood flowed. Disarmed, he withdrew his fangs. Before he could renew his attack, Sonia ripped Gimello away from him and held Victor back with a steellike arm.

"You're wasting your energy," she said. Sonia put her hand on his cheek and pressed her body against him. "Why make this difficult? You were on your way to join the Dark Kingdom. You wanted my kind of life. No more racing the sunrise. No more running from authorities, preying on derelicts. Always alone. No one to understand your life. You think you have found someone now. Just as I once found someone."

"Then there really was a Regina?"

"Yes," Sonia said, kissing his cheek. "My love cost her her life. You cannot have him. The Dark Kingdom protects its own, but when its children violate immutable laws, you leave us no choice."

"So you're the Dark Kingdom?" Victor felt warm and weak against her lovely body.

"No. My power is superior to yours because—contrary to what I've told you—I finally entered that realm, where a vampire's strength reaches full maturity. Impersonal spirits govern the Dark Kingdom. They chose me as their emissary. Your action has frozen all life in our world. Until you rectify your violation, our citizens pay the price. I will pay the price since my freedom from their frozen state is temporary. Listen to me, Victor. Avoid the next step. We love our own. But my family in the Dark Kingdom is calling out to me even in their icy silence." Sonia whispered now. " 'Restore us,' they say. 'Restore order.' And what else can I do?"

Victor tried to concentrate. "What is the next step?"

"I will take Paul's life if you do not leave him."

"I don't believe you. You would have done it by now."

"We love our own." Sonia's mouth found Victor's neck. With a quick jab she pierced his flesh and sucked. The sensation of warmth increased and spread through his body like bathwater.

The room spun around him. His thoughts took on the quality of a dream. Sonia's naked flesh, her round breasts and snowy belly moved softly around him. His excitement was intense and sweet, but just before he reached the heights, an image of Paul's pale, glassy-eyed corpse shook him from his ecstasy.

"No!" he shouted.

When he opened his eyes, he stood alone on the dark street outside Calloway Manor.

SACRIFICE

If then true lovers have been ever crossed,
It stands as an edict in destiny.
Then let us teach our trial patience
Because it is a customary cross,
As due to love as thoughts and dreams and sighs,
Wishes and tears, poor fancy's followers.
—*A Midsummer Night's Dream I, 1, 152–156*

11

The pristine structure enshrining Lincoln reminded Victor of Rome's great temples. The strong columns, perfectly spaced around the perimeter, announced the sort of order emanating from Rome, world order. He and Paul climbed the marble steps, turned back, and gazed at the white obelisk reflected in the rectangular pool at the temple's base, with the obelisk itself rising stark and unyielding against the night sky. Beyond it the illuminated Capitol dome shone a mile away. Large square museums, like structures from the Roman forum, lined the grassy mall between the Lincoln Memorial and the Capitol.

At eleven-thirty, they stood alone in the temple to Lincoln. But Victor could discern a few tourists moving near the Vietnam Memorial, off to the side of the reflecting pool. The solemn wall of polished black granite attracted viewers night and day, many searching for the engraved name of a son or father or brother slain in Vietnam. Perhaps he and Paul could wait to pounce on a pilgrim after he had finished making a rubbing or attaching a photograph or flower to the wall. Respect had nothing to do with his restraint. The wall was well lit. But once viewers left the memorial area they walked across the dark edges of the mall to their cars. The night would shield Paul and him as they fed.

The warm air smelled of cut grass and flowers from the garden near the centennial castle, the Smithsonian's trademark. It was a potentially intoxicating night with his lover. Victor watched Paul as he gazed out at the dark Mall. He wore his long hair in a ponytail. In his tie-dyed T-shirt, jeans, and Birkenstocks he looked like a sexy San Francisco hippie from the sixties. He calmly smoked a cigarette, without a worry in the world.

He didn't know. Victor had told him nothing. Not yet. Maybe never. Maybe it was all a ruse.

Paul had no memory of their entombment. It was as though the powers had protected him from reliving the terror. And if Sonia was right, if the powers loved their own, why would they take his life? Besides, Paul had not violated the rules. If anyone was in danger of destruction, it was the transgressor. Even Kyle had been spared from knowing of his comalike state.

Still, Victor was hypervigilant. For days he'd accompanied Paul whenever he fed. He scanned the faces of pedestrians on the sidewalk. He steered him away from alleys and unlit areas—except for the brief moments when they fed. And then he stood like one of the president's secret service agents, his back to Paul and his sentinel eyes roaming the environs. Usually, he declined to feed when Paul cleared away from the victim's throat. The distraction would leave Paul unprotected, especially if his own lust for blood got out of hand. He had attributed his abstinence to a general need for vigilance against the powers. Paul had not questioned him.

With every passing day since the encounter at Calloway, his caution had increased, lest the Dark Kingdom's emissaries use a stalling tactic that put him off guard. *Delay acting until he thinks we've disappeared. When he relaxes, attack.* So Victor never relaxed. Every muscle was taut and ready to propel him into action. His attention to every sense had never reached such an intense level. Sensory overload could result, but his keen mind screened all irrelevant stimuli. It was as though he knew exactly what he listened and looked for. This experience of certainty assured him, but that assurance must not be permission to relax his vigilance.

Now they gazed at the marble likeness of the seated Lincoln and read the passages from his speeches etched on the walls of the temple.

"Freeing the slaves," Victor scoffed. "Modern sentimentality explains why there are no empires today."

"So the Roman Empire owed its existence to enslaving human beings?" By now, Paul should have gotten over the shock of Victor's views, but they clearly troubled him still.

"Enslaving them. Instilling fear in them. It's the way of power." Victor darted a glance toward the stairs when he thought he heard a footstep. No one was there.

"The way of power. It is that." Paul followed Victor's glance. "But isn't the price of power constant fear for the ones in control? Every ounce of energy goes into defending turf."

"You sound like a Marxist."

Paul smiled. "Maybe I am," he said ironically. "You, too. We're rising against the powers that be, aren't we? The oppressive powers of the Dark Kingdom."

Victor was not amused. "We're the ones with the power. Don't forget that." He walked to the marble steps and stared out across the terrain that once was swampland. Nothing appeared to interrupt the quiet nobility of the scene. But he knew better than to trust appearances. Rome had radiated splendor even as Barbarian tribes approached the city walls.

They left the shrine to Lincoln and made their way to the protective cluster of trees between the granite wall of the Vietnam Memorial and Constitution Avenue. Within twenty minutes, a silhouette of a man approached them across the grounds. He was tall and well built with a shaved head. He carried himself like a soldier, shoulders back, his stride confident and determined. The challenging prey enticed Victor. Ascertaining with a quick inspection of the area that no danger threatened Paul, he decided to enjoy the victim himself. They stood behind a tree and waited. When the man was within arm's length, Victor lunged for him, throwing him to the ground.

"Mother fucker!" the man muttered, shoving Victor with impressive strength.

Victor wrestled with him for his own pleasure, rolling on the ground with him as the bruiser tried to get to his feet and gain ascendancy. Fortunately, he was too much of a he-man to call out for help. Victor finally put an end to the game, plunging his fangs into the man's throat and willing him to surrender, which he instantly did. Sweet nicotine and the yeasty smell of beer rose from the man's shirt. Pressed against the victim's solid chest, Victor swallowed greedily. Feeling something beneath his shirt, he stopped and pulled out a chain with dog tags. Focusing his vision in the darkness, he read the embossed name LIEUTENANT ROBERT BEYER.

"Dog tags?" Paul said, squatting next to Victor and examining the tags. "The year of birth is 1948. The tags must have belonged to the guy's father. His name's probably on the wall." Paul touched the victim's square jaw. "Looks like he's in the military himself."

"The bastard fights like it," Victor said. "Go on. I'm through." He stood up to guard Paul while he fed, scanning the dark ground like a security camera.

Suddenly the victim groaned and struggled against Paul. He managed to clutch Paul by the throat before Victor fell on him and in one quick motion snapped his neck. His muscular limbs stiff, he lay lifeless on the ground, like one of the G.I. Joe figures Paul received for Christmas when he was little. He'd told Victor that they were the only dolls his redneck father would permit him to have.

"Jesus, Victor." Paul got to his feet. "Why in the hell did you do that? He just regained consciousness. Doesn't that ever happen?"

Victor stood and glanced around. "No. Never." This was a lie. Occasionally over the centuries, an exceptionally strong victim would rally and fight. The remedy was pressure on the throat and a reassertion of willpower. But no one who attacked Paul now would get a second chance. Who knew what kind of control over victims the Dark Kingdom might exert?

"He came to pay his respects." Paul fumbled in his pocket for a cigarette to calm him. He lit it and exhaled in frustration. "How can you be so cold-blooded?"

Victor kept to himself the words that came to him. *Because I'm a vampire. And I won't let anyone hurt you.* Better not to disturb Paul any more than he had. "Come on," he said.

"We're just gonna leave him here?"

"He'll be found and properly buried. Don't you want that? If we hide him somewhere, he won't." He hoped the response would appease Paul. The real reason for not moving the body was the risk they would incur in the city light. Leaving him was in their best interest. No one had seen them with the man. No one would trace them to him.

After surveying the area beyond the trees, they walked silently across the dark portion of the Mall to the dark jogging path along the river. Then they turned toward Georgetown. An occasional car passed them on the nearby parkway, including a patrol car sounding its siren, which sent them to the shadows well away from the path until it passed. When they had climbed the steep incline to M Street, Paul finally spoke.

"You're scaring me, Victor."

"This is our life. We kill. Especially when there's a threat."

"But what threat was he? I could have restrained him if you'd just given me half a chance."

"I don't take chances. You can't either. Your conscience will eventually conform to reality."

Paul seemed to yield. There were no arguments on the rest of the walk home.

As he unlocked the front door of their townhouse, Victor listened for any strange noise within. Satisfied that there was no danger awaiting them, he entered the house, Paul following him in. They went up to Paul's studio, where Victor occupied himself with tarot cards while Paul painted. He'd experienced a series of nightmares featuring Gimello and Paul, and he couldn't shake the vivid images from his head—Gimello's hairy, naked body spread out on Paul, like an incubus sucking the breath from his victim; Gimello standing behind Paul as he painted, his long nails like talons on Paul's shoulders, inching closer and closer to Paul's exposed throat; Gimello kneeling over Paul's bloody neck, his goatee dripping with the red fluid. Unsettled, Victor sought solace in the cards. Over the centuries, he had learned to trust the wisdom they conveyed to readers truly attuned to the forces of the universe. Michael had been such a reader, instructed in the art of interpretation by his Creole grandmother Jana, a voodoo practitioner. Michael was a monk at the monastery of St. Thomas in the Appalachian foothills, where five years ago Victor had posed as a monk visiting from England. Victor had been taken with the dark, intensely spiritual man. He had pursued him, and stupidly disclosed his true identity—hoping against hope that love would conquer Michael's abhorrence for a predator's life and accept Victor's blood, live as a vampire, in solitude for two hundred years on the earth, and finally join Victor in the Dark Kingdom.

When Victor looked back now, the audacity of the fantasy astounded him. How could he expect even the most exceptional human to agree to such terms—barring an imminent danger that made even such a life a better alternative, as had been the case for him? Even if obsessive love moved a human to accept a ghoul's life, the same obsession would terrify the lover at the prospect of separating for two hundred years from his vampire creator. Humans could not fathom the speed with which two centuries can fly. At any rate, Michael had balked in the final hour. Enraged, Victor had forced him to witness his own bloody killing spree in the streets of Knoxville, where the police had fired upon the innocent hostage, killing him.

The episode had taught Victor two important lessons. First, after centuries of disillusionment because of his betrayal by Joshu, he could love again and hope for an eternal partner. Second, it was mad to believe that a prospective lover would agree to a vampire's life without a transitional period as a thrall. Such a period had not only prepared Paul for this life, but it had also produced in him a lusty impatience for it.

The tarot cards only heightened Victor's sense of foreboding. Again and again he turned up distressful cards from the suite of swords. First came the three of swords, a heart pierced with blades, indicating the heartbreak of lost love or betrayal. Did this bode his ultimate loss of Paul? Surely not betrayal—for how could even the Dark Kingdom force Paul's love of Victor from him? The eight of swords turned up twice. It displayed a figure blinded and bound amid swords that formed a fence. The message was restriction, confusion, and powerlessness. Merely a reflection of his current state—as much as he hated to admit it? Or a reflection of his future state—after he was deprived of Paul? The nine of swords also appeared twice, a man sitting upright in bed, his face buried in his hands, a series of horizontal blades rising above him. The card might indicate brooding of the sort that now occupied him. But it might also bode anguish and despair. His sure fate if he were to lose Paul.

No cards opposing these gloomy cards turned up—no lover card to counter the broken heart in the three of swords, no hopeful magician or chariot to counter the bound figure in the eight of swords, no consoling star or ten of cups to counter the nine of sword's anguish. Instead, the dark cards were reinforced by other cards boding pain and bondage, including the most foreboding cards of the deck: the crumbling tower, indicating a downfall, and the horned devil, the embodiment of disaster.

Of course, alternate interpretations existed for these cards. They could bode temporary ignorance and a period of danger. If so, his restlessness would cease as the events of the future unfolded themselves. But he put little stock in utopian dreams. His understanding of evil had served him well through two thousand years, and he could not let down his guard for a moment. If anything warranted believing in ultimate victory, it was his own cruel strength.

Just before dawn, after Paul had crawled into his coffin, Victor inspected the house from top to bottom—every closet, every dark corner, every kitchen cupboard. He even patrolled the small patio outside the kitchen door, peering up into the fading night sky. Nothing unusual caught his attention. The house was in order, the patio quiet—as was the street, which he scanned before bolting the doors and descending to the basement. He'd had a double bolt installed in the wine cellar's steel door. The irrationality of the measure did not eliminate his compulsion to take it. And maybe the measure was not totally irrational: a double bolt would not stop powers like those of the Dark Kingdom, but it might frustrate an intrusion by the Kingdom's human agents. Satisfied that all was well, Victor climbed into his resting place.

They both arose at dusk and spent an uneventful evening in Paul's studio. Then, during a midnight storm, Victor sensed a presence in the house. He climbed to the playroom, now painted black and streaked with brilliant red. The implements of torture gleamed on the table near the bed—handcuffs, clamps, chains, stainless steel dildos, and giant marble anal beads. When he approached the table, he noticed something had been moved. A knife with an ivory handle, purchased for the pleasure of a few extreme masochists, now rested on a pile of beads rather than on the table. Fresh blood coated the blade. He brought it to his tongue. The blood did not belong to Paul, nor to Horatio or Mark—this flavor he did not recognize.

Clutching the knife, he examined the closets. Silk dressing gowns and transparent black negligées dangled from hangers. Leather halters and assorted lingerie filled the shelves. Finding

Palace. Victor usually took such outlandish claims with a grain of salt. His guests loved to play roles and often guarded their real, bland identities. But when Giles Edmundson appeared downstairs in the club, Victor could imagine the tall, good-looking man in the uniform and fur hat of a Buckingham Palace guard. In a turtleneck and leather slacks, he chain smoked, and assumed a proprietary air around several of the club's female members, all pale and waiflike. Among them, one stood out: a dark-haired, statuesque woman, who eyed Edmundson with contempt. She looked remarkably like Sonia, even dressing in a low-cut dress, like the ones Sonia preferred. Every now and then, Victor left his computer to watch her chatting at the bar with men from her club or drinking with a group of women in the lounge area.

At midnight Paul joined him, and they went downstairs to hear the band that Mark Seepay had booked, a heavy-metal Goth group of three men in their twenties. The lead singer's bare chest was tattooed with a heart full of daggers, like macabre images of the Madonna in Italian villages—or like the three of swords from the tarot deck. The performer at the keyboard wore a black hood over his head. Hair crawled up his belly from his low-slung jeans. The drummer wore a vampire cape and a black jockstrap. Strobbing red lights flashed on the band. The S and M guests gyrated around the stage. Victor and Paul watched from their table.

The woman who resembled Sonia climbed to the stage, stripped off her dress, and danced in her black bra and bikini panties, her white body jerking and rocking, her red lips parted and her tongue licking them. She danced with the singer, caressing his chest, sinking down to his crotch to pantomime fellatio. Then she pointed at Edmunson and motioned for him to join her. He eagerly obeyed. On the stage he peeled off his shirt, and moving to the beat of the music, thrust his middle finger at the crucifix high on the reredos. The woman smiled in approval. Teasing him, she patted his buttocks and crotch, but as he moved toward her, her expression hardened, clearly commanding him to keep his distance. The little game seemed familiar to both of them. He stopped in his tracks, looking like a puppy reprimanded by his master. Then for his benefit, she turned her attention back to the singer, caressing his chest as he screamed "Take my body. Take my blood. Take my soul." The red light strobed on his flesh like a visible sign of his heartbeat. The heavy metal bass rattled the windows. The woman drew the singer to the floor, pulled off his jeans, and mounted him, facing the audience whose cheers barely cleared the music. Her red panties evidently created for frolics in bed, she maneuvered his penetration of her without removing them. As she rode him, Edmundson knelt before her, his chest heaving in excitement.

Suddenly her gaze shifted to Victor, who watched her through a gap in the crowd. Her eyes were at once seductive and defiant. His excitement turned to anger. It was Sonia who stared at him now, not a strange woman. Sonia's cruel gaze. Sonia's scarlet lips, now mouthing words lost in the ear-shattering noise but discernible in his mind, like a whisper that overpowered all sound. *Come to me. You belong with me. You don't belong here. Save Paul. Save him. Save him.*

"You bitch!" He lunged toward the stage, shoving a burly male guest so hard that he crashed into a table and knocked it over. When a big-eyed woman in a spandex top tried to calm him, he backhanded her.

Suddenly Paul had him by the arm. "What in the hell are you doing?"

"Let go of me."

Paul shook him. "Come on, Victor."

Paul stared at him, confused and frightened. Victor recovered control of himself. When he glanced at the stage, all traces of Sonia in the face of the groaning woman were gone. The crowd around him eyed him cautiously. Two women were assisting the woman he had struck. One wiped her bloody nose with a napkin. The burly man's friends were holding him back.

Victor took Paul's hand. "Let's go."

"He's sorry," Paul shouted, his words lost in the blasting music. "What the fuck is going on?" he said when they were out on the quiet street.

"Sonia."

"What?"

"Nothing. I can't explain."

Later, when Paul got up from his easel and rubbed his neck, Victor led him down to the bedroom. With every touch of his lovemaking, he reassured himself that Paul was safe, that there was nothing they could do to him.

———

Exhausted, Victor slept through sunset the next evening. When he woke up nearly an hour later, he immediately inspected Paul's coffin. It was empty. Adrenaline rushed through him. *Calm down. He's up painting.* He restrained himself from racing up to the studio. He had to steel his nerves for both of their sakes. Two millennia ago, in the Roman army, he had honed the discipline instilled by his father in all of his sons. With other officers, he had bathed in the Tiber in the middle of winter. He had marched for ten miles across the frozen northern front. Without hesitating a second, he had snuffed the life out of soldiers mortally wounded on the battlefield—as his father had mercifully snuffed out the life of his afflicted brother Justin, whom he loved more than any of his four brothers. He had successfully summoned Stoic discipline for every kind of occasion except one—the icy, unbearable separation from anyone whom he desired. Joshu's rejection had sent him on a campaign of violence that forced him to flee from the very Roman authorities he once represented. Michael's rejection of him had set off a rage that caused Michael's death, the destruction of innocent monks at the monastery of St. Thomas, and his own flight for safety—once again. Now the threat of losing his beloved came from outside forces more powerful than he. Every atom of his being wanted to lash out at unseen hands manipulating him as though he were a puppet on a string. Cool restraint evaded him. But he must exert himself. Paul's life and their future together depended on it.

Testing himself, he went to their room instead of to Paul's studio. He would shower and change and then go to check on Paul. His heart raced as he stood under the stream of hot water, toweled himself, and changed into a white linen shirt and pleated trousers. His beard felt rough, but Paul liked it that way, so he didn't bother to shave. Then he calmly climbed to the studio. He hesitated at the door, then flung it open. The room was empty.

He could detect no progress in the canvas on the easel, which displayed a penciled stylized sketch of Lincoln's shrine on the Mall. The cat jumped off the couch and brushed against his leg. Its dish in the corner of the room stood empty.

Victor took a deep breath. He went to the window and glanced down at the dark sidewalk. As he watched a young couple with backpacks make their way down the street, the familiar sense of a presence within the house rose in him. He recalled the image of Sonia on Paul's canvas: the devilish gaze, the satyrlike erection and cloven feet.

"Sonia," he shouted. "Show your face!"

The lights flickered, but the house remained still and Sonia invisible. What had she done with Paul? Victor imagined Paul drugged by some mysterious potion produced in the Dark Kingdom and locked in a storage room with large windows to let in the dawn's fatal light.

"Where is he?" he shouted again into the air, clenching his fists, ready to pounce, but deprived of a victim.

Aware of the futility of searching the house, he did it anyway, every room and every closet. He followed the same procedure through Dies Irae, checking the playrooms, kitchen, and utility closets in the basement before moving upstairs to the confessionals and niches of the church, empty at this early evening hour. Then, he headed for the guest house, opening each and every door. In one room, a man and three women had collapsed on a king-size bed, a naked tangle of arms and legs. Drug paraphernalia was strewn on a table in the room, near empty tumblers and half-empty bottles of bourbon and gin. He heard groans in another room and pounded the door. The sounds subsided and a hairy, bearded man appeared at the door in black briefs that barely contained his erection. Pushing past him, he found a blond woman, bent over the side of the bed, her hands tied behind her back.

"Hey, man, if you want some action, I'm cool."

Victor shoved him aside and left the room. In two other rooms, guests were innocently watching television when he pushed his way in. The rest of the rooms were empty, the beds made, clothes hanging in the large wardrobes that served as closets.

Despite the futility of interrogating anyone about Paul's whereabouts, Victor nonetheless decided to drill Horatio, who jumped up from his Soloflex bench when Victor charged into his apartment. His sweaty tank top clung to his chest. His short bleached hair was drenched. No, he had not seen Paul since the night before. No, he'd heard nothing strange during the day. Victor's worst fear was a daytime intruder who could have exposed Paul to the sunlight. Of course, such an apprehension made no sense. Victor would have seen signs of destruction in Paul's coffin. Moreover, Kyle, his watchdog, would have seen something. He was instructed to make regular rounds to the cellar during the day.

"Is Kyle in his room?" Victor said.

Horatio nodded. "I think he just got back from shopping." Whatever questions he had about Kyle's changed appearance and new relationship with Victor he kept to himself. He had learned to see nothing at a place like Dies Irae.

Victor glanced around the room. Horatio, insatiable in his need for changing his surroundings, had redecorated. His new waterbed was covered with a magenta duvet. Above the bed hung a new poster announcing Judy Garland's final performance in Carnegie Hall and a new poster featuring the buff character Rocky from the *Rocky Horror Show*. Victor remembered the day he and Paul had barged in on Horatio and Kyle in bed and preyed on their beautiful flesh.

Victor climbed to the third floor of the guest house and opened the door to Kyle's room. Kyle looked up from a maroon sofa, a rosary in his hand.

"Have you seen Paul anywhere?" Victor said.

Kyle looked alarmed. "No. What's wrong?"

"When did you last check the cellar?"

"An hour before sunset."

"And you noticed nothing strange during the day?"

He shook his head.

Victor left him without another word and rushed down the stairs and out to the street. The warm air smelled of rain. He inhaled deeply to calm himself.

Maybe it was all a ruse. Maybe Paul had gone out of his own

free will. Maybe there was nothing to do but wait. But he was too restless for that. And whether Sonia had harmed Paul or simply wanted to taunt Victor, her presence haunted the premises. Victor had to stay on the move. Futile or not, he could not resist the compulsion to go on searching for Paul.

He walked to the art store that sold Paul's paintings, a corner row house painted yellow, just a block from the Georgetown University campus. A bell on the door jingled when he entered and from the counter a plump man gazed up at him over half-glasses. Portraits in gold frames cluttered one wall. On the opposite hung an eclectic mixture of unframed temperas and watercolors. The small back wall displayed Paul's work, a dozen canvases depicting scenes from Rome and Washington. There was also one small painting he had never seen. He recognized his own face in the abstract image formed of bold black lines.

"Can I help you with anything?" the man said attentively, taken with Victor's looks.

"You have some of Paul Lewis's paintings," he said, nodding to the back wall.

"Yes. Aren't they wonderful? People love the Roman scenes. They're not the typical tourist stuff." The man removed his glasses and let them dangle by their chain.

He was right. The light and shadow in the Colosseum painting gave it an almost surreal appearance. The same was true for the painting of the Forum, in shades of purple and blue. But his portrait intrigued him. Why had Paul never told him of it? It conveyed his aggressiveness in a strangely sympathetic way, almost as a kind of sadness. The sight made him long for Paul. *Where the hell is he? Where have they taken him?*

"I'd like to buy the small one."

"Good choice." The man's gray eyes glowed at the sale. He waddled over and lifted the painting from the wall, apparently making no connection between the image and the customer. At the counter he wrapped it in brown paper and accepted four hundred dollars from Victor, surprised by the hundred-dollar bills that Victor pulled from his wallet.

"Does the artist bring in new paintings very often?" Victor said.

"Occasionally. He just brought this in today. He'll be thrilled to know how quickly it sold."

"Today? You mean tonight?"

The man shook his head. "I found in on the counter when I came in this morning. The artists have keys to the shop. He left a note on it. Good thing. I don't think I would have recognized it as his. It's so different from the other paintings."

So Paul had actually dropped it off late last night, which meant he had slipped out when Victor went to his office. Victor's vigilance had made Paul resort to sneaking. Now he had stepped into a trap set by Gimello.

Victor left the shop and hurried home, dropping off the painting in his office before trudging all the way to the fountain on Dupont Circle, where Paul sometimes sketched. Three drunken vagrants argued on a bench. On the opposite side of the fountain, a shaggy-haired man strummed a guitar, his German shepherd on the bench next to him. No sign of Paul.

Victor soared to Congressional Cemetery, one of Paul's favorite places. He liked to stand over the bold headstone engraved with a pink triangle and the words *They gave me a medal for killing two men and a discharge for loving one.* He liked to see dog owners walking their pets through the sunken, lozenge-shaped stones. He liked to imagine President Lincoln—the great emancipator of slaves—presiding over the burial service of the nineteen women killed in an arsenal explosion during the Civil War. Marking the burial spot was a tall monument topped with a statue of a long-skirted woman. Victor gazed across the field of headstones and sculpted angels, as though his lover might be wandering among them. *Where are you, Paul? Where are you?*

Despite his frantic search, a persistent intuition told him that Sonia had not hurt Paul. Not yet. This disappearance was just a warning. *You want to bargain? Bring him back to me. Bring him back to me now!* The words seemed to roar across the graves, though he did not open his mouth.

City lights cast a greenish hue on the cloudy sky. The stones and monuments glowed eerily beneath its illumination. But patches of sheer darkness lay beneath the cemetery's trees, rustling in the warm wind. The burial vault of George Watterston, the first librarian of Congress, was wrapped in shadows. The gated, brick façade of the mausoleum abutted a grass-covered mound that stood five feet tall. As Victor stood at the door, gruff laughter echoed through the cemetery. Across the grounds, fifty yards away, a figure in white glided through the headstones.

"You want him back? Back? Back?" The hollow, reverberating voice and the trailing laughter belonged to Sonia.

Just across the gravel road, under a shaggy pine, another figure stirred. His face, white as a moon, rose above a Roman collar and cassock. Gimello. He laughed and pointed to the mausoleum.

On the turf mound rose a wooden cross and on the cross Paul hung by nails driven through his wrists and his feet, exactly as they had been driven through Joshu's body two thousand years ago. And he was naked, as Joshu had been. Plaited thorns ringed his head, as they had Joshu's, and when he peered down, blood streamed into his eyes, making him blink. Blood dripped from his wounds to the turf. Victor salivated despite himself, suppressing the impulse to lick greedily the wounds that tortured Paul.

He reached for Paul's feet. They were warm, as though human blood once more circulated through them.

In excruciating pain, Paul yelled when Victor tore the nails from his hands. When Victor braced him against the wood and wrenched the nail from his feet, he passed out. He drifted in and out of consciousness as Victor dislodged the thorns and gently lapped his bloody body.

The wounds healed the instant that the causes of torture were removed, but Paul continued to moan in pain. He was dehydrated and exhausted. Victor took him to feed and led him to the bedroom where he slept fitfully at first, screaming out Sonia's name, but finally calming down and sleeping soundly. Victor stationed himself in a chair near the bed, alert to any strange noise or movement, ready to shield his beloved from any intruding force.

The night passed without event. Just before dawn, Paul woke up, weak but no longer hurting. Victor lay next to him and described the encounter at Calloway Manor. "They gave me an ultimatum. I follow the rules or you pay for it."

Paul stared at him, panic-stricken. "Why believe them? If you leave me, what's to keep them away from me?"

"What motive would they have to hurt you once I'm gone?"

"Sure," he snapped. "No big fucking sacrifice for you. What's two hundred years for someone who's been around as long as you have? Especially when you've got plenty of company in the old DK. But what about me? I wander around like some Bela Lugosi parody. Give me back my mortal life any day of the week. It might be short. But it's a life." He got up and started dressing.

Victor climbed out of bed and grabbed him by the shoulders. "We can't watch our backs every second. I can't live like that. And you can't either. I have to go."

"No!" Paul said.

"We have no choice."

"I have a choice," Paul said. "Let them take me if they want. I can't do this alone. I'm not cut out for it."

"You could find someone else."

Paul bristled. "You don't care if I find another lover?"

"Human lovers don't scare me."

Paul stared solemnly at him. "If you leave me, I'll kill myself."

Victor ordered Kyle to guard their coffins while they slept. A thrall's power against Sonia was doubtful, but it was better than nothing.

When Victor awoke, he found Kyle asleep on a blanket near Paul's coffin. The coffin was empty.

Victor fell on Kyle and grabbed his throat. Kyle's eyes flashed open. His face turned red. He tugged at Victor's hands.

"I'll deal with you later," Victor said, releasing him.

He searched his buildings before hurrying out to the street. Angry, Paul had probably left of his own accord, perhaps heading to Wisconsin Avenue's busy bars and restaurants in order to stay close to home and in a very public area—whatever safety that might bring him. Victor walked up to Q Street and followed it to Wisconsin Avenue. He walked uphill, past a corner flower market with its doors still open and flowers still displayed outside on a little patio. Beyond that an Ethiopian restaurant buzzed with people. Next door at a coffee shop, he scanned the faces of customers seated at the counter by the window. Paul sometimes liked to sit at the counter with an untouched cup, watching pedestrians or sketching.

He crossed the street and walked downhill, peering through the plate glass of brightly lit boutiques and a dark, cozy pub. Several young, well-dressed couples on the sidewalk ahead of him glanced up, alarmed by his frantic pace and intensity.

This was foolishness. Paul could be at any of his favorite haunts: Capitol Hill, Dupont Circle, Eastern Market, or the Mall—a particularly easy place to feed on stray tourists making their solitary pilgrimage to the Vietnam or Lincoln Memorials. The best strategy would be to go home and wait.

When he returned, he found Paul in the studio at his easel, Kyle standing guard over him.

"I had to get out," he said before Victor could open his mouth.

"You must want to die."

Paul glared at him. "What do you care?" He went back to painting. "I couldn't feed," he said quietly.

"What do you mean?"

"Every time I tried, I puked." Paul looked at him. "I finally had to stop. The nausea was violent. I thought maybe the blood was contaminated somehow. But then, Jesus, what are the chances that three unrelated people in a row have contaminated blood?" Paul's gaze drifted back to the canvas.

Victor grabbed the brush from his hand. "We have to go out again."

They needed easy targets. If Paul was reacting to certain blood, or blood types—not unheard of in vampire lore—they might need to try several victims. They soared the short distance to Georgetown Hospital, entering through the emergency room doors, and easily slipped into a corridor that led to the neurology ward. In the third room, they noticed a motionless man on a ventilator. According to the chart outside the door, the man had suffered a stroke. From what Victor could decipher, he was brain dead, but since he was not classified as a do-not-resuscitate patient, the hospital obviously had to keep him breathing.

The corridor, brightly lit with fluorescent lights, was empty. The nurse's station was a hundred yards away. The top of a woman's head was visible behind the desk. She appeared to be reading.

Victor nodded to Paul. They entered the room and closed the door.

"Go ahead," Victor said. "I'll stand here by the door."

Paul looked out of place in the sterile white room. His shaggy hair, baggy jeans, untucked shirt, and new goatee made him look like a beach bum. And his full lips, sensitive eyes, and large, beautiful hands—like the hands of Michelangelo's David—projected a sensuality at odds with the corpulent, lifeless body on the bed. The man had plump cheeks and a recessed chin that sank into the folds around his throat. Paul leaned over him, jabbed his throat, and began drawing blood. Immediately, he gagged. He drew back to catch his breath and tried again, apparently straining to keep to task. He managed to swallow a good portion of blood. But as soon as he raised his head, he clutched his stomach and vomited on the bright linoleum floor.

Victor approached the patient and applied his mouth to the wound on his throat. He tasted nothing unusual in the blood and felt no unusual effect.

"It's me," Paul said. "Jesus. What has Sonia done to me?"

"Let's try another patient."

"I can't do this again."

"Just one more," Victor insisted.

They moved down the corridor until they found an old woman sleeping. According to her chart, she was being observed for seizures. She had fine, white hair, so thin in places that her pink scalp was visible through it. Her eyes flashed open when they entered the room. She opened her mouth to speak, but before she could utter a sound, Victor clasped his hand over her mouth. She struggled until Paul bit her throat. Then she became limp.

For a minute, he drank successfully. Victor concentrated his will on Paul, as though by sheer volition he could ward off the nausea. Suddenly Paul drew away and vomited profusely. The blood splattered the sheets.

"That's it," he said. "It's not working."

With no other choice, Victor remained silent, attracted to the regurgitated blood despite its horrible implications.

Was it too late to save Paul now? Was he past the point of no return?

Nightmares haunted Victor's sleep that night. Then, just before rising, he dreamed of Joshu, standing on a rocky hillside outside Jerusalem surrounded by crowds of people seated on the ground. He recognized the scene not because he had witnessed it, but because Paul had painted it for the Bible at San Benedetto. It was an illumination of the multiplication of the loaves and fishes. Only Joshu did not look like Paul's version of Joshu—a rugged, Middle-Eastern-looking man with a wild mane. He looked like the real Joshu, strong, but graceful, his deep brown eyes gleaming playfully. He walked among the crowd offering them a basket. They reached in with both hands and scooped out blood, raising it to their lips and swallowing contentedly. With no trouble at all.

12

What it's like to stop feeding? Sitting listlessly on his studio couch, Kyle reading a book next to him and Victor pacing, Paul imagined trying to explain to Becky what he was feeling now, on the second night without human blood. His throat felt taut, the way it used to feel before the scratchy stage of a sore throat. He felt depleted of all energy. It was as though he had low blood sugar. Well, literally he did. Or at least it was a condition very like it. His own blood lacked essential nutrients for his physical maintenance. His organs—stomach, intestines, brain, and, finally, his heart—all designed to endure for eternity when properly maintained, would gradually cease to function. He had forced that information out of Victor, who had followed it by uttering, "It won't happen," as though he were issuing Paul a command, rather than reassuring him.

Victor had guided him first to a house with children, then to a woman dumping garbage in the alley behind a restaurant. The idea was to experiment with victims. Maybe some kinds of humans resisted contamination by the powers that be. Maybe children were too pure to be touched. Maybe estrogen made women immune. Maybe Asian people had a resistant gene. As preposterous as it sounded, they were both willing to try everything. But the results were always the same. Profuse vomiting.

He got up and adjusted the thermostat. Although the temperature read seventy, the air-conditioned room felt like the inside of a refrigerator. Normally, his body temperature a good ten degrees below that of humans, he thrived in external temperatures in the low sixties. But his cool skin was noticeably cooler now. *Before long I'll be dead, instead of undead.* That joke kept running through his mind.

"How long can I last without feeding?" he asked Victor.

"You're going to feed again," Victor said. He stood by the window.

"What if I don't? How long do I have?"

"A week," Victor said quietly. "Maybe ten days. Unless I leave."

"It's too late."

"We don't know that."

Paul moved the cat and stretched out on the couch. *He'll have to do it now. He'll have to leave me.* The solution was obvious. But he'd be damned if he'd let Victor go. He was better off dead than alone in this fucking ghoulish life. He looked at Kyle, his head buried in *Imitation of Christ*, a tract by the Medieval acetic Thomas à Kempis. A monk used to read aloud from it during meals at San Benedetto. The book advised against "particular friendships" and "impure thoughts." *Impure thoughts. Jesus!*

"What's the point?" he said to Kyle. "You read that garbage like it will save your soul. A little late, isn't it?"

"I don't believe that." Kyle looked tired from watching with him, but his eyes were earnest. His azure polo shirt made them look blue instead of gray. "God is master of the whole universe. Heaven and earth and everything in between."

"But you're in hell." Paul's condition made him edgy, cruel.

Kyle shook his blond head. "Hell is forever. And souls get there by exercising their free will."

The phrase must have come from a catechism book. Paul smiled and closed his eyes. "Then that's where you'll go. For sucking Victor off—so to speak. For guarding someone who makes a meal out of human beings. God is keeping score on the big tally sheet in the sky."

"God will save me. He can save you, Paul."

"What makes you think that God has any say about this realm?" Victor blurted. "You know how long I've lived—no help from your God. He's impotent."

"That's not true."

Paul found himself wishing that Kyle was right. Considering the ruthless Sonia, the Dark Kingdom sounded more like a hell than a heaven. Especially if it robbed him of Victor. And if that happened his life would be hell on earth.

If only Victor had never taken his natural life away from him—and at the youthful age of thirty-two. Years and years had stretched ahead of him. Years of painting, travel, screwing around the way normal, healthy young men do. And all of it in the daylight. Surrounded by his friends. And his family. He and Victor could have stayed lovers, apart by day but together at night, making love in the moonlight.

Maybe his illness was messing up his mind. Maybe this idyllic dream was ludicrous. How long could he and Victor have remained lovers on unequal footing, Victor the ultimate master and he a slave? In sex, the roles might be a turn-on, but in life they spelled disaster. At least they would for him, as he aged while Victor stayed forever the studly Roman officer. All the same, he'd take that sad reality any day over the prospect looming before him now: two hundred years of solitude. An eternity.

He closed his eyes. "I hope you're right," he said.

"Can I . . ." Kyle whispered to Victor. "Can I pray over him? For healing."

Victor laughed scornfully. Paul was touched, but he smiled at the weirdness of the scene: a ghoul in prayer. *Hey Jesus, I'm not so bad. I just feed on people. Do me this favor!*

"I'm still a priest," Kyle said. "Once you're ordained, you're ordained forever."

"Do it," Victor said.

Paul felt Kyle's thumb trace a cross on his forehead. "Lord Jesus," he prayed, "you healed the blind and the lame, for you desire wholeness. Bring your forgiveness and healing to Paul, beloved child of God. Relieve his pain. Relieve his hunger with your own abundance. For you live and reign with the Father, in the unity of the Holy Spirit, forever and ever. Amen."

Kyle laid his hands on Paul's head, then on his belly. Warmth rushed through his body, like a stream from a hot spring suddenly undammed. Was he imagining new energy? New strength? Did he want it so badly that his own will was producing it? But the changes were unmistakable. The tautness in his throat had vanished. The chill had left him. His limbs felt solid. He opened his eyes and found Kyle gazing tranquilly at him. Victor stood behind him, his arms folded, unbelieving.

"I can do it now," Paul said to him.

They went out to feed. The air, though heavy with humidity, invigorated Paul. He inhaled the scent of freshly mowed grass and gazed with pleasure up the charming street of bay windows, turrets, painted brick, and bright shutters.

"An old woman lives in this house," Kyle said. The bricks of the corner row house were painted lemon yellow and the shutters deep green. Ivy climbed all the way to the roof. "I take her communion everyday. I consecrate the hosts when you and Victor are asleep. I know you won't hurt her."

Paul and Victor followed Kyle through the wrought-iron gate and up the painted iron steps above the entrance of an English basement. Kyle took a key from his pocket and opened the door.

The house was hot and stuffy. According to Kyle, the woman never used air-conditioning and never opened her windows. They entered a narrow hallway, which ran through the middle of the house. Kyle softly shut a half-open door. "The nurse," he whispered.

Kyle opened the next door and listened. Paul followed him to a hospital bed in the corner of the dark room. The old woman, her mouth sunken, must have weighed eighty pounds. She smelled of urine, but the odor did not dampen Paul's appetite. He leaned over and tore into the frail skin. He savored the initial mouthful of blood before swallowing it. He paused, waiting for a reaction. Nothing. He continued drinking, pulling away only at Kyle's urging. Paul owed him. He had to spare the woman.

At home, Victor commanded Kyle to consecrate the cellar. "Now," he said, when Kyle hesitated, uncertain whether to believe him.

"What are you doing?" Paul said.

Victor did not answer.

Kyle collected the necessary things from his room. When he returned to the living room, he wore an alb and a purple chasuble. He had combed his wavy hair, wet now, as though he had stuck his head under a faucet to purify himself. He carried a black valise with his initials on it in gold.

They followed him down the basement stairs. In the wine cellar, he removed a linen cloth from his valise and unfolded it on the table. He added two glass cruets containing water and wine, a gold plated chalice and paten, a communion wafer, candles, and a red lectionary. He apparently offered secret masses in his room or elsewhere, afraid of Victor's response. Paul and Victor perched on their caskets as Kyle mumbled the liturgical prayers. Through the rite, he squeezed his eyes shut—opening them long enough to read the epistle and Gospel from the lectionary. Paul assumed that their presence, leering from grotesque coffins, disconcerted him. He assumed that Kyle silently uttered prayers for the salvation of all of them.

Victor watched the performance with interest. But when Kyle withdrew a silver sprinkler from his valise and began strewing holy water around the damp cellar, he slid from his coffin.

"Not on me," he said.

Paul let the drops shower his flesh. Who knew what kind of power the sprinkling held? The *asperges*. He had learned the Latin word at San Benedetto. As the drops of water struck his face, he prayed. *Don't let him go, Joshu!*

But the prayer was useless. After the ritual, Victor turned to him. "It's time."

Paul made no attempt to plead. The decision was made. When he took Victor's hand, it wasn't because of desperation. It was because he knew the end had come.

Under Victor's orders, Kyle put scarlet satin sheets on Victor and Paul's bed. As a reward, Victor tore open his wrists and offered him the fresh blood. As Kyle drank, he bore his head into Victor's crotch. Victor might have given him what he wanted, as he sometimes did after he fed, the bloodletting arousing the host as much as the drinking aroused the thrall. But tonight he performed perfunctorily. Paul absorbed all of his attention.

"That's enough," he said, nodding to the door.

Disappointed, Kyle left the room. When he glanced back, his eyes flashed red, like the eyes of people in some photographs. Thralls were prone to the strange look.

Victor lit the thirteen candles of a pewter candelabra. It showered a fountain of light on the game table in the corner of the room. He lit candles on the bed tables and on the mantel. He called down the stairs for Paul.

Paul appeared, silent and pale. Victor kissed him and undressed him slowly, pressing his lips to Paul's shoulders, throat,

and chest. Lifting Paul's hands to his mouth, he kissed his palms
and his long, knobby fingers.

They made love on the cool sheets—shifting, straining, lifting,
rolling. They bit into each other's flesh and tore at each other's
hair, creating pain to express pain. When Victor entered Paul,
Paul stretched his arms and groaned, as though he were once
again crucified—like one of the hundreds of insurgents Victor
had witnessed on the highway to Jerusalem. Like Joshu himself.
Victor blocked the thought. At the moment of orgasm, tears
rushed down Paul's face. Victor kissed Paul's wet cheeks.

"Two hundred years is like a month for us," Victor said.

He spoke the truth. As much pain as leaving Paul would cause,
his sense of perspective prevented despair. But he feared for Paul.
Predators thrived in the solitude they abhorred because feeding
on others required detachment, if not absolute cruelty. Paul resisted his own predatory nature. He craved association beyond a
lover's bond. Victor was uncertain whether time would change
him or whether his struggle would continue for two centuries. He
ran the risk of losing Paul to dangerous liaisons forged from
loneliness. He ran the risk of losing Paul to another lover. But he
must save Paul's life. This compulsion was new to him, at least
this sustained experience of it. In the final desperate moments
with Michael, the feeling had flared. Then, it was inseparable
from his own sense of loss. Now, he was even prepared to lose
Paul if it meant saving Paul's life.

"What will happen to Kyle?" Paul said, stroking Victor's chest.

"He can't survive without me."

"He'll suffer?"

"Yes. That's why I'll kill him before I go."

Paul stared sadly at the ceiling. "Can someone cross over?" he said. "From our kind of eternity to another?"

Victor studied him. *Why in the hell would they want to?* he wanted to say. But he spared Paul his bitterness. "I don't know," he replied.

"What about us?" Paul said. "Can there be any communication at all between us?"

"No. It would only make it worse."

"You're wrong," Paul said.

"It can't happen. I'm sure." He wasn't sure, but he was right about making everything worse. The best breaks were clean breaks. "This is what you have to do. Go down to the cellar and go to sleep. Once you're asleep, I'll leave."

Paul stopped stroking Victor's chest. "I want to be there."

"You don't. I told you about Tiresia." When Victor's creator entered the Dark Kingdom, her flesh had shriveled and darkened like a piece of rotten fruit before disintegrating. Paul knew that an image like that would stick in his mind. He didn't insist.

"All right," he said. "But I can't go to the cellar. Dawn's two hours away. I won't sleep."

"You will. Go on."

"Victor." Paul threw his arm over him and wept.

Victor held him. "I love you."

Paul climbed out of bed, put on a pale blue robe, and slowly left the room without looking back.

One last time, Victor wandered out into Georgetown, where a gentle wind stirred. The full moon had begun its western descent. The Gothic façade of Dies Irae glowed, white as bone. The row houses up and down the street basked quietly in the light. This was not the ideal place to end everything. Rome would be better. His home. Where their life together had begun.

He walked to Calloway Manor. The windows glowed, and strains from the piano drifted to the front lawn where Victor stood.

He mentally summoned Sonia's face. *You know my intentions. Do they satisfy your requirements? I want confirmation. It's the least you can do for me. You say you love your own.*

The wind swelled, violently shaking the two giant magnolias in front of the mansion. The large, shiny leaves spun from the trees. In the house, the music stopped. The lights flickered and vanished. Victor opened the front door and entered the large hall. The dark, bare room showed no signs of recent habitation.

As he passed his home on the way to the guest house, he cast a final glance at the place where Paul lay. Where his own heart lay.

With Paul, he had learned he was capable of making a sacrifice for love. But there were limits. He was no martyr. He could not banish himself to a place full of inhabitants like Sonia. And who knew? Perhaps, there were ways around the powers and their laws, ways to reunite him with Paul that he had yet to discover.

His separation from Paul would appease the Dark Kingdom for now. It would bring an end to the forbidden consolidation of power. And in the calculations of spirits ruling the Dark Kingdom, it was a matter of time before the isolated renegade turned homeward. Let the spirits think what they would.

In the foyer of the guest house, a large crate rested on the floor. Kyle sat on it. He jumped up when Victor entered.

"Is everything taken care of in New Orleans?" he said.

Kyle nodded. "My flight arrives in the morning. I'll be at the house hours before the delivery." Suddenly he dropped to his knees before Victor. "Please, free me. Don't make me go on in this kind of life." He placed Victor's hands around his throat.

A wave of pity passed through Victor, and he started to choke Kyle. But pragmatism brought him back to himself, and he stopped. "Have the crate carried to the cellar. And make yourself scarce when it arrives. I don't want your face to be the first thing that I see there."

Kyle hugged Victor's legs, sobbing.

Victor slept fitfully on the flight to New Orleans. In the cold belly of the plane, his new coffin sealed in a crate, he felt uncomfortable and vulnerable. The crate had been loaded in the dark when he was still wide awake and his keen senses sharper than ever in the precarious situation. He had smelled the deodorant of the airline workers and the nicotine that clung to them. He had even smelled their blood and imagined breaking through the barrier to feed on them. But there would be opportunity enough for that when he arrived.

As the noon sun pounded the fuselage, Victor half awakened to the sound of Joshu's voice. *No greater love, Victor. No greater love.* Even in his drowsiness, he recognized the reference in the

Christian scriptures to laying down one's life for one's friend. A dream. Too drained to scoff at it, he drifted back to sleep. But when he awoke in his new home, he felt something in his grasp. He brought a chunk of wood to his face. It smelled of Joshu's blood. He crumbled it as though it were a clod of earth.